PREY FOR A MIRACLE

AIMÉE AND DAVID THURLO

THORNDIKE PRESS

An imprint of Thomson Gale, a part of The Thomson Corporation

Detroit • New York • San Francisco • New Haven, Conn. • Waterville, Maine • London

THOMSON
GALE

™

LIBRARY OF CONGRESS CATALOGING-IN-PUBLICATION DATA

Thurlo, Aimée.
    Prey for a miracle / by Aimée and David Thurlo.
      p. cm.
    "A Sister Agatha Mystery" — T.p. verso.
    ISBN 0-7862-9038-2 (hardcover : alk. paper)
    1. Nuns — Fiction. 2. Catholics — Fiction. 3. New Mexico — Fiction.
    4. Large type books. I. Thurlo, David. II. Title.
PS3570.H82P74 2006b
813'.54—dc22
                                            2006025486

U.S. Hardcover:
ISBN 13: 978-0-7862-9038-3
ISBN 10: 0-7862-9038-2

Published in 2006 by arrangement with St. Martin's Press, LLC.

Printed in the United States of America on permanent paper
10 9 8 7 6 5 4 3 2 1

To Carol and the folks at the
Roswell Animal Humane Association,
who, over the years,
have brought us some of
our most beloved canine companions

AUTHORS' NOTE

Angels, heavenly visitors — we've always been fascinated by this subject and have researched it on our own for years. Then one day, the basis for a new storyline came to us and we couldn't wait to get started.

As usual, this book unfolded in stages, not all at once. We sat in our den, tossing ideas out, letting our partner improve upon it or shoot it down altogether. (Just so you know, this is the fun part of a book, and the most stressful!) David and I have worked out a system so feelings aren't hurt. We work by playing off each other's ideas until the right one comes along and then build on that. Of course, that doesn't preclude a throw pillow being hurled at someone's head every now and then. After thirty-six years of marriage, we've learned play is important, too.

Prey for a Miracle turned into one of our all-time favorites. The underlying theme mirrors our belief that no one is ever alone, despite what the eye can see. It's a story about strength of conviction, about serving God, and the power of innocence. Mostly, it's a story about trusting God and the blessings that brings.

I hope you'll enjoy the story and remember — God's universe is filled with possibilities!

ACKNOWLEDGMENTS

A special thanks to Diane and Phillip Uzdawinis for answering a gazillion questions, especially during those occasions when the hour was late and the information was crucial.

PROLOGUE

If they reached St. Augustine's, she and her daughter would be safe. Her brother Rick was the priest there. Before he'd become Father Mahoney, Rick had been a pro wrestler — stage name Apocalypse Now. Rick could handle any threat to her or Natalie; she was certain of it. She and her daughter would find sanctuary at St. Augustine's Church until they could leave New Mexico for good. It was the only answer.

The heavy pounding of rain on the windshield of their old car had eased, but the road was still incredibly dark, and her range of vision only extended a few feet beyond the glow of the headlights. Ever since they'd left the house she'd had the feeling that they were being followed, but the lights in her rearview mirror had never come any closer. Another false alarm, that's all.

Wishing she'd contacted the district attorney the instant the threats and calls had begun instead of playing it cool — quietly planning their escape — Jessica began to recite another prayer under her breath. Sometimes running away *was* the right answer. She'd just hand over the evidence to her brother. He'd know what to do with it after she and Natalie were long gone.

"Mom? Are you scared?"

Jessica looked over at Natalie, her eight-year-old daughter, trying to manage a smile. She was afraid to speak in a normal tone, knowing her voice would crack and her tears would start again, so she just shook her head.

"You sure?"

Jessica swallowed, determined not to cry. "Just another ten minutes, maybe less," she muttered in a barely audible voice. Then the nightmares would be over — or at least postponed for a while longer.

"Huh? Mom, what's in ten minutes?" Natalie said, poking her head out of the hooded jacket to look around, then sitting up to glance out the side mirror.

That's when Jessica saw the vehicle following them closing the gap. The glare from the high beams was blinding now, but she didn't dare take her hand off the wheel to flip that thing on the rearview mirror that would deflect the light.

She sneaked a look over at her daughter. "Let's play a game, Natalie," she said, surprised that she'd managed to make her voice sound so calm. "Scrunch down and pretend you're hiding."

Natalie started to turn in her seat to look behind them. "Huh? Hiding from what?"

"Just do it!" Jessica yelled as the car on their tail started to go around them.

Jessica eased off on the gas, desperately hoping she'd been worried about nothing. If the car was just trying to pass, it couldn't possibly be *him.*

Hanging onto the wheel with both hands, Jessica prayed, looking straight ahead and focusing on doing what was necessary to protect herself and Natalie. "Come on and pass me. The road is clear," she whispered.

Out of the corner of her eye, she saw that the vehicle nearly beside them now was a pickup. A *tan* pickup! Her heart nearly stopped as she caught a glimpse of the driver's baseball cap. The light was bad, but she now knew who it was.

Refusing to admit defeat, she let off on the gas, hoping he'd shoot past her, but the truck stayed even with her. Prayers forgotten, she concentrated solely on survival. Nothing else mattered now.

Then the pickup accelerated and swerved

into their lane. Jessica hit the brakes instinctively. "Hang on, Natalie!" she screamed. The loud, metallic screech that followed drowned out the sounds of their terror.

The car trembled and they ricocheted off to the right, onto the shoulder of the road. Jessica fought the wheel, afraid they'd turn over on the soft ground. A heartbeat later they hit something hard and the car jumped, then skidded through brush and crashed through a wooden fence. The wild bouncing seemed to go on forever, then the car came to an abrupt stop.

Jessica's head slammed into the steering wheel, and bounced back painfully. An all-encompassing darkness threatened to overcome her, but she fought it back, knowing what was at stake. Something warm was running down her face — not rain. Her nose was numb and probably broken, and her lips were starting to swell.

The headlights were still on, though the engine had stopped, and she saw a figure pause in front of their car. Recognizing the face in the glare helped her summon up her courage and she strained to move her head, looking for Natalie.

"Mom? You're hurt. There's blood on your face."

"Natalie, get out of the car. Now! Run and hide."

"Mom?"

Hearing the fear in her child's voice tore at her very soul, but there was no time to comfort her. "Run and hide, Natalie. Now!" Jessica's head almost exploded as she moved, but she reached out and pushed Natalie.

Even as the pain came to her in waves too powerful to fight, the darkness called softly to her. The sudden breeze that told her Natalie had opened the door helped her hang on a moment longer. "Run!" Jessica managed once more, her voice thick.

Hearing a thud on the windshield Jessica forced herself to look back. A hand was pressed against the glass, and she heard her name being called. But the voice quickly blended with the sounds of the night and began fading away. Blackness awaited, and within that was peace — and silence.

1

Silence defined the monastery — except during recreation. The hour before Compline, the concluding canonical hour of the Divine Office, was a time of community togetherness. Pictures and letters from family and friends, parts of the lives they'd each left behind, were passed around freely. Over the years, the names and faces had all become part of a bigger family here at Our Lady of Hope Monastery.

Tonight, Sister Maria Victoria had photos of her new baby niece to show, and Sister Gertrude had received a letter announcing that her cousin had entered the priesthood. On the outside, these bits of news might have been glossed over, but here they were savored and relished as gifts from an ever present and good God.

Sadness, too, was more bearable a burden when shared by the entire community. After Sister Clothilde's sister had passed away at another monastery few months ago, everyone had taken part in an all-night vigil. Through their shared prayers, the pain of one had been borne by many shoulders, lessening its crushing weight.

Now laughter rose easily among them almost in defiance of the storm brewing outside. The windowpanes rattled as the wind whistled through the cracks, announcing the rain that would quickly follow. As was the custom among long-time New Mexico residents, the nuns walked to the open back door to watch the rare event. Pax, the monastery's large, white German shepherd, remained behind, content to sleep through the commotion.

"We're in for a gully washer tonight," Sister Bernarda said. The former Marine turned nun had a delivery that made even the simplest of sentences sound like an order.

"This should help ease the drought a bit. It'll be a blessing, providing the rain doesn't evaporate before it hits the ground," Sister Agatha said quietly. Truth was, she didn't like thunderstorms.

"This storm *will* bring a blessing," Sister Ignatius said excitedly. "Look! Do you see it?"

"What?" Sister Agatha asked, glancing

over Sister Bernarda's massive shoulders.

"There! That cloud looks just like an angel with huge, feathered wings. This morning at prayer I asked the Lord to send us an angel as a sign that the monastery's financial problems would soon be over, and there it is! And just to make it perfect, the angel has appeared to us in the middle of a storm!"

Sister Agatha looked up at the clouds and tilted her head, trying to discern the shape Sister Ignatius was describing. As she brought her cheek down and pushed it against her shoulder, a form began to take shape — but she couldn't swear that it wasn't a giant rabbit.

Sister Bernarda looked at Sister Agatha and shrugged.

"Maybe the angel won't appear to us externs," Sister Agatha told Sister Bernarda with a ghost of a smile.

"It's the price we pay for not taking a vow of enclosure — we become too affected by the world," Sister de Lourdes, their newest extern said, joining them.

"I suppose it's all in how you look at it, but in my opinion we externs have the best job of all," Sister Agatha said with complete conviction. Extern nuns were part of the contemplative life of the monastery where prayers and a lifetime spent in service to

God defined who and what they were. But externs also ventured into the outside world. The monastery relied on them to run errands, escort a plumber or an electrician onto the premises, and to be the liaison between the monastery and the community. It was that duality Sister Agatha loved the most, and she couldn't imagine any greater blessing.

Sister Agatha glanced at Sister de Lourdes.

The petite young woman had been known as Celia just two short years ago, a postulant headed for a life as a cloistered nun. But now she was an extern nun, having placed her own wishes aside to answer the needs of the monastery. Celia had been her godchild, and Sister Agatha hadn't exactly welcomed her into the monastery. But there was no doubt that Sister de Lourdes's calling was genuine.

Sister Agatha's musings were interrupted when the bell announcing Compline rang. The sisters stepped away from the door, heads bowed, and began walking silently toward chapel. The stillness that surrounded them now as they entered the chapel provided a comfort all its own. It was the serenity and quiet that helped make Our Lady of Hope Monastery a spiritual fortress. Body and soul had to be at peace before the heart could attain union with the Divine.

As they began chanting the Divine Office, Sister Agatha felt a clear sense of God's presence. Compline meant "to make the day complete" and that was precisely what the liturgical hour did. The prayers being chanted now were a daily reminder that He whom they served was faithful.

"And under His wings shall thou find refuge." The words of the psalm said it all. Here at Our Lady of Hope, she'd found the "pearl of great price" that had required her to give up everything to possess it. A woman surrendered much when she answered God's call. Turning her back on the right to have children and a family of her own, Sister Agatha had embraced another life, one where the spirit was fed daily, but human needs had to be set aside. Yet this was precisely where she belonged.

After Compline, the Great Silence began. Except for a grave emergency, it wouldn't be broken until after Morning Prayers the following day. Listening to the storm raging outside, Sister Agatha lingered in chapel after the cloistered sisters had left. The two other externs, whose duties often prevented them from having time for silent meditation, had also chosen to remain.

Sister Agatha's gaze focused on the sanctuary light flickering over the tabernacle. The flame was a symbol of the living presence there — of the One they loved. Though rain continued to fall outside and the rumble of thunder shook the windows, the menacing gloom couldn't disturb the blessed serenity of their chapel.

As the rain peaked in intensity, Sister Agatha heard one of the branches of the cottonwood tree outside hit the roof with a heavy thud. Flat roofs — old flat roofs — had a tendency to leak, particularly during downpours like the one they were experiencing now. She made a mental note to check things out tomorrow morning.

Focusing once again on her prayers, Sister Agatha's gaze shifted to the statue of the Blessed Mother. The stand of votive candles before it cast a maze of dancing shadows on the wall, but it was the liquid shimmer there that drew her to her feet and in for a closer look.

As Sister Agatha reached the far corner, her fears were confirmed. Water was trickling down from the ceiling. The light from the candles played on the drops, making them sparkle with a benign grace that was dangerously deceptive. A water leak here in the chapel could do untold damage.

She felt a hand on her shoulder. Turning her head, she saw Sister Bernarda standing there with a worried frown. Sister de Lourdes approached a moment later from the sacristy, flashlight in hand. After using a bright light to examine the rivulets of water running to the floor, Sister de Lourdes pointed to the ceiling, which was bowed slightly in one section. Sister Bernarda looked back at Sister Agatha and, without breaking the Great Silence, pointed with her thumb toward the chapel doors.

It was obvious that she wanted to go up to the roof now and not wait until morning. Sister Agatha nodded in agreement. The water would have to be drained immediately to prevent the ceiling from collapsing.

Sister Agatha went to the front doors and stepped outside. Lightning was only visible behind the mountains now, and there was no more rain. The downpour had been typical of New Mexico storms — impressive but short-lived.

Sister de Lourdes and Sister Bernarda came out to join her a moment later. After seeing that the *canales,* the protruding gutters, were clogged and the water wasn't draining properly, Sister Bernarda and Sister de Lourdes followed her lead and walked to a storage shed to retrieve a long ladder and more flashlights.

Once the ladder was in position, Sister de Lourdes climbed up while Sister Bernarda held it steady and Sister Agatha aimed a flashlight. But as Sister de Lourdes reached the highest safe rung, it was clear she was too short to hoist herself up onto the roof.

Sister Agatha took a deep breath then signalled for Sister de Lourdes to come down. A few minutes later, trying to ignore the way her arthritic joints screamed with pain in this kind of weather, Sister Agatha stepped onto the ladder. Sister Bernarda's fear of heights was something she'd never quite mastered, and making her climb up now with only the glow of a flashlight for guidance seemed uncharitable. It was up to her.

Sister Bernarda tapped her on the leg, signalling for her to come back down. Sister Agatha came off the ladder and stepped away. Before she could figure out what was going on, Sister Bernarda grasped the sides of the ladder and climbed up.

With a sigh, Sister Agatha helped Sister de Lourdes steady the ladder and aim the flashlights. So many people thought that they lived loveless lives here in the monastery, but she'd seen more genuine affection since her arrival at Our Lady of Hope than she'd ever known on the outside. Love here often took the form of small, selfless acts of courage like what Sister Bernarda had just done.

Sister Agatha placed her flashlight in a pocket, forced her swollen hands to grip the sides of the ladder, and climbed up to join Sister Bernarda. Two could work faster than one. As she hoisted herself up onto the roof, she saw Sister Bernarda's grateful smile.

The *canales* were clogged and blocked by branches, leaves, and plant debris. Oblivious to the light drizzle that had started, they cleared the *canales* and soon were ready to go back down. Sister Agatha went first. Sister Bernarda was a large woman and it would take two of them on the ground to steady the ladder for her.

Once the signal was given, Sister Bernarda went down slowly, feeling her way with each step, but as her foot touched the last rung of the ladder, she slipped and fell unceremoniously to the ground.

Hearing Sister Bernarda moan softly as she reached for her ankle, Sister Agatha looked over quickly at Sister de Lourdes. The younger nun nodded and ran inside to search for Sister Eugenia. The infirmarian was needed now.

Sister Bernarda struggled to her feet and, grudgingly accepting Sister Agatha's help, hobbled back inside the chapel. As they stepped through the massive wooden doors and entered the cloistered side, Sister Eugenia suddenly appeared, pushing an empty wheelchair.

Sister Agatha recognized it instantly as the one Sister Gertrude had been using since her second heart attack. Here, everything was shared as the need arose.

Seeing the wheelchair, Sister Bernarda took a wobbly step backward and shook her head in protest. However, Sister Eugenia's formidable stare left no room for objections. Mortified, Sister Bernarda sat down and allowed herself to be wheeled out of the chapel.

As soon as they entered the infirmary, Sister Eugenia spoke. "The vow of charity takes precedence over the vow of silence, so speak freely and tell me what happened," she said.

"It was my fault," Sister Bernarda whispered, making sure her voice didn't carry. "I was so relieved to be close to the ground again that I hurried — and slipped."

Sister Eugenia took off Sister Bernarda's *alpargates,* the rope-soled sandals they all wore, then removed her wet woolen sock.

As she did, they all saw the tattoo above her ankle that read, SEMPER FI. The dagger between the words almost looked like a cross.

Seeing it, Sister Eugenia laughed. Noticing the uncomfortable look on Sister Bernarda's face, she added, "I'm sorry, Your Charity. I just didn't expect the tattoo."

Sister Agatha smiled widely. Somehow that didn't surprise her at all. "At least the words that go along with that tattoo seem appropriate to our life here, too. Do you have any others?"

"You'll never know," Sister Bernarda answered with a trace of a smile.

After rubbing ointment over the ankle area, Sister Eugenia stepped back to evaluate her work. "All you have is a minor sprain. The ointment will help the swelling and the pain," she said. Refusing to let Sister Bernarda leave the infirmary, Sister Eugenia led her to the cot. "Tonight, Sister, you'll remain here."

Assured that all was well, Sister Agatha stepped to the door and nearly collided with Sister de Lourdes. "I found some more leaks in the chapel," Sister de Lourdes whispered at the infirmary doorway. "I've placed buckets beneath them, and brought towels to absorb any splashing or spills."

"There's nothing more we can do tonight. We'll have to call in a roofer tomorrow. For now, you should go to bed. I have a feeling tomorrow will be a very long day."

Sister de Lourdes bowed her head and hurried silently down the corridor. Sister Agatha continued more slowly to her own room, known as a cell. She was incredibly cold and the wet fabric of her habit felt as heavy as chain mail. Quickly slipping into another dry habit, she looked wistfully at her bed, where Pax was snoring contentedly, then hurried back to the chapel.

Sister Agatha entered through the side door leading from the enclosure. Only candles illuminated the interior now, but even in the flickering glow she could see fresh leaks everywhere. She was nearly finished positioning more buckets beneath the drips when she heard a rustle of cloth from somewhere behind her. Glancing back, she saw Reverend Mother watching her.

Sister Agatha shook her head imperceptibly, letting the abbess know that the situation was grave. She was considering breaking the Great Silence and going up to talk to her when she heard a new plopping sound. Spotting a new leak near the second station of the cross, she hauled out another bucket from the sacristy and positioned it beneath the steady drip.

After wiping up the water that had collected there with a towel, she was ready to call it a night, but just then a loud ring sounded. It was the telephone in Reverend Mother's office, down the hall.

Sister Agatha's heart began to beat faster. There were only two phones in the monastery — one in the parlor, and a separate phone line in Reverend Mother's office. As their abbess, it was necessary for Reverend Mother to maintain her own link to the outside. Calls from the archdiocese and the Mother House usually went directly to her. But nothing except an all-out emergency would have caused that phone to ring at this hour. Glancing down the hall, she saw Reverend Mother hurrying to answer it.

Sister Agatha followed Reverend Mother to the office, ready to serve if needed and preparing for the worst.

2

Sister Agatha raised her arm to knock, but at that instant Reverend Mother opened the door. Seeing Sister Agatha, she whispered, "Praised be Jesus Christ."

"Now and forever." Reverend Mother's breach of the Great Silence shattered her hope that the telephone call had been a wrong number.

"Come in, child," Reverend Mother said quietly.

Sister Agatha entered, her heart racing. For Mother's sake, she was determined to appear calm, but that took willpower.

Sister Bernarda appeared at the door a few seconds later and Reverend Mother gestured for her to come in. As she did, Reverend Mother gave the ex-Marine a concerned look. "I know about your accident, child. Are you sure you should be walking?"

"I'm fine, Mother," Sister Bernarda said,

ing lot was rolling toward a man in a wheelchair. Natalie saw it and yelled 'stop'—and the car suddenly came to a complete standstill. There was no one at all in the car, and though there were several witnesses, nobody could explain why the car stopped. One of the TV shows picked up the story after that and ran a sensationalist feature claiming Natalie's angel had saved the day."

"That would have made a good story, all right."

"Of course the church hasn't made an official statement and probably won't in a case like this. But this whole thing has sure put Father Mahoney in a difficult position."

Less than fifteen minutes later, they arrived at the rectory behind the town's adobe and brick Catholic church near the center of old Bernalillo. The rectory was a small building with desert landscaping all around it.

Sister Agatha helped Sister Bernarda out of the sidecar, then walked with her to the front door. "I'll make sure Sister de Lourdes picks you up in the Antichrysler after we're done here," Sister Agatha said, using the nickname they'd given the monastery's ancient car.

Mrs. Frances Williams, the rectory's

housekeeper, answered the door. "I've been expecting you two. Reverend Mother called a little while ago."

Sister Bernarda explained their plan, then added, "I'll free you up here and that way you can join the search."

"That would be great. I'll need you to call the names on the list that Father Mahoney gave me. They're mostly friends of Natalie, teachers, and parishioners who live in the general vicinity of the accident site. Ask if they've seen her, and relay any messages that come in."

"No problem," Sister Bernarda said briskly. "Now you two need to go help find Natalie." Sister Bernarda took the list that Frances handed her. "I'll do what has to be done here."

"I really appreciate this, Sister. A girl that age alone . . ." Frances's voice trailed off and she wiped an errant tear away with a shaky hand. "Just follow me on the motorcycle, Sister Agatha, and I'll show you where the sheriff has set up his command center."

Sister Agatha followed Frances out of town, driving south. It felt colder now than when she'd started out. The rain was nothing more than a mist, but it clung to her clothing like plaster, weighing it down. Forcing her discomfort aside, Sister Agatha focused on Natalie and tried to remember their conversations. Maybe if she thought about those hard enough, she'd recall something that would tell her where the girl would likely go if she was afraid or in trouble. However, the harder she tried, the more she blanked out. The same switch that kept her fear under control had apparently put a tight lock on her thoughts, as well.

After following Frances for five minutes they arrived at the makeshift command center — an abandoned roadside fruit stand less than a hundred feet from where Jessica Tannen's car had skidded off the road. The vehicle, surrounded by yellow crime scene tape, still hadn't been moved, and its front tires were suspended in midair over a muddy arroyo.

Floodlights powered by a portable generator illuminated the wreck and the wood-framed fruit stand. Sheriff Green was speaking to a group of people in various styles of rain gear holding lanterns or large flashlights.

She'd just climbed off the cycle and was attaching a leash to Pax's collar when Smitty, the owner and manager of the largest independent grocery store in town, came up to her.

"I thought you'd show up soon, Sister,"

he said. "We have a good turnout of volunteers anxious to help out so I'm sure we'll find Natalie — if she's still in the area."

"So they haven't ruled out kidnapping?" Sister Agatha managed through the fist-sized lump in her throat.

"Not yet," he answered in a soft voice. "The sheriff found footprints that were probably Natalie's leading into the brush, but the trail fizzles out after a few yards. The rain's really creating a problem for the police."

Smitty was tall and lean. His thin brown hair had long disappeared on top, giving way to a shiny skull that had people wondering if he buffed it. Even now, in this weather, he was meticulously dressed. Water beaded up on his warm-looking black raincoat, and his tan boots held a coat of polish despite the muddy ground.

"In addition to the search and rescue people, several local businessmen, including Joseph Carlisle, Jessica's boss, have shown up, ready to help. And everyone on the Interfaith Council is here as well," he continued. "When a child goes missing, we all take it personally." He paused, then added, "It's just a shame that it takes an incident like this to pull everyone together." He took a step back as Pax shifted.

Noticing Smitty's reaction, Sister Agatha said. "Relax. He's harmless."

"Oh, sure. Those teeth are just for show."

"He's smiling at you," she said, then looked ahead at Tom Green, their sheriff, who was speaking to someone on his hand-held radio and reading a note one of the deputies had handed him. Tom had a son Natalie's age, and, no doubt, this case hit a bit too close to home for him. He'd want any child lost on his turf found — and fast.

"Looks like they're dividing up all the large fields and sections of the bosque leading in every direction," she noted, looking at the map Sheriff Green had tacked up on the back wall of the fruit stand. "I assume all the major roads are being covered by deputies and law enforcement agencies. Is anyone searching the little side roads, the one-vehicle dirt tracks? A frightened kid running away from here might not stick to the roads, especially if she thinks someone's after her."

"Sounds like you've got some good ideas. Better talk to the sheriff when he's finished," Smitty suggested.

"Father has some real friends here," she answered gently.

"He's a good man," Smitty said. "And right now he's determined to do whatever's

39

necessary to find Natalie."

"I didn't see Father when I pulled up. Is he here now?"

Smitty shook his head. "He went out with the first search team. I don't think he could bear to stand still."

Before she could reply, Sheriff Tom Green approached. "Sister Agatha, I'm glad you're here and that you brought the Harley. That cycle can go where cars can't in this weather, and I've got a grid along the edge of the bosque I want you to search. Good thing you brought Pax, too. If you end up having to do some walking, the dog will be an asset. He'll let you know if someone else is around."

"We figured he might be useful," she said.

"I want you and Smitty to team up. No one searches alone tonight. The roads are slick and dangerous, and if we're dealing with a kidnapper, we don't want anyone else at risk."

"Were there any skid marks or other indications that this was more than just someone running off the road in a rainstorm?" Sister Agatha asked.

"The dual skid marks we found, and the damage to Mrs. Tannen's vehicle on the driver's side, indicate she was sideswiped. We haven't determined if she was forced off the road or lost control after the collision," he said in a barely audible voice, "but a witness saw someone in another vehicle fleeing the scene." His gaze strayed along the roadside as various search teams got underway and additional volunteers arrived. "I've got to tell you, whether we're dealing with a carjacker, kidnapper, or simply a drunk driver, I sure hope one of my officers finds him first. The community volunteers are angry as . . . well, you know. They won't be gentle bringing him in, especially if he's got the girl and she's been injured or mistreated."

Tom led them to the map and indicated a section on the east side of the river. "I want you to concentrate your search where the tree line begins. The bosque, especially during the rain and wind, might have looked too dark and frightening to Natalie, but it's possible she ducked beneath the trees along the edge. Or maybe she's scared and has holed up somewhere. That motorcycle will take you into places most cars can't go, and you can also search for a trail on foot. I see a big flashlight in your jacket pocket, but did you bring along the cell phone I gave you for emergencies?"

She nodded, then brought it out. "Right here, fully charged and turned on."

"Good. I'll give the number to my deputy in case you need to be contacted."

As Sister Agatha walked back with Smitty to the motorcycle, she noticed him giving Pax uneasy glances.

"How am I supposed to share the sidecar with *him?*" Smitty finally asked. "He's an ex-police dog. What if I make a wrong move and he goes for the closest body part?"

Sister Agatha laughed. "Pax isn't vicious or temperamental. Besides, he's a civilian now, retrained so he could live with us. Just tell him to sit and stay."

"I'm a cat person, and this animal's nearly the size of the Great White Buffalo. Are you sure he's trustworthy around someone who's not wearing a habit or a badge?"

"Absolutely. Stop being such a sissy," she teased.

"Easy for you to say," he muttered.

Smitty stepped into the sidecar and sat down on the small bench. Pax jumped in, sitting right between Smitty's outstretched legs, looking right into his face. "What if he smells Preacher, my cat? He might suddenly remember he's descended from predators," Smitty whispered.

"He likes cats."

"Grilled or deep fried?"

With a reassuring smile, Sister Agatha

maneuvered away from the maze of vehicles alongside the fruit stand command post and drove directly to the area that the sheriff had mapped out for them. They began at the southernmost path leading toward the thickly wooded area on both sides of the Rio Grande, their route lit by the single headlight of the Harley, and Smitty searching to the side with the flashlight. Sister Agatha realized she'd have to move carefully to avoid being stuck, and only stop on firm ground.

Smitty called out, "Why are we searching here? From what I've been told, Natalie wasn't the outdoorsy type. She'd rather be in a library than alongside a ditch bank."

Sister nodded slowly. "You're right. But we have to rule out every possibility. A scared kid doesn't always opt for the logical, especially if someone's chasing her. Let's see if we can find any sign that she came through here," Sister Agatha said, parking on a grassy area that looked well drained. "If not, we'll head back and get a new assignment."

With Smitty to her right, and Pax heeling on her left, they walked along the tree line of the bosque, flashlights in hand, heading north and occasionally calling out the girl's name.

"We should have been able to spot foot-prints even if she came here during the worst of the rain, especially on my side where the trees begin and the ground is drier," Smitty said. "But what if she's been taken by some desperate parent or religious fanatic? That story on television was really something. They made her look like a kid with a direct line to the spirit world and an angel for a sidekick. I'm surprised Father Mahoney didn't see this coming."

"We all assumed people would realize that Natalie's just a kid — admittedly, one with a terrific imagination," Sister Agatha said, defending the monastery's chaplain. "That show, I'm told, has also run features on UFOs and werewolves. Their credibility fac-tor is pretty close to zero."

"I'm not so sure. That segment about Na-talie was impressive. No one could explain how that car managed to start rolling, or what made it stop in time if it wasn't because of Natalie or her angel. And there's another story going around about the girl, too. Apparently Natalie warned a classmate to watch out for a fire at her home, and the house *did* catch fire later that same night. The family managed to escape because Na-talie's friend had remained watchful, though she never told her parents about the warning until afterwards."

"The church is looking into all that, Smitty, but nothing's been sanctioned. If I were you, I'd take everything you've heard with a large grain of salt." Sister Agatha paused for a moment, then continued slowly. "I may be wrong about this part, but I get the feeling that Father Mahoney doesn't buy any of it."

"I know he's asked Natalie not to talk about it anymore."

Sister Agatha wasn't surprised by how much Smitty knew. Smitty genuinely liked people and always took time to talk to them when they came into his store.

"Father doesn't want the stories to mislead people. As Catholics we believe in saints and angels, but God is the only one who should be worshipped."

"We differ on that saint business," he answered with a smile, "but I agree with the rest." He paused for a long moment, then exhaled softly as they continued to look for a trail. "Poor Jessica. Things just seem to go from bad to worse for her lately. More than anything she wants her daughter to be treated like a regular kid again. That's why she refuses to let Natalie do anything that sets her apart. She even pulled her out of art class, though Natalie's a first-rate sculptress. Natalie's teacher was really upset about that decision. She's from our church, so I heard all about it. When I ran into Jessica at the store, I did my best to get her to change her mind about that, but I didn't have any luck."

"Jessica's worried and with reason. Let's face it, the world's seldom kind to anyone who's different," she said, carefully searching the ground.

They continued for two hours, covering their area from one end to the other and calling out until their voices were hoarse. By then Smitty was sneezing every few seconds and was shivering from the cold despite his raincoat.

"I'm going to drop you off at the command center. You need a hat and something warm to drink," Sister Agatha said at last. "We've searched our area completely and Natalie obviously never came this way."

"If she's on her own and scared, my guess is that she'll head someplace familiar to her — someplace dry," he said, coughing.

"There are people at the rectory, her home, and even her school just in case she goes there," Sister Agatha said.

Smitty shook his head. "No, I don't think she'd go to any of those places. School is locked up tight at this hour, and the other places are too far away. I think she'd head someplace closer. Maybe the monastery."

"I sure hope so. If Natalie goes there, she'll be safe and Sister de Lourdes will notify everyone here immediately."

As Sister parked the motorcycle, Smitty climbed out stiffly. "I'm going to get myself a big mug of hot coffee. Want some?"

"No, thanks. I need a chance to think things through. I have a strong feeling that we're missing something."

"The search grids are meant to make sure we don't miss anything. They even overlap. Sheriff Green's being thorough."

"I know, but . . ." She shrugged.

With Pax in the sidecar, curled nearly into a ball to stay warm, Sister Agatha took a quick pass down the road that led to the monastery. Something Smitty had said kept playing over and over in her mind. If Natalie was alone and frightened, she'd go someplace where she'd feel safe. The monastery was one possibility, of course, but surely she had her own special places. Kids always did.

Turning around, she went back to the command post. Hector Mondragon, the town's barber and one of the most plainspoken men she'd ever met, was talking to the deputy at the radio table when she walked by. He looked up, catching her eye.

"Hermanita," he said bowing his head. "Heckuva night."

She nodded somberly. "No one's had any luck?"

"Not yet. We've taken all the right steps, but I think we need more help," he said, and pointed upwards. "Smitty led some of the others in prayer a few minutes ago. Then Reverend Peterson, from the Baptist church at the north end of town, decided that the Presbyterians and Catholics shouldn't be the only ones petitioning God at a time like this, so he started a prayer group at his church. The Good Lord said he had many sheep, and I reckon tonight he's gonna hear from all of them."

"Good. The sisters are starting a vigil, too. We'll storm the kingdom of heaven with prayers until Natalie's found."

"I sure hope we find her, and soon. If we don't, it won't be long before people will start throwing blame around. The mayor will take heat for not fixing our bad roads, then the police will come under fire for not keeping reckless drivers off the streets, and the list will go on and on." Hearing someone call his name, Hector strode away quickly.

Sister Agatha watched him go, unsettled by the truth in his words. He was right —

unity during a crisis seldom carried the seeds of permanence. Time was working against them on every imaginable level.

3

After a fruitless night of searching, Sister Agatha finally returned to the monastery. Sister Bernarda had caught a ride with Frances an hour earlier and was waiting for her in the parlor, hoping to hear some positive news. Sister Agatha shook her head in response to her unspoken question, noting at a glance that she hadn't slept a wink either.

Sister Agatha stopped by the provisory, the pantry, and offered Pax a bowl of kibble. The dog took a few bites, then lay down, opting for sleep instead.

Breakfast was in the refectory, the monastery's dining room. It was a simple meal — mostly bread, today toasted and with homemade apple butter — plus tea or coffee. A somber mood had settled over everyone. Sister Ignatius was staring at the wall, where a large wooden cross had been hung over a small table that held a skull. Its purpose was to remind the sisters of the shortness of earthly life. Looking over at Sister Ignatius's plate, Sister Agatha couldn't help but notice that it was empty. Although fasts were common here, she hated to see the older nuns follow that practice.

With a sigh, she listened as Sister Gertrude, their only speaker, read from the martyrology, following the rule that required them to feed their spirits, not just their bodies, at mealtime. This morning, however, the heroics of the saints failed to give her any comfort.

Morning Prayers followed breakfast. Sister Agatha went to the parlor, giving Sister Bernarda the chance to attend Divine Office in chapel before trying to grab a few hours of sleep for herself. As the soft sounds of chanting filled the empty corridors, Sister Agatha called the rectory, hoping for some good news.

"I was just about to call you, Sister," Frances said. "Father Mahoney asked me to tell the sisters that because of the circumstances, he wants to celebrate Mass at a different time today. He was hoping to be there at nine thirty."

"That's fine. I'm sure none of us expected him to say Mass this morning at all, though the truth is that we need it more than ever," she answered softly. "How's he dealing with the pressure? I never did see him last night."

"He's a strong man, but even Father is starting to wear down a little," she said. "Is Sister Bernarda planning to return to the rectory today so I can go back out and join the search?"

"Yes, I'm sure she is. But we both need a couple of hours of sleep or we won't be any good to anyone."

"Me, too," she said. "Why don't I save you some trouble and pick her up after Mass?"

Sister Agatha placed the phone down, and after Morning Prayers, went to tell Reverend Mother about the schedule change for Mass. The abbess would give the others the news after Terce, which was said at eight, and commemorated the third hour, when the Holy Spirit descended on the apostles.

Back on duty at her desk a few minutes later, Sister Agatha searched for the leather-bound book that listed the companies the monastery did business with, and found it in the bottom drawer of the desk.

Sister Bernarda came in a moment later. "Don't forget to call the roofing company. Some of the leaks in the chapel seem to have gotten worse. There's still too much water on the roof, apparently. I wanted to go up there myself, but Sister Eugenia stopped me."

"I'll call the roofers and have them take care of the problem. Right now you and I need to get some sleep, then we'll attend Mass and go back out," she said, telling her about Frances's call. Hearing a soft knock, they glanced up as Sister de Lourdes entered the parlor.

"Praised be Jesus Christ," she said.

"Now and forever," they both answered.

"I've come to work as portress. Both of you need some rest."

"You look very tired yourself. Did you get any sleep?" Sister Bernarda asked her.

"Some, but since I won't be going out to search, it's not as critical for me."

"The desk is yours, Sister. Will you call the roofer for us?" Sister Agatha asked, giving her the book and pointing out the firm.

"I'll make all the arrangements. Don't give it another thought," Sister de Lourdes said. Before Sister Agatha could go inside the enclosure, she added, "Sister Eugenia said that you're to take the pills she left for you in your cell."

Sister Agatha nodded, grateful for the ever attentive Sister Eugenia, who best exemplified the high ideals of every nun at Our Lady of Hope Monastery. Though her work as infirmarian could be brutal, she'd faithfully devoted herself to it. Mixing duty with all the love she had to give, Sister Eugenia's heart was never far from her Lord's.

"If there's any news of Natalie, wake me up immediately," Sister Agatha said as she headed into the enclosure.

"Me, too," Sister Bernarda added.

The moment she entered her cell, Sister Agatha saw the pills Sister Eugenia had left beside a cup of water on the dresser. She swallowed them all at once, then went to lay down, pulling the blanket over her. Exhaustion overruled the pain and stiffness in her joints and she drifted off into a deep sleep.

It felt as if she'd only just closed her eyes when she was awakened by a hand on her shoulder. Sister Agatha opened her eyes and saw Sister Bernarda standing over her.

"Did they find her?" Sister Agatha asked quickly, sitting up.

"No, Sister, but Reverend Mother needs us."

Sister Agatha rose and checked her wristwatch. She'd been asleep almost three hours. "I've missed Mass!"

"So did I, but Reverend Mother insisted that no one wake us. Since Natalie hasn't been found, we'll need to set out again shortly."

"Natalie's missing, the roof is practically on its last legs . . . It can't get worse than this," Sister Agatha said.

When Sister Agatha and Sister Bernarda arrived at Reverend Mother's office, they found Father Mahoney there. Although he was a former wrestler and had the constitution of an ox, the priest looked as if he'd aged twenty years.

"Did you get any sleep at all last night, Father?" Sister Agatha asked, her heart going out to him.

"How can I sleep? My niece is missing, maybe the target of a kidnapper, and my sister is in a coma. Jessica had been getting threatening letters and phone calls, and had even made plans to leave town and start over in another community. If I'd paid closer attention and pressed her to leave sooner, this might not have happened. And now I keep thinking that there's someplace I should be looking, and if I could just figure out where that is, I'd find Natalie."

She'd felt exactly the same way last night. Maybe it was just a way of coping with their helplessness and fears. "We'll do all we can to help you but you have to rest," Sister Agatha insisted.

"I'm resting now. Sleep is out of the question."

"All the sisters are praying for your niece, Father," Reverend Mother said softly. "She *will* be found. Despite the report of another person at the scene, and the threats that obviously have been causing a lot of concern, there's no evidence to confirm that someone took her. She might have been dazed and just wandered away on her own."

"Father, why don't you lie down in the room off the sacristy for just a little bit," Sister Agatha suggested, afraid that he was in no condition to drive.

"I can't afford to rest now, but I'll take a few minutes to pray in the chapel before I go."

As he stood, Sister Bernarda gave him an encouraging smile. "I'll go with you, Father. We'll pray together."

After they'd left, Reverend Mother looked at Sister Agatha. "Go out and look for Natalie. Do whatever's necessary. This situation . . ."

"I'll do everything I can, Mother." Sister Agatha walked to the door, then glanced back. Reverend Mother was standing in front of the statue of the Blessed Virgin, rosary in hand, already in prayer.

Her duty clear, Sister Agatha went to the

kitchen and woke up Pax. Half of his food still remained, so she fed him by hand until he started eating on his own. "You have to keep up your strength, buddy. We have another long stretch of work ahead of us."

Sister Clothilde, in her eighties and the eldest among them, came out of the kitchen just then, and leaned down to give the dog a slice of cinnamon bread. Pax ate it in one gulp.

"Thank you, Sister," she said, not expecting an answer. Sister Clothilde hadn't broken her vow of silence in over thirty years.

The elderly nun then handed Sister Agatha a small loaf of cinnamon bread covered in plastic wrap.

"Oh, this isn't necessary." She knew that Sister Clothilde baked the small cinnamon loaves as a treat for Reverend Mother and Sister Gertrude. But Sister Clothilde refused to take it back, and gently ushered her out of the kitchen.

Sister Agatha ate some of the bread as she went outside to the motorcycle, then, as a sign of hope, stuck the remainder of the loaf in her pocket.

Pax looked at her hopefully. "No. That's for Natalie. When we find her — and we will — she'll be hungry."

As Sister Agatha drove down the long gravel road that led away from the monastery, she moved slowly, searching for footprints down the single-lane paths that intersected the main road. Most eventually led to farmhouses or, in a few cases, small businesses of one variety or another.

In the light of a new day the search went easier, but clouds were massing again, and from the looks of it, it would rain again by midafternoon. Although their prayers for rain had been granted, what would have otherwise been a blessing now spelled potential disaster. Even if she was safe from harm, Natalie was bound to be cold, miserable, and hungry. Another downpour would not only worsen her condition, it would obscure what was left of her trail.

Worried and not at all sure what to do next, Sister Agatha pulled to the side of the road and let the engine idle. Realizing Pax was looking at her quizzically, she reached out to pet him. "It's okay," she assured him. Bowing her head in prayer, she whispered, "Lord, I know you're trying to tell me something. This feeling that I'm missing something just won't go away. But you're going to have to speak louder."

Suddenly a bright flash of lightning cut across the base of a gray, flat-based cloud, followed by an earth-shaking crash of thunder. Sister Agatha swallowed, then took an unsteady breath, struggling to lean on logic. It had been coincidence, of course, but still a bit unnerving. Then, as she stared at the cloud that the lightning had emanated from, she suddenly remembered something important. The old adobe church that had been deconsecrated and sold several years ago lay in that direction. These days it was closed — the efforts to restore it were on hold until the local historical society came up with the funds to complete the project.

Natalie had told her once in passing how much she liked the angels that had been carved into the wood over the tabernacle area. If Natalie was on her own and scared, she'd head there. Sister Agatha put the motorcycle in gear and took off again at a quick pace, wanting to reach the old church while the weather held. Hope swelled inside her even as she tried to caution herself against expecting too much. They'd all prayed hard for Natalie's safety and had asked for God's blessing on their search — surely it wasn't out of line to believe they'd received an answer.

Although the old church was quite a way

from the accident scene — at least five miles — it wasn't an impossible distance for Natalie to have walked. If the girl had been afraid and trying to reach safety, she might have remembered that place, especially because of the angels.

Sister Agatha couldn't ignore the hollows and bumps in the tree-lined lane so she kept her speed slower than she would have liked because of Pax, who was getting jostled around a bit in the sidecar. A few minutes later, she skidded to a stop in the loose gravel at the front of the old church. Even at this distance she could see that the entrance was chained and padlocked. Fighting a wave of disappointment, Sister Agatha got off the bike. As she glanced at Pax, she saw him sniffing the air.

"Let's go, boy," she said, giving him the signal to join her.

Pax jumped out of the sidecar in one fluid motion, and ran around to the north side of the church. Looking back at her, he stopped beneath one of the long, narrow, double-hung windows, then began his rapid-fire barking that signalled someone was inside.

The window was open about sixteen inches, ample enough for a girl Natalie's size to wriggle through, but not an adult. Sister Agatha tugged at it, hoping to widen the opening so she could fit through, but it stuck after moving another foot and refused to budge.

Sister Agatha looked at Pax and considered her options. It didn't seem likely that Natalie was being held there against her will, but if the girl was inside alone, Pax might scare her. Praying that she wouldn't get stuck, Sister Agatha decided right then to force her way inside. She was relatively thin — with a bit of luck, she'd manage it.

Two minutes later, feeling bruised and scraped, but grateful to have made it in, she allowed Pax to scramble through, then put him on stay and glanced around. The only light source in the building came through the windows, but between the gloom of the gathering storm and the dirt that had accumulated on the windowpanes, everything looked dim and gray. A dozen or so old pews were pushed against one wall, and the area where the altar had stood was now an empty platform.

"Natalie, are you here?" Sister Agatha called out, hearing a scraping sound coming from the pews.

A head popped up from behind a backrest, and in a heartbeat, a little girl with waist-length brown hair and delicate features came rushing up. She launched herself into Sister Agatha's outstretched arms, nearly knocking her backwards.

Recapturing her balance quickly, Sister Agatha cupped Natalie's face in her hands, looking into her large hazel eyes. "Are you all right?" she asked, checking her for injuries.

"Yes, but my mom bumped her head and got cuts all over her face! The man who'd hit us was coming up to the car and Mom told me to run and hide. I did what she said, but then I got lost in the dark. I was so scared! Then my angel led me here and told me to wait. She said someone nice would come and take me back to my mom."

Despite the warmth of the old chapel, Sister Agatha felt a chill, knowing that someone had threatened the child. She led Natalie closer to the window for another good look at her. "Are you sure you're not hurt?"

"I'm okay, but we have to go get Mom!"

"She was taken to the hospital, and is getting the care she needs, Natalie. You don't have to worry anymore, but everyone's been out looking for you. We couldn't figure out where you'd gone," she said, continuing to check Natalie for cuts and bruises as she spoke. Finding none, she added, "Now we need to get back to the others and let them know you're safe. Are you warm enough?"

"Yes, Sister. I sat in front of the window when it was sunny earlier and let the sun dry off my feet. My raincoat keeps me warm on top."

Natalie tugged at Sister Agatha's hand, forcing her to look directly at her. "Is Mom really okay?"

As Sister Agatha saw herself reflected in those large innocent eyes, her stomach tightened. Natalie wanted answers she just couldn't give her. "You don't need to worry. You mom's in good hands," she said, side-stepping the question.

Natalie's eyes lowered as she pulled back her hand. "She was right," the girl said softly.

"Who?" Sister Agatha glanced around quickly, making sure they were alone.

"My angel," Natalie said, then looked down at the floor.

Sister Agatha caught only a glimpse of the emotion that had shimmered in Natalie's eyes before she'd looked away, but she had no trouble identifying it. Natalie had seen her evasion for what it was. In an attempt to protect the girl from the hard facts, she'd created a new problem. Trust could be almost unassailable under the right circumstances, but once broken it was nearly impossible to repair.

"Things are very complicated right now, Natalie." Sister Agatha tried to use her cell phone to let the others know that Natalie was all right, but she couldn't get a signal. "Your mom *is* getting the care she needs, but your uncle has been going out of his mind with worry. We have to get back quickly. People from all over town are out looking for you. You're a very lucky girl to have so many friends who care about you and want to help you and your mother."

Natalie held Sister Agatha's gaze for a moment, then shook her head. "People in town don't *really* like me. They think I'm weird. They just want me back because they think I can get my angel to help them."

Her words hadn't been bitter. Natalie had only stated the facts as she saw them. The reality of Natalie's situation hit Sister Agatha hard. For someone so young, she'd already seen way too much of the dark side of human nature.

"You're wrong to think that no one really cares, Natalie." Sister Agatha looked at the entrance doors and sighed, remembering they were chained shut on the outside. "We'll have to go back out through the window. Pax is over there waiting for us."

As they entered the small room, Pax's tail

wagged. "Okay, boy," she said, releasing him from stay. "Up, Pax." Sister Agatha touched the windowsill and Pax jumped out easily.

Natalie looked up at Sister Agatha and smiled expectantly. "He's a really cool dog. Are you on the motorcycle? Can I ride with Pax in the sidecar?"

At that precise moment, Natalie looked and sounded just like an ordinary eight-year-old, and the realization made a wave of relief sweep over her. Even the desperate circumstances hadn't stolen Natalie's excitement for life and new experiences. "Yes to both. Now let's go," Sister Agatha said, lifting Natalie up to the windowsill.

Once Natalie and Pax were safely nestled in the motorcycle's sidecar, Sister Agatha gave the girl a big chunk of cinnamon bread and said a quick prayer of thanks for Natalie's safety. Checking her cell phone, she was relieved to find that it was receiving a signal, so she called in, then started up the Harley and headed to the sheriff's station in Bernalillo. EMTs would check out Natalie there and make sure that she was as okay as ˙˙ to be. A clinic was just down ˙˙ became necessary.

˙ made a mental note to ˙˙˙˙ ˙ as soon as she reached the ˙uld relieve the minds of all there when they learned that Natalie had been found safe and sound. Maybe she could get permission to remain with Natalie while Sheriff Green questioned her. It was inevitable now, considering Jessica's last words to her daughter — "Run and hide."

Natalie would have to answer tough questions about the collision and the man who'd caused it all. The child would be forced to relive what had undoubtedly been the most traumatic experience of her life. Tom would be gentle with her, but that wouldn't really lessen the impact.

Sister Agatha glanced at Natalie and saw that she had her arm over Pax and, for now, seemed at peace. Her own innocence protected her. But innocence was fragile and no match for the evils in the world.

Thinking about Natalie's affinity for angels, she whispered a prayer to Saint Michael, her soft words masked by the thunderous engine and the roar of the wind. "St. Michael, Prince of the Heavenly Host, be our safeguard against wickedness . . ."

4

Although Sister Agatha's gaze remained on the road ahead, her thoughts stayed on Natalie. She'd been about Natalie's age, give or take a year, when her own mother had died. Although her father had found ways to deal with his loss, none of them had involved a relationship with his daughter. The worst part had been that feeling of aloneness — not loneliness, exactly, but a horrifying certainty that, from that time on, she'd have only herself to rely on, that no one would ever come to her rescue again.

Her brother Kevin had helped her more than anyone. Working on his motorcycle with him, playing basketball in the driveway, though she could never shoot worth a hoot, all these had helped her survive that time. But Natalie would have no such comfort if the worst came to pass. The tension and pressure of the days to come would try the girl to the breaking point, and if somebody had actually tried to kidnap Natalie, there was real physical danger to her, as well. Knowing that, Sister Agatha prayed all the way to the station.

They arrived less than ten minutes later. Trying to avoid the press gathered by the front doors, Sister Agatha parked among the official vehicles in the back parking lot. Natalie was just removing her oversized helmet when Sheriff Green came out of the door.

"Natalie?" Seeing her nod, Tom led her quickly inside, hurrying to avoid two reporters with accompanying cameramen who'd come around the building after spotting the cherry red Harley with the nun and big white dog. Pax and Sister Agatha remained behind, running interference at the doorway until Tom and Natalie disappeared from view.

The next several minutes went by in a hurry. Using an officer's desk phone, knowing it would be a more secure line, Sister Agatha called Reverend Mother and received permission to remain for as long as necessary. While she was on the phone, the EMTs passed by, heading for Tom's office, where he'd taken Natalie. Then Father Mahoney arrived.

Fifteen minutes later, as Sister Agatha

waited in the hallway, Sheriff Green came up to her. "Father's with Natalie now, but before I question her any further, I need to know if she already told you what happened."

She recounted briefly what Natalie had said about the man — and her mother's order that she run and hide. "I didn't ask her for any details, though. I figured you'd want to hear all that firsthand."

"Yeah. I still haven't been able to determine for certain whether this was an attempted carjacking, kidnapping, or just a drunk driver who collided with them, went over for a look, then took off when he saw someone else approaching the scene. Footprints indicate another person was moving in Natalie's direction as she fled the accident, then reversed course when the third car approached. But Mrs. Tannen obviously thought Natalie was in danger, or she wouldn't have told her daughter to run for her life. According to Father Mahoney, mother and daughter were planning on leaving town as soon as possible because of threats and harassing calls. We can't afford to rule out kidnapping — the circumstantial evidence is there for such an attempt."

Father Mahoney came out of the room before she could comment, a frustrated look on his face. "I've told Natalie about her mother's head injury," he said. "But she's convinced that Jessica's going to be just fine. I didn't have the heart to take away that hope, but the truth is, Jessica's condition could go either way."

"Natalie's only eight years old and may not be ready for tough love. For now, let her cling to whatever hope she has," Sister Agatha said softly.

"But that's just it. It's not hope — it's utter conviction. And if Jess never wakes up again, what then?"

"Father," Tom interrupted. "I understand all the girl's going through, but I've really got to speak to Natalie now. The more time goes by, the less clearly she'll remember the details of the incident, and right now she's my only real eyewitness. If the man who hit them is a predator, or has singled out your niece, he may strike again."

Father nodded. "Okay, but please be gentle with Natalie. She's a lot more fragile than she seems. Shall I go in with you?"

Tom considered it. "I understand that you and Natalie have been at odds about the angel she claims to see."

Father Mahoney glowered at him. "She's a kid with a great imagination, but there are desperate people out there trying to make her into some kind of pseudo-saint. I had to step in. Imaginary playmates are one thing, but this angel thing of hers has gotten way out of hand. Now she and her mother are victims."

Tom nodded. "If there's tension between you two, you're not going to be much help to me. Let me take Sister Agatha with me instead. Are you okay with that?"

Father Mahoney looked at Sister Agatha, then nodded. "Take care of her, Sister," he asked wearily.

"We all will," Sister Agatha assured the priest, then looked back at Tom. "But you should know that she doesn't completely trust me. I hedged when she asked me how her mother was doing, and she picked up on that right away."

Father Mahoney exhaled softly. "She's too perceptive for her own good sometimes. Natalie's always been able to tell when Jessica or I try to keep something from her," he said, rubbing the back of his neck with one hand.

"Well, if she's as perceptive as you say, that may turn out to be a big help to me," Sheriff Green said. "I need to put the perp who did this behind bars."

Sister Agatha followed Tom into the lunchroom and found Natalie sitting by the table closest to the vending machine, sipping a Coke. The woman EMT who'd remained with the girl nodded, patted Natalie on the arm, then left the room

"Natalie, I have a few questions for you," Sheriff Green said.

She nodded. "I know. Uncle Rick said that you'd want me to tell you about what happened."

"That's right. So why don't we start at the beginning. When you left the house, where were you and your mom going?"

"I don't know. I was playing in my room when Mom came in and told me we were leaving. It was raining really hard and I didn't really want to go anywhere, so I told Mom I was too tired. But she was really upset and told me to put on my raincoat and get into the car. There was lots of lightning, so I wanted to take Gracie with me. But Mom just grabbed my hand and pulled me outside."

"Gracie? Who's she?"

"Gracie's my angel doll."

"What I need you to do now is try to remember what happened next," Tom said. "When you were riding in the car did your mom say anything about where you were going?"

Natalie shook her head. "Mom was upset

and she never talks much when she's like that. She just mumbles to herself."

"Does your mom usually go for drives when she's upset?"

Natalie thought for a moment, then shook her head. "No. When Mom's upset, she cooks. She makes lots and lots of spaghetti sauce. We always have tons of it in the freezer."

Sister Agatha bit her lip to keep from laughing out loud. Seeing the intent look on Tom's face sobered her up quickly. He was like a dog with a bone. He'd keep asking questions until he had answers.

"So she took you for a drive instead of cooking. Did that help calm her down?"

Natalie shook her head. "I don't think so. We drove for a while, but I could tell she was getting scared. She kept looking in the rearview mirror and saying Hail Marys. I knew something bad was going on, but she wouldn't talk to me. Then I saw the bright lights of the car behind us. I started to turn around and look back, but Mom yelled at me to scrunch down in my seat and pretend I was hiding. I ducked down real low, then this pickup came up right beside her window and bumped us real hard. It made a scary scraping sound and Mom screamed. I think I did, too. Then our car went bouncing off the road. I thought we were going to turn upside down, like on TV. But we didn't."

"Did you see the driver of the pickup?"

She shook her head. "It was dark and rainy and I was really ducking down. All I saw was his hat when he came over to the car."

"Cowboy hat or baseball cap?"

"Baseball. When our car stopped, I sat up. Mom was lying back and she had scratches on her face. Her nose was bleeding. I was really scared, then we saw the man getting out of his pickup. Mom tried to sit up, but she couldn't. That's when she told me to run and hide."

"Run and hide from the man?"

"I guess so."

"What did you do?"

"I told Mom I wanted to stay with her. She was hurt, but she just told me to go, and kind of pushed me out the door. I just ran. I could hear the man using swear words, like he was mad at us. But I didn't stop or look back."

Huge tears welled up in Natalie's eyes and spilled down her cheeks. Tom handed her a tissue from the table, and waited.

Sister Agatha wanted to comfort the girl, but experience told her that might lead to more crying and Tom needed answers.

A few minutes went by, then Natalie looked up. "I shouldn't have left her. I should have stayed in the car."

"You did the right thing obeying your mom," Sister Agatha said gently.

Tom looked like he wanted to reach out and hug the girl, but instead he sat up straight and cleared his throat. "The man didn't call out your name or your mother's name?"

"He yelled my mom's name, I remember — Jessica. Then he said a lot of those bad words. Do I have to say which ones?"

"No, I don't need to hear them. What happened after that?"

"I heard a car horn and saw lights. Another car was coming, but I kept running like Mom said."

"Was the person in the pickup tall or short, fat or skinny?" Tom Green asked.

She considered it for a moment. "He wasn't real tall, or short. And he was wearing a big jacket so I don't know if he was fat or not."

"So the figure was a he?"

Natalie began crying again. "I don't know! Maybe it was a woman with short hair. But the voice sounded like a man."

"You're doing okay, Natalie," Tom said,

his voice gentle. "I just need to know what you remember."

Natalie sniffed, then wiped her face. "It's so hard!"

"I know. But I need you to help me, okay?" Seeing Natalie nod, Tom continued. "What color was the pickup?"

"Tan. Like sand. Our house is that color, kind of."

"What did you do next? After running away from the man?"

"I found a road beside a big ditch and kept walking just like my angel said. Then, after practically forever, I saw the church way across the fields. When I got there the front doors were locked, but I walked around and found a window that was open just a little. I used a stick to open it enough to crawl inside, and went in. I was only going to stay until the rain stopped, but my angel said that I should wait there. I laid down on one of the pews and I guess I fell asleep. Then Sister Agatha came."

Sister Agatha could tell with just one look that Tom wasn't exactly thrilled to hear Natalie mention the angel. If Natalie saw things that weren't there, then her testimony wouldn't be worth much in court, if it ever came to that.

"Do you think that your mom knew the

person in the pickup?" Tom asked. "You said he knew her name. Do you think that's why she told you to run and hide?"

"I don't know. But she was always pulling me away from people who wanted to ask me questions. Mom doesn't want me to talk to strangers, even if they call us by our names. We were on TV, you know. Lots of people know who we are now. Mom wants us to move away. She didn't tell me yet, but I heard her talking to Uncle Rick — Father Mahoney, I mean."

Tom nodded. "Right. Could the man have been a neighbor or a relative, like your father?"

"Maybe Mom knew who it was, but I didn't. I . . . ," Natalie sobbed and looked over at Sister Agatha. "But why would my dad come back and make us have a wreck? He doesn't want us anymore. He left a long time ago when I was just a baby."

"Sorry, Natalie, I didn't mean to get you upset. I'm just trying to help," Sheriff Green said softly. "If you remember anything more about the person from the pickup, will you let me know?" He reached into his pocket and handed her a business card.

She took the card and nodded, running her fingertip over the embossed gold star in the center. "Sure."

Sheriff Green bought Natalie a candy bar, then stepped outside with Sister Agatha. Father Mahoney was waiting for them. "How did it go?" he asked.

"I'm not sure," the sheriff said honestly.

"Tom, I really think she's told you all she knows," Sister Agatha said.

Father Mahoney clenched his jaw, then expelled his breath in a slow hiss. "If you press her for answers she doesn't have, she'll . . . remember things that never happened."

"You mean she'll make it up?" Tom asked.

"Yeah," he said reluctantly. "And that could slow down the search for whoever's after Natalie."

Tom considered it for several moments. "I can't rule out the possible involvement of Natalie's father yet, not until we track him down. Or it could simply be the work of a carjacker — more or less random. But this angel idea has generated a whole batch of potential suspects, as well, and I've got to look into it. Just how aggressive *are* the people who try to get Natalie to help or intercede for them?"

"According to Jessica, it runs the entire spectrum. The good ones take no for an answer. The bad ones are rude, aggressive, pleading, insistent, and prepared to do whatever it takes," Father said, shaking his head. "But after that TV segment aired, people really went nuts. People started showing up from all over the area, even out of state. That's why Jessica was planning to move away. According to Jessica, one man cornered Natalie at Smitty's grocery store and offered her and Jessica a blank check if they'd come and talk to his sick wife. But I don't know who it was."

"I'll talk to Smitty, and if he doesn't know, maybe his video cameras picked it up," Tom said.

"I still don't understand why people are jumping to the conclusion that Natalie is capable of healing anyone. She's never claimed that she can. But I suppose it's to be expected. After Natalie said that her angel stopped the car in the parking lot, stories continued to spread — and grow."

Tom said nothing for a moment, then continued. "I understand Jessica told Natalie not to discuss her angel with anyone. Do you think Natalie did as she was told?"

Father Mahoney nodded slowly. "Yeah, I do. After she realized that she couldn't go anywhere without people coming up to her and asking her for favors, she became wary of people. I don't think she has many friends left at school, either, since no one knows what to make of her, so she stays pretty much by herself. The only place I know she feels comfortable is at the monastery. That's why I'd take her to Mass with me whenever I could. She thinks she has something in common with the nuns."

Sister Agatha looked at Father Mahoney in confusion. "I don't follow you."

"She said that nuns hear God's call inside them. It's not something that other people can hear, too. According to her, that's the way it is between her and her angel."

"That's tough to argue against," Sister Agatha said with a rueful smile.

"No kidding," Father said with a weary sigh.

"Folks, we need to stay on track here. If someone is willing to risk killing Natalie or themselves just to contact her, that girl is in serious danger."

"I learned a lot about publicity and promotion when I was a pro wrestler," Father Mahoney said. "What we need to do is plant the idea that it's all television hype. We'll insist that Natalie's angel is just an imaginary playmate. We can point out that she has had a thing for angels for years — angel dolls, angel pins, angel candles — you name it. She and her mom made a game of it, but then it got out of hand."

"Are you so sure that's all there is to it,

80

Father?" Sister Agatha asked.

"Yes, I am. Look at it objectively. Joanne Ulibarri, the owner of the car involved in the parking lot incident, couldn't remember putting it in gear or setting the brake. The car is thirty-five years old and barely operable with its sloppy manual transmission. The parking lot is sloped away from the building for drainage, and if the car slipped out of gear, it could have started rolling. Another bump could have put it back in gear. But that possibility was never even considered on the TV show. I heard that very rational explanation at Mr. Gonzales's garage, and it makes sense to me."

"What about the other story going around, about Natalie warning her friend about a fire *before* it happened?" Tom asked.

"I talked to Natalie myself about that. Louann Madison had told Natalie the day before in school that her family had just installed a wood stove. That turned out to be the source of the fire," Father Mahoney said. "Face it, it wouldn't have taken much for a girl with an active imagination like Natalie's to mention the dangers of a fire."

Sister Agatha said nothing. She knew that the archdiocese had put pressure on Father Mahoney to stop the rumors — at least until they could be verified or debunked.

"My sister has had a very hard life," Father Mahoney continued, looking at Tom, then at Sister Agatha. "Her husband Henry took off and hasn't shown his face around here since Natalie was born. Forget about child support. He never stays in one place long enough for anyone to track him down. For the past few years, Jessica's been holding down two jobs just to make ends meet. By the time she gets home, my sister's dead on her feet. Natalie hasn't been getting the attention that she needs, and that's what started this mess. When Natalie began talking about her angel, she got exactly what she wanted — more attention from Jessica."

"Be that as it may, we have to deal with this current situation," Tom said flatly. "Natalie is an eyewitness to a crime — maybe a hit-and-run, maybe much more. She was a target before, but it'll be even worse now. She needs to stay out of the public eye for a while in some kind of protective custody."

"I'd love to keep her with me at the rectory, but most people know that I'm her uncle. That's the first place anyone would look," Father said. "Especially someone who knows the rest of the family, like Henry."

"I can arrange to have a social worker find a suitable foster home away from here," Tom said. "Perhaps in Rio Rancho or Albuquerque."

"Bad idea. That's going to expose her to even more strangers," Sister Agatha said. "And to Natalie, all they spell is trouble. If you're hoping she'll remember something that'll help you with your investigation, you need her in an environment where she'll feel safe. She won't be able to think clearly unless she can relax."

"Any suggestions?" Tom asked.

"The monastery," Father said. "It's the only answer."

"*Our* monastery? But —"

"I know what you're going to say, Sister, but there are uncloistered areas there, and if you think about it, you'll see that it's perfect," Father said. "The monastery is out of the way, secure behind walls and locked doors, and has few visitors. There's no safer haven for her, and since Natalie feels a special kinship to the nuns, she wouldn't be frightened."

"Reverend Mother would have to give her permission, Father. I have no authority to make that decision. Also, you should know that we're going to need our roof repaired. That means we'll have workmen around."

"They'll be on the roof and Natalie will be inside. It'll still work." He looked at Tom.

"May I use your phone? I'm going to ask Reverend Mother myself."

As Father Mahoney went back to Tom's office, Sister Agatha gave the sheriff a skeptical look. "I'm not so sure Reverend Mother's going to agree to this. We have other pressing problems at the monastery right now."

"What could be more appropriate than nuns helping a child?" Tom countered.

"That's not the point. The monastery separates the sisters from the world so they can pray for it more effectively — like a doctor who has to distance himself emotionally in order to work for his patients. We're there to achieve union with God and to pray for a world that very often forgets Him. There are plenty of orders that remain active in the outside world, but that's not the role of our monastery."

She paused, then smiled slowly and continued. "All that said, I hope Reverend Mother says yes. Even if the cloistered sisters can't come out and meet her, they'll be able to visit her from behind the grill. I think they'd all really enjoy having Natalie around."

Father Mahoney came out a moment later, smiling. "Mother agreed to take Natalie in. She'll stay with the externs, of course. Mother said that the reception area adjacent to the main parlor can be turned into quarters for her."

"Okay, that part's worked out. But the key to this plan is to make sure no one else knows where Natalie is," Sheriff Green said. "That means Sister Agatha can't drive her back to the monastery in the motorcycle."

"I'll take her and make sure we're not followed," Father Mahoney said. "That'll also give me a chance to talk to her."

"Father, we have a lot of reporters out there and Natalie's a hot story. You'll never even make it to your car without drawing their attention. We'll need a diversion," Tom said, then paused thoughtfully. "I'll meet the reporters and issue a statement that Natalie has been found. I'll add that kidnapping could have been the motive, and because of that she's being placed in protective custody in a nearby community. This should throw some of the cranks off the trail. While this is going on, I can have one of my deputies smuggle my eight-year-old son Brent out beneath a blanket. He came to visit and is with Sergeant Miller right now, the head of our motor pool. I'll make sure the reporters get a glimpse of the action during my talk, and they'll assume I'm the diversion and Brent is Natalie. They won't know whether to follow the figure under the blanket or stick with me a bit longer. Either way, that'll buy you some time, Father — but not a lot."

"I'll be away before they know it," he said resolutely.

"I'll leave now and make sure that they all see me leaving alone," Sister Agatha said. "Then, once I'm sure I'm not being followed, I'll stop by Jessica's house and get some of Natalie's things."

"Whoa, Sister," Tom said. "I don't want you going in there alone. Jessica's place may hold a clue that'll tell us what really happened on that highway, and who might be responsible for the attempt on her. I'll make arrangements for a deputy to meet you there shortly. Wait for him."

As Father Mahoney went inside the lunchroom to join Natalie and Tom left to set up the plan, Sister Agatha called Pax and left immediately. Several reporters spotted her, including some she recognized, but when they realized that she didn't have Natalie, they returned to the front lobby.

It didn't take long for her to reach Jessica's home. As she pulled into the driveway of the tan, pueblo-style stucco house she admired the flower bed of multicolored cosmos that ran along the front of the house. Two large sunflower plants grew next to the front door, brightening up the entrance with its large yellow flowers. Everything was well tended and it was clear at a glance that Jessica loved her home.

As she approached, Sister Agatha noticed that someone had painted a second, smaller doorway behind the giant sunflower on the right. Over the faux entrance were the words, GOOD ANGELS ONLY.

Sister Agatha smiled. There wasn't a lot of wealth evident here, but there was love in abundance.

As a deputy sheriff's car pulled up, Sister Agatha waved at the officer. Although everything had appeared normal from the outside, the minute they stepped into the living room, her breath caught in her throat. The place looked like it had been struck by a tornado.

"Wait here, Sister. I'm going to check —"

Pax, who'd come in with them, suddenly shot down the hall.

The deputy raced after him, Sister Agatha a step or two behind. The second they entered Natalie's room, they found Pax braced beside the open window, snarling and clinging to someone's pant leg.

5

"Stop! Sheriff's deputy!" he ordered, trying to reach around Pax to grab the intruder.

Suddenly the fabric tore and there was a thud as the burglar fell to the ground outside, then the sounds of footsteps as he took off running. After failing on his first attempt, Pax jumped onto the window ledge and then outside in pursuit.

Sister Agatha moved out of the way as the deputy rushed past her, heading out the window behind the dog.

Gathering her wits, she pulled out her cell phone and called the station. "We just surprised a burglar," she told the emergency operator after identifying herself. "A deputy and a police dog are in pursuit." From the window Sister Agatha could see Pax leaping up into the air next to the six-foot-high fence on the property line, growling and trying to get over, but not quite making it. On the ground was the swatch of fabric from the intruder's pant leg. Then the officer jumped up and over the fence, out of her view.

Realizing that she was still on the line, she added, "The deputy and Pax are now searching for the burglar, who was last seen heading east."

"We'll send a unit over right away," the dispatcher said. "Just stay in the house."

"I'll be here." But not idle. She wouldn't touch anything, but maybe if she took a look around, she'd be able to figure out what the intruder had been after.

Screaming sirens announced Sheriff Green's approach less than five minutes later. The burglar was long gone and Sister Agatha was sitting on the front step with Pax as Tom came up.

Tom spoke to the deputy, who handed him the swatch of fabric from the intruder's pant leg as evidence, then came over to meet her. "I need you to tell me exactly what you saw," Tom said.

After giving him a quick rundown, she added, "I'm sorry I didn't get a look at his face, just his legs and rear end."

"Same with Deputy Riley. That's not a win for our side." Tom walked inside with her as another deputy who'd just arrived began to take photographs of the room. "Did you touch anything?"

"You know me better than that, Tom. All I touched was the floor with my feet. I didn't even have to turn on the lights because the curtains were already open."

"Did you get any of Natalie's clothes or toys yet?"

"I never had the chance."

"Good. If you still want them, you'll have to stick around until I release the scene."

Tom walked to the kitchen counter, then stopped to play back the messages on the telephone answering machine. There was only one: "Jessica, we have to talk about this, but not at the office. Call me as soon as you get home."

Sister Agatha glanced at Tom. "I don't recognize his voice. Do you?"

"No, but it's obviously one of her coworkers. I'll find out what that was about soon enough," he said.

As Tom walked away, Sister Agatha stepped back out onto the porch and used her cell phone to call the monastery.

"Natalie got here a little while ago," Sister Bernarda said in answer to her first question. "I took her to the chapel and she just loved the angels in our stained glass window. We've already started turning the reception area into suitable quarters. Father Mahoney left to go get her a box of instant hot cocoa and a safe coffee pot to warm water. She likes instant cocoa at night and Father wanted to make sure she had some available. Frances at the rectory has a supply, so he'll be coming right back."

"Frances knows?"

"Father considered it a necessity and he trusts her with his life."

"The fewer who know, the safer she'll be," Sister Agatha said in a barely audible voice.

"I think it'll be fine," Sister Bernarda assured. "But Natalie could really use some of her own toys."

"I'll gather what I can as soon as possible." She gave Sister Bernarda the highlights of what had happened.

"I wonder what the intruder was after."

"I have no idea, but from the looks of it Jessica and Natalie are in more trouble than we suspected. My guess is that this is related to the incident that put Jessica in the hospital."

"It's too coincidental to be otherwise. We better make sure Natalie stays away from the windows and doorways, particularly after the roofers arrive."

Soon after Sister Agatha hung up, Tom came back outside and took her statement.

Once that formality was over, he led the way to Natalie's room. "Nothing is obviously missing, like a television set or jewelry, and we have no way of knowing if the intruder actually got what he came for, if anything. You can take whatever you need for Natalie, but do it quickly and discreetly. I don't want my people to know what you're doing. I trust them, but they don't have a need to know," he said softly, then shut the door, leaving her there alone.

Sister glanced at the books that had been scattered around on the floor. They were mostly animal stories, and the now famous series about the boy wizard. Even one of those books, which appeared to be the size of a bible, would keep Natalie busy for a long time. She picked up one volume, seeing the dog-eared page near the middle, and figuring that Natalie hadn't finished reading it yet. Placing it beneath her arm, she moved to the closet, picked up a small athletic bag, and filled it with a few changes of clothes.

Seeing a pair of fuzzy slippers shaped like mice, she decided to take them, too. She was forcing them into the overstuffed bag when they suddenly squeaked. Sister Agatha jumped, then laughed. Thinking of that squeaking sound every time Natalie took a step, particularly during the Great Silence, made her hesitate, but then, with a smile, she packed them anyway.

"You almost ready to clear out?" Tom asked, stepping back into the room.

"Let me grab a toy first."

"Take only what you can stick in the bag. And keep an eye on anyone who shows an interest in your coming and going." He paused thoughtfully, his gaze taking in the condition of the room. "I sure wish Jessica could tell us if anything's missing. I'm tempted to bring Natalie here, but I can't risk that right now."

"Tell me something, Tom. Do you think we're looking at this wrong? If they're after Natalie, why come here and toss the place like a burglar? Everyone knows Jessica's in the hospital, and this would be a terrible place to hide Natalie."

"I don't know. But I suppose it's possible that the incident with the vehicles and this break-in *are* unrelated. Sometimes burglars watch the papers to try and find out when a house will be unoccupied."

Sister Agatha nodded. "Like the deceased's home during their funeral service, or the news coverage of the accident. I'm certain the incident the other night made the local news." Her experience as a journalist years ago still served as an asset at the oddest times.

"All the local papers and TV stations covered the incident, especially with the kidnapping angle. I've pretty much ruled out drunks or a carjacking because the perp knew Jessica by name, but exactly what the motive was for the confrontation isn't clear at the moment," Tom confessed. "We're checking her vehicle for prints, and will be comparing them with any we find in the house, in case the same person is responsible for what's been going down. But we have to assume Natalie's still in danger. Be very careful with her."

"We'll guard her with our lives."

Tom nodded, then left the room to go though the house once more.

Unable to stick any of Natalie's toys into the already overstuffed bag, Sister Agatha made a quick exit. Walking toward the Harley with Pax, she turned her head at the sound of Tom's voice.

"Here," he said, walking toward her and handing her a large pillowcase. "Maybe this will do," he said, grinning sheepishly.

She peered into the pillowcase and smiled. A large doll dressed up like a queen, complete with crown, was inside. "Can I tell Natalie you picked it out yourself?"

"If you say anything, I'll deny it," he grumbled.

Sister Agatha had Pax climb into the sidecar first, then pushed the pillowcase and bag under the cowling where they'd be protected.

Bag and pillowcase under each arm, Sister Agatha walked into the monastery's entry hall, Pax leading the way. As she reached the parlor, Sister Agatha heard the scuffling of furniture being dragged across the brick floor in the reception room to the left. Sister de Lourdes and Sister Bernarda were adjusting the placement of a small three-drawer oak dresser. Seeing her, they both smiled.

"Good thing you're back," Sister de Lourdes said. "We've been trying to make it a little more like home in here for Natalie, but we need toys. What did you bring?"

"All the sheriff would let me take was one small bag, and I stuffed it with clothes and a book. But then he handed me this." She took the doll out of the pillowcase. "He picked it out himself."

"Looks brand new. It has probably been on a shelf since she got it for her birthday. He should have picked the rattiest looking doll instead," Sister de Lourdes said, smiling. "That would have been the one she's played with the most."

"It's the thought that counts." Sister Agatha opened the bag and started putting clothes away. "Where's Natalie?"

"Father Mahoney and she went to the chapel. Then he's going to try and explain why she has to stay here for a bit," Sister de Lourdes said.

"Natalie's a bright kid. I have a feeling she knows exactly why she's here," Sister Agatha said. "But things aren't so clear for the sheriff. He's not sure what the motive for the incident was, but he still fears for her safety. The fact that the other driver knew Jessica by name is significant, especially because it appears more and more to have been an attempt on Jessica or Natalie and not merely an accident."

"Natalie's taking it well," Sister Bernarda said. "I expected her to be a little bit apprehensive, but she acted completely at ease, asking a million questions about the monastery."

"I've heard the stories about her," Sister de Lourdes said. "Maybe she has a vocation."

"Right now she's just a kid with a lot of problems," Sister Agatha said. "Don't let *her* imagination run away with you," she added with a smile.

Sister Agatha finished putting away Natalie's things. A simple cot with comfortable blankets was against one wall, and on the opposite side the dresser. Atop the dresser was the coffee pot for heating water, Natalie's hairbrush, her book, and the elaborately costumed doll. The rest of the room remained as it had been, with two wooden chairs and a large wooden crucifix on the wall. Except for the out-of-place doll, it looked like a monk's vacation home. "This room needs some warmth. I'll go back to her house once the police are gone and get more of her toys."

Sister de Lourdes checked her watch. "Mother has asked that everyone meet before collation," she said, referring to the monastery's evening meal, "to discuss the financial crisis we're facing. But one of us will have to stay with Natalie. I think that should be me since I've got to call the pharmacy with questions from Sister Eugenia about Sister Gertrude's new pills."

"All right then," Sister Agatha said. "If Father Mahoney returns with Natalie while we're gone, assure him that we'll take excellent care of his niece and that he shouldn't worry."

Sister Agatha and Sister Bernarda entered

the enclosure and made their way quietly to the large room at the other end of the cloister where their chapter meetings were held. The other nuns arrived at almost the same time, but their soft-soled shoes scarcely made a sound as they entered the room and took seats in the simple, straight-backed wooden chairs. Reverend Mother was the last to arrive, and as she entered, they all stood.

After leading them in a brief prayer, Mother gave them a nod. "Sit down, children." Reverend Mother always called the nuns her children, as was the custom of their order, because her position required her to provide for them spiritually and physically.

There was a pause as Reverend Mother quickly studied the notes she'd brought along. At long last, she looked up. "Some of our best scriptorium customers have stopped sending us work. That's cut our income considerably and now we've taken another serious blow.

"A secular company mass-producing altar breads is taking over the business. They've sent free samples to every parish in the state, and as a result we've lost customers. The bottom line is they charge less than we do and give their customers more choices.

We have some loyal customers who'll remain with us, but in the long run we won't be able to compete. What it all boils down to is this — we need a new source of income for our monastery."

"Until we find one, we'll learn to do with less, Mother," Sister Gertrude said.

Reverend Mother smiled sadly. "We do with very little as it is, child. But we have temporal needs that have to be met — a new roof, for one." She paused, then saw Sister Gertrude rubbing her temple as if in pain, and added, "Child, are you sure you're up to this meeting?"

"I'm supposed to rest, Mother, but how much more restful can I be if all I do is sit?" Sister Gertrude answered. "Sister Eugenia has made sure that old Ironsides and I" — she pointed to the wheelchair — "are practically inseparable."

Sister Eugenia smiled. "Sister Gertrude has been a good patient, Mother. She's even stopped doing zoomies down the hall to the chapel," she teased.

The idea of Sister Gertrude doing "zoomies" anywhere made everyone laugh. Of all of them, she was the most methodical about guarding the silence of the cloister. Her entrance into any room had been almost undetectable until her heart condition had forced her to use a wheelchair.

Reverend Mother continued. "We need a substantial sum for our roof, so today we need to come up with some fund-raising suggestions."

"Can the roof be patched again?" Sister Agatha asked. "I know Mr. Martinez keeps saying we need a new roof, but perhaps he can just fix the leaks one more time?"

Reverend Mother shook her head. "We've put it off too long as it is. Some of the sheeting is beginning to rot and we can't risk weakening the structure and having it collapse through the ceiling."

"What about our sinking fund?" Sister Gertrude, their former cellarer, asked.

"It won't be nearly enough to cover the roof," Reverend Mother said. "We could take out a loan, but the truth is I'm not at all sure we can handle the monthly payments."

"The roof *was* damaged during a storm," Sister Bernarda said. "Can't we collect on our insurance?"

Reverend Mother sighed. "Unfortunately we missed two payments in a row and that part of our coverage lapsed."

Sister Ignatius was the first to speak. "The Lord has always provided for our needs. We should bring this matter to Him and let

Him handle the problem for us."

"We do need prayers, child, now more than ever," Reverend Mother agreed softly.

"We'll get started on that immediately. This might seem insurmountable to us, but nothing is insurmountable to God," Sister Ignatius answered, her voice as firm as her faith. "And remember the angel-shaped cloud we saw the night of the storm. That was a sure sign that we're being watched over."

Sister Eugenia, ever practical, looked at the others, then at Reverend Mother. "Sister Maria Victoria's quilts are popular and always sell for a good price. Is it possible she could do another one?"

Sister Maria Victoria looked at Sister Eugenia. "Sister Ignatius, Sister Gertrude and I have been working on a pictorial quilt that shows Our Blessed Mother. It think it's one of our best and it should be finished soon."

"That's wonderful," Reverend Mother said. "As soon as it's ready, make sure Sister Agatha or Sister Bernarda places a photo of it on our Web site. But we'll need more than this quilt can raise."

"We can bring back our Rent-a-Nun project. People like the idea of hiring one of us to pray for them," Sister Bernarda said. "We'll post suggested donations for each rental time frame — a day, week, or month. We did this a few years ago during another crisis and it helped."

"We'll do it again. Does anyone else have any other ideas?" Reverend Mother asked.

"There's one other way to raise funds quickly — and maybe it'll give us a new source of steady income, as well," Sister Agatha said slowly. "Whenever I go into town, people always ask me if they can buy some of our Cloister Cluster cookies. Smitty the grocer, in particular, never fails to do that. I think he'd carry them in his store if we asked, and other merchants might be willing to do that, too. If we could start baking the cookies on a regular schedule I think we'll be able to turn it into a good, steady business."

Reverend Mother glanced at Sister Clothilde. The elderly nun spoke through hand signals only, but by now most of them could communicate easily with her.

Sister Clothilde nodded, then pointed around the room and back to herself.

"Yes, we'll all be happy to help. You won't be doing this alone," Reverend Mother said. "Any more suggestions?" When no one else spoke, she nodded once and continued. "Then let's set our plans in motion." Reverend Mother looked at Sister Agatha. "I want you to come up with some estimates. Figure out what it would cost us to mass-produce the cookies and what kind of profit we could expect to make."

"Mother, you want a profit and loss statement," Sister Gertrude said. "I know how to do that. Please let me help."

Reverend Mother shook her head. "Not yet. You're still recovering." Seeing Sister Gertrude's downcast expression, she relented. "On second thought, we do need your help. But let Sister Agatha do the preliminary work. Your job will be to check her work."

"Yes, Mother. And thank you!" Sister Gertrude said with a bright smile.

"I'll get the paperwork to you as soon as possible, Sister," Sister Agatha said.

As the bell sounded signalling time for the Angelus, Reverend Mother stood and led the prayer. "The Angel of the Lord declared unto Mary . . ."

". . . and she conceived by the Holy Spirit," the sisters answered, their words echoing softly as the peals of the Mary bell resonated in the distance.

When Sister Agatha returned to the parlor, Natalie had already eaten and Sister de Lourdes was at the desk. Across the entry hall, in Natalie's new quarters, Father Mahoney was giving his niece one last hug.

"You'll be okay?" he asked.

"Sure! I like it here already," Natalie said cheerfully.

"As you said yourself, Father, there's no safer place in the world for her," Sister Agatha reminded him gently as he stepped through the doorway.

He nodded. "Well then, I'd better go back to my duties." With one last glance at Natalie, who was across the room, book in hand, he left through the outside door.

"I think we better say some prayers for Father, too," Sister de Lourdes said softly.

As Sister de Lourdes left to ring the bell for Compline, Natalie came across the hall and into the parlor. "Is she gone to ring the bell again?"

Sister Agatha smiled and nodded. "That's her job — well, one of her jobs." Glancing at the book in Natalie's hand, she added, "Did I bring the right book?"

She nodded. "I like this story a lot, and I'm glad you brought my queen doll, Regina. But I wish I had Gracie, my angel doll. Can we go get her?"

Sister Agatha shook her head. "No, not yet, but soon, I hope."

Natalie sighed. "Even though my angel

always keeps me company, I'm kind of homesick already. Having Gracie around would help."

"We may have a teddy bear in St. Francis's pantry. Shall I go look?"

She shook her head. "No, thank you. It wouldn't be the same."

Making a mental note to try and get her favorite doll as soon as possible, Sister Agatha helped Natalie into her nightclothes then explained the nighttime routine.

Seeing the apprehension in her eyes, Sister Agatha gave her a reassuring smile. "You can come to Compline then the blessing with me." After that, she was sure Natalie would sleep peacefully.

At four thirty the next morning Sister Agatha heard the wake-up call. She had thirty minutes before Matins, the canonical hour said before daybreak. As she opened her eyes, she fought a sudden sense of disorientation. Why was she sitting in this uncomfortable chair? Her joints were on fire. Then, seeing Pax at her feet and Natalie asleep on the cot, she remembered.

In spite of her quick acceptance of the monastery, Natalie had experienced a rough first night. She'd stayed with externs as they'd joined the others at Compline and then *asperges,* a ceremony where holy water was sprinkled upon them in a symbolic cleansing from sin. Then she'd attended and taken part in the last blessing of the day, the *noctem quietam,* asking the Lord to grant them a "quiet night and a perfect end." Even after all that, sleep had not come easy for Natalie.

Natalie hadn't wanted to be alone, and at the first sign of a silent tear — for Natalie hadn't broken the Great Silence — the externs had decided to take turns staying with her all throughout the night.

Spending time with Natalie and responding to the homesick little girl who hadn't wanted to be left alone last night, had made her realize that her maternal instincts were still very much alive. Pushing back a momentary twinge of sadness for what might have been, she took a deep breath, walked to the door, and sent Pax outside.

As soon as Sister Bernarda arrived to take her place, she went to Matins. This morning, more than ever, she needed the comfort that would provide. The heavenly Father's love would sustain her. Life came with precious few guarantees, but knowing His promises were kept was enough.

At the close of Morning Prayers, Sister Agatha relieved Sister de Lourdes. After *Lectio Divina,* Sister Bernarda arrived at the parlor, and stepped across the hall into what had become Natalie's room. "Natalie, why don't you and I take turns reading to each other from your book while Sister Agatha takes care of some monastery business?"

"Okay," Natalie said.

Sister Bernarda ushered Natalie toward the chairs and closed the door behind them.

Alone, Sister Agatha checked the entrance doors at the end of the hall and made sure they were locked. Although normally the doors were unlocked during the day while a portress was on duty, for the duration of Natalie's visit the front doors would only be open when a visitor came. That extra precaution would insure that no one came upon Natalie by chance. If anyone asked about the change in policy, they'd be told that it was a security precaution because of the presence of workers on the monastery grounds.

Sister Agatha made the necessary calls to get price quotes on the flour, nuts, and the other Cloister Cluster ingredients. Then, leaving the parlor in Sister Bernarda's care, she went to the scriptorium and used one of the computers to make out a spreadsheet for up to six months of production. Once finished, she took the papers and went to find Sister Gertrude.

The elderly nun rechecked all the values and entries carefully, adding up everything in her mind. "These figures are correct based on your estimates," Sister Gertrude said at last. "But I think there's one problem you didn't factor in."

"What's that?" Sister Agatha asked, looking over her shoulder and trying to guess.

"The cookies take eight to ten minutes to bake. And that doesn't factor in the time needed to mix and place the dough on the cookie sheets. The quantity you have here will require hours of baking — possibly the entire day. The only way we can meet this schedule is with three or more ovens."

"We have two, although, admittedly, one is very old. But these are hard times. Our equipment has to work for us. If worse comes to worse and one breaks down, Sister Bernarda and I will do our best to repair it ourselves. We can always cut our production, too, if sales drop off."

"Then you're all set," Sister Gertrude said. "You can take these figures to Mother whenever you're ready, with my blessing."

Sister Agatha was mulling over Sister Gertrude's warning when she heard the dinner bell. This was their main meal at the monastery and she was hungry.

Lost in thought, Sister Agatha went to the refectory. Although she was sure that the cookies would give them the funds they needed, the venture would require that all the nuns pitch in and sacrifice their time — and possibly some sleep — during the months to come. The prospect of possibly working round the clock was daunting, but there was no other way.

After the meal, Sister Agatha knocked lightly on Reverend Mother's door, then went inside. "Praised be Jesus Christ."

"Now and forever," the abbess answered.

"Sit down, child." Reverend Mother waved to the chair by her desk. "I hope you're bringing me good news."

"Good and bad, Mother," she said candidly. "Sister Gertrude and I calculated the figures for various sale levels and it all looks good. But there's a downside. With our current equipment, we may need to work round the clock in shifts. It'll be hard work, but I think we can handle it."

"Most of us can," she agreed. "But we'll have to make sure that Sister Clothilde and Sister Gertrude get very short shifts and lots of breaks. I would refuse to allow Sister Gertrude to help out at all, but I think that would do her more harm than good."

Hearing the sound of distant thunder outside, Reverend Mother sighed. "Call Mr. Martinez as soon as possible, child, and authorize the work. I've put this off long enough." She met Sister Agatha's gaze and held it. "But it will be up to our externs to make sure that the workmen respect the rules of our cloister. *No one* can wander inside, and if they're going to work near our enclosure windows, we need advance notice so the drapes can be closed."

"We'll take care of that, Mother," she said.

Reverend Mother exhaled wearily, and for a brief moment, Sister Agatha got a glimpse of what Reverend Mother would look like when she reached her eighties. "And our young guest . . . how is she?"

Sister Agatha filled Reverend Mother in on the break-in at Jessica's home and what had transpired since Natalie's arrival. "I need to get her doll, the one she really plays with, but otherwise she seems to be adapting well."

"I understand why the girl feels a spiritual bond to those who've received a calling. The logic is there. But these visions of hers . . . unsettle me."

"Father believes that Natalie's angel is simply her imaginary playmate," she said.

"The whole thing may be nothing more than a child's game."

"Then, for now, don't encourage her to talk about that." Reverend Mother reached for her rosary and ran the beads through her hands. "I'm very worried about all the sisters right now. These outside influences — our guest, the fund drive, the unbearable racket the roofers will make as they work — will take a terrible toll on everyone. It's going to be very difficult for any of us to focus on our prayers."

"But we've already received one very tangible blessing," Sister Agatha said. "You saw it last night during our chapter meeting. Everyone came together as one, ready to weather the hard times ahead. We'll come through this just fine, Mother."

The abbess rewarded Sister Agatha with a smile. *"Deo gratias."*

Sister Agatha left Reverend Mother's office. As she entered the parlor, she saw Natalie lying down on her stomach on the brick floor, reading her book and eating a cookie from a plate beside her.

Sister Bernarda smiled. "A gift from Sister Clothilde. All the sisters have come by to visit Natalie, though they stayed behind the grate, of course. Sister Ignatius presented our guest with a holy card depicting Our

Lady and the Angel Gabriel, and Sister Gertrude brought her a needlepoint bookmark."

Sister Agatha smiled. Natalie couldn't have come at a worse time, and yet having her here among them had renewed all their spirits. Innocence cast its own special light even during the darkest of times.

6

It was after None, the liturgical hour said at three commemorating the ninth hour when Christ died. Natalie was still reading, but looked a bit restless from what Sister Agatha could tell from across the narrow hall. For the past hour, she'd been watching the girl without seeming to do so. To be here, without friends her own age, or being able to use the computer, telephone, or television, would have been unbearable for most kids her age. Yet Natalie had accepted the situation without fuss so far. In some ways Sister Agatha suspected that solitude had become her most trusted companion, or maybe it was because she'd only been here less than a day.

"Do nuns have TV?" Natalie asked, closing the book and standing in the doorway.

"No, I'm sorry. But I'll see if Father can provide one for you, if you'd like."

"Or some games," she said with a shrug.

Hearing a car coming up the drive, Sister Agatha went to the window and glanced outside.

"Shall I close my door?" Natalie asked.

"No, it's not necessary. It's Sheriff Green and he already knows you're here."

Sister de Lourdes came into the parlor just then and smiled at Natalie. "Are you getting cabin fever? You've been reading for a long time. I thought you might enjoy a walk outside in our garden. I have Reverend Mother's permission to take you through the cloister, and out the back so no one can see you."

"Cool!" Natalie said, scrambling to her feet and turning to smile at someone — or something — only she could see.

Sister Agatha felt a shiver course up her spine. Natalie's gaze had been focused and centered. It hadn't been the diffuse look of someone pretending to see what wasn't there.

That's when she had a sudden troubling thought. In their eagerness to discount Natalie's visions, it was possible they'd overlooked one important possibility. Perhaps the girl was seeing something dark and evil masquerading as good.

Looking back at Sister Agatha, Natalie asked, "Can Pax come, too?" She glanced at the dog who'd been lying at the opposite end of the parlor by the enclosure door.

"I think that Pax would love a chance to go for a walk." Then, to her own horror, Sister Agatha found herself disobeying Mother's orders and voicing the question foremost in her mind. "Does your angel have a name?"

"She said that it was Samara, which is Hebrew for 'under God's rule.' " Natalie paused as if listening to someone, then smiled. "She says you're afraid but you shouldn't be." Her eyebrows knitted together as if trying to listen to something that confused her. *"Laudamus Dominum,"* she said. "Did I get it right? She said if I told you that you'd stop worrying."

Sister Agatha dropped down into her chair. No angel that had fallen into darkness could praise God. The words *laudamus Dominum* meant "we praise God," meaning the angel with Natalie was one of the heavenly host. But skepticism was part of her nature, and it was impossible for her not to see the other side of the argument. Natalie's uncle was a priest and it was very possible Natalie had heard the name and the phrase from him.

A knock on their door diverted her thoughts. "Go have some fun," Sister Agatha told Natalie as she stood.

Sister de Lourdes left with Natalie and Pax, and Sister Agatha opened the door and invited Sheriff Green inside. "Come in," she said, her voice strained.

"Everything okay here?" he asked, picking up on her tension.

She nodded. "We're in the midst of a financial crisis, that's all. Anything new on the case?"

"We're still talking to people, and running fingerprints found on the vehicle and in the house. The perp may have left a handprint on Jessica's windshield but it's too smeared to get any usable fingerprints — just a man-sized outline. I'm also checking on known DWI offenders to see if any of them owns or has access to a tan truck. The night of the accident, Jessica's boss, Joseph Carlisle, called her. That was him we heard on the answering machine. He apparently was pretty upset when he found out Jessica was moonlighting. I spoke to him and the office staff over at Grayson Construction, where Jessica works as an accounts receivable and payable clerk, but so far I've turned up nothing that'll help me close the case. Which brings me to the reason why I'm here. I need you to do something for me."

"Name it."

"Do you think you can get her to open up? My detectives have spoken to some of Natalie's teachers, and they've all commented on how observant she is. I'm willing to bet that the kid saw more than she realizes the night of the accident."

Tom paused, then continued slowly. "The thing is, I'm afraid to question her myself again this soon. If I push her hard I'll become the bad guy, too, and she'll lock up on me. Kids do that — I know, I have an eight-year-old of my own."

"I'll see if she gives me an opening, but if I press her, I won't get anywhere, either."

"Start as soon as you can. Remember that it won't be long before people start guessing she's here." He looked around. "Speaking of Natalie, where is she?"

"She's in the back garden with Pax and Sister de Lourdes."

"I thought that she couldn't go into any cloistered area."

"Ordinarily, no, but Natalie's an innocent and the vow of charity takes precedence over all the others." She paused and exhaled softly. "Before Vatican II anyone who admitted even a doctor into the enclosure without permission from the bishop could be excommunicated. But things are different now. Granted, until very recently, Mother still preferred to follow the tradition of asking the bishop. But last year our new bishop told Reverend Mother that she should make those decisions herself, since she's the one best qualified to judge the circumstances."

Tom stood. "One last thing. What had you so upset when I came in?"

"I wasn't upset," she said, smiling. Tom had an amazing radar. He could always tell when someone was holding out on him. But she didn't want to discuss Natalie's angel with him right now. "A small problem took me by surprise, that's all."

Reverend Mother leaned back in her chair. Telling her about the sheriff's request had been easy, but Sister Agatha had also been obligated to tell her what had happened with Natalie. "You made a mistake by asking her about the angel, child. Your motives were good so I'll forgive you. But I have no idea what to make of what she said."

"I've been trying to figure it out myself, Mother. Truth is, Natalie could have found the name Samara in a baby book, or on the Internet, or maybe she heard Father mention it. But I checked all our references and there's no record of an angel by that name. The phrase *laudamus Domino* isn't uncommon and Father has a Latin-English dictionary in his computer, so it's possible she found it there."

Reverend Mother steepled her fingers, staring thoughtfully past them at an indeterminate spot across the room. "Whether or not Natalie really sees an angel is not for us to decide. We have to let that go for now. But let's do our best to honor the sheriff's request. As a former journalist, you're the best person to try and unlock whatever secrets Natalie's memory holds, so do whatever you have to do. If you succeed, it would be a blessing to everyone — Natalie, Father Mahoney, and all of us here."

Sister Agatha nodded. "I'll do my best but, Mother, Natalie needs something to do while she's here to keep her mind and body occupied. I've been told she's quite a sculptress. Maybe we can persuade Sister Ignatius to let her help with the ceramic figures she makes for the Christmas bazaar."

When Sister Agatha returned to the parlor, Natalie was in her room across the hall with a pencil and pad sketching Pax, and Sister de Lourdes was back at her desk.

Seeing her enter, Sister de Lourdes looked up, a worried expression on her face. "Will you take over now, Your Charity? I need to go help Sister Clothilde before Vespers," she said.

Sister Agatha worked at the desk for a while and answered calls. Sometime later she glanced into the next room, and saw Natalie looking up at her. "Bored?" Sister Agatha asked.

Natalie nodded. "Kind of."

"You prefer sculpting over sketching, don't you?" Seeing the girl nod, Sister Agatha continued. "You do wonderful work. I've seen the beautiful angel sculpture you made for Father Mahoney."

Natalie smiled. "That was Uncle Rick's birthday present." Then she wrinkled her nose, and added, "But angels don't look like that, you know."

"They don't?" If Tom and Reverend Mother wanted her to build a rapport with Natalie, she would have to allow the girl to speak freely.

"No — well, it's not like I've seen them *all*. But mine doesn't have wings. I asked her about that, and she said that she could get some if I wanted, but she really didn't need them."

Sister Agatha smiled at the girl. "Could be she's allergic to feathers."

Natalie laughed. "I didn't think of that. Do you think anyone sneezes in heaven?"

"I guess I'll find out when I get there someday," Sister Agatha said, then added,

"Natalie, how would you feel about making some ceramic angels to help with our fund-raising?"

The smile that suddenly covered Natalie's face was like the sun breaking though the clouds after a storm. "I'll take that as a yes," Sister Agatha said, chuckling. "Come on. Let me show you our crafts room. Sister Ignatius normally does all our artwork, but she's probably not there right now, so we won't be bothering her."

Sister Agatha led the way down the corridor, mindful of the time. The bells would ring for Vespers soon, so this would have to be a short outing.

"Sister, do you think I can go see my mom soon?" Natalie whispered, mindful of how quiet it was around them.

"I'm not sure," Sister Agatha answered honestly, also at a whisper.

"I miss her," she said.

"I know you do," Sister Agatha said gently.

The crafts room door was open just a few inches, and as they approached they could hear the low hum of the potter's wheel. A moment later they entered and Sister Agatha saw Sister Ignatius shaping a bowl.

Looking up, Sister Ignatius smiled at Natalie then at Sister Agatha. "I saw Reverend Mother in the corridor and she told me that you two might pay me a visit."

"I didn't realize that you'd be working here this late."

"Everyone's doing their best to raise money and I know these bowls sell well, so I thought I'd give them to Sister Bernarda to take to our booth at the Harvest Festival."

While Natalie watched in fascination, Sister Ignatius finished the bowl she'd been working on, switched off the electrically powered wheel, then lifted the bowl carefully, placing it on a tray by the counter.

Seeing the unworked clay that had been left beside the wheel in a plastic bowl, Natalie looked up at Sister Ignatius. "May I use this?" When Sister Ignatius nodded, Natalie began molding the brown lump.

Minutes ticked by as they watched the girl shape the clay, the soft mass taking form under her confident hands. "You have a gift," Sister Ignatius whispered.

Natalie didn't reply. Once she'd begun to work, it was as if she'd shut everything else from her mind.

7

Sister Agatha knew she was trying too hard. The more she attempted to get involved with Natalie and show an interest in the work the girl was crafting, the more Natalie pulled away emotionally. Yet when Sister Ignatius arrived after their time for private prayers, Natalie greeted her as warmly as she would have an old, trusted friend. Their gift for sculpting and their affinity for angels meant they spoke the same language. Sister Agatha sensed the connection between them almost immediately. They were kindred spirits.

"Your Charity, I just heard a truck pulling up. Will you be okay with Natalie?" Sister Agatha asked.

Sister Ignatius nodded. "Take whatever time you need. We'll be fine."

Sister Agatha left the room and, as she walked down the corridor, heard loud voices coming from outside. The unsettling sounds echoed harshly in the hall. Silence was the natural order of things here in the monastery, but for as long as the workmen were around, that would be nothing more than a memory. As she imagined the canonical hours sung to the beat of a hammer — or many hammers — she shuddered.

Sister Agatha hurried into the parlor and saw that Sister Bernarda had closed the door to Natalie's quarters. Hearing a radio outside blaring loud country-western music, Sister Agatha cringed.

"If you can attend to the roofers and make sure they understand the need to keep noise at a minimum," Sister Agatha said, "I can make sure Natalie remains out of sight, away from any windows."

"I'll speak to the workmen," Sister Bernarda said in her brisk, no-nonsense tone. "But I have a feeling they'll be the least of our worries. I just heard that the bishop will be sending his chancellor over to talk to Natalie later today or tomorrow."

When Sister Agatha returned to the crafts room, she found Sister Ignatius and Natalie working on the angel together. Sister Agatha drew the blinds just in case a workman wandered near, silently noting their easy rapport.

"Angels come in all forms," Sister Ignatius said. "They've appeared as fire, and light, and even ordinary people."

"I think they're whatever they want to be," Natalie said.

As Sister Ignatius moved away, Natalie smiled up at Sister Agatha. "I like it here."

"In the crafts room or in the monastery?" Sister Agatha asked.

"Both. But especially in the crafts room. Things are simple here. I mean, when you make something it's either pretty or not. There's no pretending."

"Do you pretend a lot?"

"Sometimes I make up my own games," she said. "When I play with my bear Diesel and my doll Gracie, I pretend they talk to me. But that's just make-believe. It's not like when my angel talks to me. That's real, but since no one sees or hears Samara but me, people don't believe she's there at all."

"But isn't it nice knowing that you're the only one who can see her?" Sister Agatha asked.

"Sometimes. But it's hard, too. The people who believe me keep wanting Samara and me to do all kinds of things for them. The ones who say I'm lying probably think that God goofed up big-time when he created me, and I'm going to go to you-know-where when I die."

"You are God's child, and He doesn't make mistakes," Sister Agatha said firmly.

"Then why is it that I'm always in trouble? *You* don't believe I can see Samara. Sister Ignatius is the only one who really understands."

"Understands?"

"She believes — in here," Natalie said, pointing to her heart. "She said that she knew an angel would come to help the sisters, that she'd seen a sign."

Sister Agatha remembered the night of the storm and the angel-shaped cloud. She'd dismissed it at first, but now . . .

Natalie's fingers danced over the clay as she shaped the figure. What had begun as crude folk art was now taking on a more delicate, expressive form.

Seeing that for the first time Natalie felt relaxed and at peace, Sister chose not to mention the impending visit from the chancellor. Deep down, she had a feeling that knowing wouldn't make any difference at all to Natalie. Her story would remain the same because, to her, it simply was the truth.

When the bell rang for Sext, the sixth hour of prayer said at noon, the roofers had already started ripping up the old roof with shovels and wrecking bars. The harsh din of metal scraping across the roof, the screech of nails being pulled, and the dragging of old roofing materials became a nightmare beyond anyone's expectations. The rich sound of the Mary bell was all but lost against the rumble of destruction up above and the crash of tar paper and debris as it struck the ground outside.

As if sensing the frustration of the others, Sister Gertrude sang louder. Others joined her, but their voices were no match for the racket outside, which only seemed to grow in intensity. It was as if the Devil himself had decided to host a concert of chaos just beyond their door. The scrapes and thuds made it impossible for them to devote themselves fully to prayer. When the "little hour" was finished, the pallor on Sister Clothilde's face, and the way Sister Eugenia gripped her rosary until her knuckles were a pearly white, said it all.

After checking on Natalie, who was still in the crafts room, this time with Sister de Lourdes, Sister Agatha followed through on an idea she'd had. Stopping by the scriptorium, she printed out some small cards that informed the bearer in a calligraphy style font that they would have a novena said for their intention. Today, she'd approach merchants in town, asking for donations, and having these with her would no doubt come in handy.

A short time later she joined Sister Bernarda in the parlor. "One of us needs to go by Smitty's Grocery and confirm that he's willing to carry our Cloister Clusters. If he places an order right away, we'll pick up the ingredients there, preferably in bulk. The two of us should go, but I really don't think we should leave Sister de Lourdes alone with the roofers in case there's an emergency. She's still too new as portress."

An ear-shattering crash sounded right outside the parlor door and Sister Agatha cringed instinctively. Sister Bernarda, on the other hand, never even blinked. "You've got nerves of steel," Sister Agatha commented.

"In the Marines I was trained to observe and direct artillery fire. I only seek cover when the rounds are incoming."

Sister Agatha looked at the unflappable Sister Bernarda. On the outside, they probably never would have met, nor would they have become friends had their paths crossed by some twist of fate. They came from very different backgrounds. Yet here none of that mattered. They were as close as sisters — sisters in Christ.

"I suggest that we bring Natalie back to the parlor for now, unless Sister Ignatius wants to watch her, and that you take Sister de Lourdes with you to town."

"That's a good idea," Sister Agatha said with a nod. "But you should consider inviting Pax into the parlor, too. I won't be able to take him with me, so he might as well make himself useful here. With all these workmen around, his place is guarding our doors."

Less than twenty minutes later, after a quick bite to eat, Sister Agatha and Sister de Lourdes left the monastery and climbed aboard the Antichrysler. The engine sputtered and coughed as she switched on the ignition and pumped the accelerator pedal. After running less than ten seconds, however, the Antichrysler died again with a strange wheeze.

Sister Agatha lifted the hood, removed the air filter, and sprayed some carburetor cleaner around the choke, then got back behind the wheel. This time it roared to life, but that was short-lived. The sound faded into a wheeze and, at last, an anemic hum.

"Will it make it to town and all the way back?" Sister de Lourdes asked, worried. "It really sounds bad today."

"The Antichrysler always sounds like it's ready to self-destruct, but it keeps going. I think ferrying us to town and back is its way of doing penance."

Sister de Lourdes smiled. "You joke now, but it won't seem like such an inconsequential thing if it poops out and we have to carry a hundred pounds of flour to the monastery on our backs."

"That won't happen. Just in case, though, pray."

They'd just turned onto the highway from the road leading to the monastery when Sister Agatha caught a glimpse of an old, faded red sedan several car lengths behind them. The driver paced them almost perfectly, never drawing too close or getting too far behind. An uneasy feeling settled over her, but when the vehicle eventually turned onto a side road, Sister Agatha relaxed.

As they continued south toward Bernalillo past fields and farmland, she cast a furtive look at Sister de Lourdes. Celia had been a reverent but enthusiastic postulant, even during the worst of times. Now she was distant and calm. The change was natural and a proper one. She was obeying the rule against forming attachments. The heart of a nun had to be emptied if it was to be consecrated wholly to God. And yet, she missed the girl that had looked to her for answers to everything when she'd first arrived at the monastery.

Sister Agatha gave her a long sideways glance, then looked back at the road. "You've done a very good thing, you know, choosing to be an extern."

"I didn't *choose*," Sister de Lourdes said quietly. "My heart didn't lead me to this — duty did. I wanted to be a cloistered nun. But when Reverend Mother asked me to become an extern, I couldn't say no," she said. "Eventually, it was Sister Eugenia who helped me come to terms with this. Did you know that she came to us from an active order? Sister Eugenia taught health classes at a community college."

Sister Agatha looked at Sister de Lourdes in surprise. "No, I didn't know that." Sister Eugenia had already been part of the monastery when she'd joined over fourteen years ago, and since then they'd never had time nor the inclination to talk much about their pasts. Admittedly, that was one subject Sister Agatha assiduously avoided. She hadn't exactly been a pillar of virtue before she got the calling. She'd had a plaque in her home that summed it all up very well — "To err is human, but it feels divine."

Mercifully, those days were a distant memory now.

"How did Sister Eugenia help you?" Sister Agatha asked, glancing over at Sister de Lourdes.

"I'd wanted to serve God as a contemplative, thinking that was the higher calling, and she reminded me of a quote from Romans that says, 'For there is no respect of persons with God,' " Sister de Lourdes said softly. "That's when I realized that there's no higher or lower calling. There's just serving God."

As Sister Agatha mulled over what Sister de Lourdes had just said, her thoughts drifted back to Natalie. Perhaps the girl, too, was serving God in her own unique way. After all was said and done, maybe her ability to see the angel would turn out to be inconsequential in comparison to her ability to believe.

As they parked in front of Smitty's Grocery, Sister Agatha caught a glimpse of the same faded red sedan she'd seen before. It passed them quickly, continuing down the highway, and although she tried, she wasn't able to get a glimpse of the driver's face.

"Is something wrong?" Sister de Lourdes asked, turning to look behind them.

"No, I guess not. Let's go inside and start our shopping," Sister Agatha said.

"But we won't know if Smitty's going to carry the cookies until we talk to him. Shouldn't we do that first?"

"Trust me."

Their list wasn't long, but it took two large shopping carts to hold all the bulk items. After they'd placed the last ingredient in the cart, Sister de Lourdes gave Sister Agatha a worried frown. "Your Charity, we don't have enough money," she whispered. "We can't possibly —"

Sister Agatha gestured for her to follow and remain silent. Locating Smitty at the back of the store, Sister Agatha went to meet him, pushing the first of the two carts.

"Good morning!" she greeted him warmly.

"Back at you, Sister!" He nodded to Sister de Lourdes, and saw the overloaded carts. He glanced back at Sister Agatha. "Are you stocking up for the rest of the year?"

"It looks like that doesn't it?" Sister Agatha let out a long, labored sigh. "Actually, we've had a bit of bad luck."

"The roof?" Seeing her nod, Smitty added, "What happened? Did the water get into your pantry?"

"No, nothing like that." She told him about their plan to bake Sister Clothilde's

Cloister Clusters to raise funds. "And we'd like your store here to carry them. Since you have another store in Albuquerque's Northeast Heights, maybe you could use some over there, too. We could make deliveries as often as you need and keep you supplied with fresh cookies."

"You don't have to talk me into this, Sister. You know how much I love them, and my customers feel the same. Consider it a done deal. I've wanted to approach you about that for a long time anyway."

"How many dozen cookies can you use, and how often will you want to restock?" Sister Agatha asked.

"How many to a box or bag?"

"I'd figured a dozen Clusters to a box," she said, sticking to the plan the sisters had already agreed upon.

Smitty considered it for a moment, then gave her the number of boxes he'd want twice a week.

When she heard it, Sister Agatha felt herself go pale. "Do you think you can sell so many?"

"Absolutely, if I'm the only vendor in town. And when the holidays come around, we'll probably increase that order by a third or more. You'll have that roof paid for before you know it," he said. "This'll turn out to be a good thing for everyone. The men who are repairing your roof are really grateful for the chance to work. With the holidays a few months away and the economy bad, everyone needs the extra cash."

"Speaking of cash . . . We're having a problem getting the funds to get our new business started. These groceries, for example . . ."

"I knew that was coming, Sister," he said with a grin. "Okay, here's the deal. You make sure that I get one box of cookies just for me every time you make a delivery and I'll cover half of what's in that shopping cart. Think of it as a jump-start."

"You've got yourself a deal," Sister Agatha said, then handed him one of the prayer cards. "And this entitles you to a novena said for your intention."

"Hey, that's terrific. Thanks. I'm not Catholic but I can always use prayers!"

As Smitty went to talk to one of his clerks, she turned to Sister de Lourdes, handing her the keys to the Antichrysler. "Can you handle things here now? I need to see about getting another stove for our kitchen."

"Go ahead. I'll be fine."

When Sister Agatha walked across the street to the used appliance store, she saw the red sedan parked at the end of the street. Uneasy, she angled toward it, but before she could walk another ten feet the driver pulled out and merged with traffic.

For a moment she stood there, wondering if she was just getting paranoid or if she'd really picked up a tail. If she saw the sedan again, she'd mention it to Tom and see if his department could figure out who it was. The honk of a horn made her remember she was still in the street, so she hurried to the sidewalk.

Sister Agatha went inside the appliance renewal center and began to look around. Sister Clothilde could use a more modern oven for her kitchen and this seemed like the perfect time to ask for a donation. Sometimes people got rid of perfectly good appliances because they'd remodeled their kitchens, or just because they'd wanted to upgrade.

Sister Agatha checked every promising stove she found, smiling often at the man behind the counter, who encouraged her to browse. She knew most of the Catholic businessmen in town but didn't recognize him, so she was pretty sure he wasn't Catholic. Saying a quick prayer, she approached him. "This is my first time in the store. Are you the owner?"

The man smiled. "That's me, Merle Hackman. I just bought this place from Larry Aker. Did you have a particular oven in mind, Sister?"

"I was impressed with the large gas stove at the end of that row," she said, pointing. "It looks almost new."

"It is. It works perfectly and is as clean as a whistle. I can even give you a full one-year guarantee at no extra charge. You couldn't get a better buy."

"It would get a lot of use, especially baking. Will it hold up?"

"Oh, yeah. Easily. That model is the residential version of a model designed for commercial use."

"Then it might be perfect for our monastery," she said, then exhaled softly. "We're starting a huge baking venture to raise the funds needed to replace our leaky roof. Have you by any chance heard of our Cloister Cluster cookies?"

Mr. Hackman smiled for the first time since she'd come in. "Yeah. My sister's a long time Bernalillo resident, and before I moved here, she'd always send me a box at Hanukkah."

"We want to supply Smitty's — the grocery store across the street — from now on, but our ancient ovens just aren't up to the task anymore. With roof repairs to pay for, we just don't have the money to buy another oven, but we desperately need a good used model like this one. Could we work out a trade? We could pray for you and your family daily throughout the coming year."

"I'm not much of a churchgoer, Sister."

"Then this is really your lucky day! Who needs prayer more than someone who has a new business and is too busy to pray for himself? Prayers can do nothing but bless. And on the temporal side, if you donate the oven to our monastery, you'd have a great write-off for your taxes! You can't lose."

"Whoa, Sister!" Merle said, laughing. "You're one fast talker, I'll give you that."

Before she could respond, he held up one hand and went to meet a delivery man who'd come to the door with three large boxes. Seeing Sister Agatha, the delivery man smiled and waved.

"Hello, Joe," she called back.

Merle signed for the order, then picked up one of the boxes and walked toward a back room.

Sister stepped over to where the remaining two boxes had been placed, then, saying a prayer, picked up one of the packages and followed Merle.

She'd only taken a few steps when a young man around twenty came rushing over.

"Sister, that's too heavy for you. Let me take it."

"I'm fine. But you can get the third box."

The young man hesitated. "Are you sure, Sister?"

"Absolutely. I can handle this." Sister Agatha took a jagged breath, then shifted the box and renewed her grip. A monstrous cramp shot through her arms, but she braced herself and continued. She was *not* crippled. As long as she refused to accept that label, arthritis would never be able to defeat her.

When she entered the back room, Merle reached to help her, but the young man who'd come in after her cleared his throat and shook his head imperceptibly.

Merle took a step back and cocked his head, gesturing to a shelf on his right. "You can put it over there, Sister."

A moment later, after she'd set the box down, he smiled at her. "You don't like to accept help, do you?"

Sister Agatha smiled back. "Not really," she admitted.

"And yet here you are, asking for help on behalf of the monastery."

"For God I'd do anything," she said, her heart in every word she'd uttered, "and right now His monastery needs an oven."

Merle studied her expression. "You have a real passion for your calling, Sister."

"I couldn't have put it better myself." She gave him a wide smile. "Does that mean you're willing to donate two ovens?"

Merle gave her an incredulous look. "*Two* ovens. A moment ago it was only one!"

"Yes, but you understand so much more now!" she answered. "And we have these little reminders of the service we'll provide for you in return." She fished out one of the prayer cards she'd made in the scriptorium and handed it to him. "And for *two* ovens, I'll personally say back-to-back novenas for you during the next twelve months."

He took the card from her hand. "What if I were to tell you that I'm Jewish?"

"Jesus was Jewish. My religion is rooted in yours and we both worship the same God. The letters *A M D G* at the bottom of the card means *Ad Majorem Dei Gloriam* — to the Greater Glory of God."

Merle laughed. "I give up. You may have *one* oven — the one you were looking at — if I can have a dozen of those cookies every week for the rest of the year."

"Deal."

"Will you be wanting to take it with you, or do you expect me to deliver it, too?"

"I'll make you a trade. Eighteen months

worth of prayers plus those weekly Clusters, and you deliver the stove."

"*Two* dozen Clusters — one for my customers here — and I'll make a special sign over the cookies saying that they were baked in one of our ovens at the monastery. We'll both get good advertising that way."

"Sounds eminently fair. And you can add the delivery costs as part of the charitable deductions on your taxes, too."

"Done deal, Sister."

As she walked to the door, Merle added, "If you ever need a part-time job, come and see me first. I can use a salesperson with your gift of persuasion."

"Thanks, but I've already got a job for life."

"Not bad, Sister," he said, laughing as he waved good-bye. "Not bad at all."

8

It had been a good afternoon and it wasn't even half over. In less than an hour she'd managed to get supplies and an oven donated. One of these days, she'd start working on one of the car dealers — the *new* car dealers. With God's help, she'd persuade them to provide the perfect transportation vehicle to the monastery. She would have started working on that today — after all, she was on a roll — but Reverend Mother would never allow them to discard the Antichrysler until the rattletrap car died permanently. It was part of honoring their vow of poverty.

Sister Agatha met Sister de Lourdes and Smitty moments later. Except for the front seat, nearly every inch of the old station wagon was filled with supplies.

"There's more in here than was in those two carts. This can't be right!" Sister Agatha said.

Smitty grinned at her. "I figured that you probably underestimated the order I'd be putting in, so to save you gas money and the trouble of coming back in a few days, I increased my donation. You owe me another prayer card."

Speechless and grateful, she pulled one out of her pocket. "Thank you so much on behalf of all the monastery, Smitty."

After the Antichrysler started up and they got underway, Sister Agatha told Sister de Lourdes about the oven.

"That's such terrific news! God certainly blessed our trip this morning!" Sister de Lourdes crossed herself. "If people understood the power of prayer, the world would be a different place."

"When people get caught up in all the pressures of their daily lives, they lose sight of God. It can be hard to focus on Him when the world is screaming in your ears."

The trip was slow, because the station wagon was heavily loaded and Sister Agatha didn't want to overtax the engine. They were close to the turnoff to the monastery when Sister Agatha once again saw the beat-up old sedan behind them. She was about to reach for the cell phone to call the sheriff when the car suddenly turned and headed down the same lane it had disappeared down earlier.

She was getting hopelessly paranoid. Someone had gone to town and back — just as they had.

They reached the monastery a short time later. The second the building came into full view, the feelings of well-being that had filled them after their successful run to town suddenly vanished.

"Oh my!" Sister de Lourdes whispered.

Other, more direct words popped into Sister Agatha's head, but mercifully her heart had leaped to her throat, making speech impossible.

Their monastery looked like it had been hit by a hurricane and a tornado at the same time. The roof — what remained of it — was mostly in ugly piles on the ground, and in the bed of an old dump truck that had been backed up close to the wall. Tar paper, torn pieces of heavy asphalt sheeting, and water-damaged plywood littered the area adjacent to the outer wall, where a workman was loading a wheelbarrow full of debris. Chaos reigned.

Parking close to the kitchen doors in the back, they hurried inside in a futile attempt to escape the agonized sound of metal scraping against wood, and the scream of power saws. Sporadic hammering inundated the abbey roof like a flock of giant wood-peckers.

Sister Clothilde gave Sister Agatha a pained smile and began to help carry the supplies into the provisory. Sister Agatha could see her mouthing the words of the Little Office of Mary as she worked: "Make haste to help me. Glory be to the Father and to the Son . . ."

After everything had been put away, Sister Agatha walked to the parlor. The thunderous noise overhead drowned out the jingle-jangle of Sister Bernarda's rosary as she paced.

"And they're trying to be quiet. Can you believe it?" Sister Bernarda said loudly, stopping in midstride and looking at her.

"It's no better around the kitchen."

"There's no escape."

Sister Agatha hesitated. Noting it, Sister Bernarda added, "What's on your mind?"

"I need to go back into town. My work's not done. I need to go talk to Jessica's neighbors. But you're working overtime in the parlor as it is . . ."

"Go, Sister, and find answers. We owe it to Father Mahoney."

Sister Agatha nodded slowly. "I'll do my best. But first I'm going to give Reverend Mother some *good* news," she said, then told Sister Bernarda about the oven and the supplies.

"That's *wonderful!* Mother will be really happy. But she can't be disturbed right now."

"What's happening?"

"The chancellor arrived from the bishop's office. He's been with Mother for over an hour."

Sister Agatha felt her stomach tighten. "And Natalie?"

"They haven't called for her yet," she said. "But that matter is out of your hands. Don't waste time worrying about it. You have other duties to attend to now," she said in her usual no-nonsense way.

Sister Agatha walked out into the garden looking for Pax, and noticed that the door to St. Francis's pantry was open. Assuming that one of the externs had gone in there for something, she turned away and continued to the far end of the garden, searching for the dog.

Then, as she considered the possibility that one of the workmen may have gone in there instead of a nun, she turned to look again. One of the sisters came out of the small building, shut the door, then half turned toward her.

From that distance, Sister Agatha couldn't

see her face, particularly because she kept it bowed down, but it had to have been Sister de Lourdes. Sister Agatha waved and tried to catch her attention, but the nun kept walking, her head down. Finally, she went around the building and disappeared from view.

"*Where* are you going?" Sister Agatha said softly to herself, picking up the pace. Hurrying, Sister Agatha reached the corner of the pantry and stepped onto the flagstone walkway which led to the open gate. The nun had vanished and there was no one in sight.

Looking down at the ground, she noticed one set of large footprints, then observed something very puzzling. The nun, who was wearing boots, had circled around the building as if trying to avoid her.

Returning quickly to the main house, Sister Agatha looked around carefully. The back gate leading to the enclosure side of the garden was open, and just beyond she saw a nun entering through the kitchen door.

Sister Agatha picked up her skirt slightly and broke into a run. She reached the kitchen in ten seconds. When she hurried in, Sister Ignatius was doing kitchen duty, sweeping the refectory floor.

"Who just ran down the hall, Sister?" Sister Ignatius asked, turning to Sister Agatha, who was now standing in the center of the room. "She sprinted past here like the devil was two steps behind her and gaining."

"I've been trying to catch up to her. I know it wasn't Sister Bernarda, but it didn't look like Sister de Lourdes from a distance, either. Too tall. I almost caught up to her, but she ditched me. I think she's wearing the mud boots, too. But none of the cloistered sisters would ever wander out to St. Francis's pantry."

"But that leaves only . . . an intruder?" Sister Ignatius said in a strangled voice.

"Or I could be wrong." Sister Agatha shook her head, walking quickly to the next doorway.

Sister Agatha hurried down the hall toward the chapel. Entering from the enclosure side, she looked down toward the public entrance. Then she heard the doors click shut. They had been locked, but could have been opened from the inside. She ran the length of the chapel, opened the doors, and nearly collided with a workman pushing a wheelbarrow full of debris.

"Whoa, Sister!" The sweating young man struggled to keep the wheelbarrow from tipping over as she slipped around him, looking everywhere for the other nun.

"Did a nun come out of here just a moment ago, sir?"

"Like a bat out of hell. Oh, excuse me, Sister. No, wait, you can say hell, right?" He chuckled. "What's going on? You have a fight or something?"

"Where'd she go?" With every passing second she was becoming more convinced that the person she'd seen hadn't been a nun at all. She looked down at the man's feet. He had on lace-up boots.

"I think the nun ran out the front gate. Fast, too."

"Thanks." Sister Agatha jogged over to the motorcycle, and hopped on. The Harley's V-twin engine sound was distinctive, and Sister Bernarda came to the parlor window. Sister Agatha saw her puzzled expression, but there was no time to explain. Wheeling the cycle in the tightest circle she could manage, Sister Agatha put on the gas and roared through the gate.

A hundred yards down the dirt road was a curve. As she eased off the gas and rounded the corner, Sister Agatha noticed something dark and familiar looking in the small drainage ditch beside the road. A habit had been discarded and left in the brush.

"That was no nun," she grumbled, braking to a sliding halt. Rising up off the seat, she looked around into the brush, hoping to see someone. A line of trees where the bosque began was less than a hundred yards away, and a fence there prevented her from following except on foot.

Motoring down the road slowly, she searched on both sides for signs of anyone, but found only birds, a few squirrels, and a cottontail. Turning around, she went back to the side of the road where she'd seen the discarded habit. Sister Agatha switched off the engine and climbed down from the cycle, then walked over to the ditch. From the habit's wrinkled appearance, she guessed it had probably been taken from a laundry basket. On the ground beneath it was a pair of rubber mud boots the sisters used for emergencies and messy garden work. That particular pair was easily large enough for a man.

"Sister Agatha?" A voice that sounded like Sister Bernarda's called from up the road.

"Over here," she answered.

As Sister Bernarda walked in her direction, Sister Agatha took time to examine the ground nearby. She quickly found what looked like a trail left by someone wearing socks. Then, after a short distance, she saw sneaker imprints leading toward the bosque. The left shoe had a diagonal slash across the heel. If she ever saw it again, the imprint would be easy to recognize.

"What are you doing, Your Charity?" Sister Bernarda's face was flushed either from the hurried walk and the extra pressure on her ankle, or consternation. "That man with the wheelbarrow told me one nun was chasing the other."

"Here's the other nun," Sister Agatha held up the dirty habit. "Or what's left of her — or him?"

"You mean we had an intruder dressed as a nun wandering around Our Lady of Hope? That sleazy . . . ," Sister Bernarda snarled.

"Whatever you were going to say, Sister, I agree. But it should probably be left unspoken."

"We need to call the sheriff's department," Sister Bernarda said. "You have the cell phone, don't you?"

"Yes. But first I'll take you back home," she said. "Someone needs to look around the monastery and make sure everyone is safe — especially our guest."

"I made her lock her door, and Sister de Lourdes is with her now."

Sister Agatha climbed onto the seat and

started the engine. By then, her companion had already climbed into the sidecar.

Ten minutes later Sister Agatha was on her way into town with Pax. The sheriff's department had been called, and because Tom Green hadn't been at the station, she'd made a quick report to the officer on duty. A deputy would be sent to the neighborhood to ask residents if they'd seen any strangers, but Sister Agatha doubted they'd be very much help, either. Later, an officer would drop by the monastery and get statements from anyone there who might have seen the bogus nun.

This time as she drove to town she remained alert for the beat-up red sedan which had taken on an all-new significance because of the intruder. But the vehicle was nowhere in sight.

Hoping to make some progress, Sister Agatha proceeded to Jessica Tannen's home and parked out by the street. The police tape was still around the house, but she hadn't planned on going inside. Getting Natalie's angel doll out in broad daylight would have been too risky. She'd come to talk to Jessica's neighbors, so, sticking to her plan, she went next door and knocked.

A woman in her late sixties or early seventies wearing workmen's overalls answered the door. "Can I help you?"

"I was wondering if I could ask you a few questions about Jessica, your next-door neighbor."

She eyed Pax with suspicion. "Is he housebroken?"

"And very well trained," Sister Agatha answered.

"Well then, you better come in and take a load off," she said, then led her to a small, homey kitchen and waved her to a chair. "I was just having something to drink. You can join me."

As she stepped into the kitchen, Sister Agatha saw a brindle pit bull curled up on a bed in the corner of the kitchen. Automatically, she grabbed Pax's collar and took a step back.

Seeing it, the woman smiled and shook her head. "Stinkerbelle's older than dirt and deaf as a stone. Don't worry about her. She probably won't wake up as long as your dog don't bother her."

Sister Agatha placed Pax at "down and stay" and kept a cautious eye on the other animal, but she hadn't even stirred.

"Sorta looks like she's gone and died, don't it? But she hasn't. If you look really close, you'll see her take a breath now and then."

Sister Agatha took a sip of the coffee she was offered and nearly gagged. It was the worst she'd ever had. Not even milk could dilute the burnt taste.

"I don't think I introduced myself properly. I'm Sister Agatha, from Our Lady of Hope Monastery. This is Pax."

The woman laughed. "Sister, you don't need an introduction. I read the newspapers. Once I saw that bright motorcycle come roaring up, I knew exactly who you were. I'm Esther Reinhart," she said, extending her hand.

"Pleasure to meet you," Sister Agatha said, shaking her hand.

"Now tell me, how I can help you."

"First, can you tell me how well you know Jessica Tannen?"

"I can't say we're close friends, but we often stand at the fence and talk. I've asked her over a few times, but she's always busy. She works long hours, and when she's home I think she spends her time catching up on the chores. But we're good neighbors. She keeps an eye on my place when I'm not home and I do the same for her."

"Do you recall ever seeing anyone hanging around the house when she wasn't there

154

". . . or when she was?"

"The police asked me the same thing, so I'll tell you what I told them. Except for her brother the priest and the occasional Parcel Express delivery man, she has no regular visitors. Truth is, she and the little girl are seldom home. On weekdays, Natalie stays with her sitter until Jessica gets off work, which is usually at around eight at night. By ten, when I watch the news, the lights over at their house are out. On weekends, they're off running errands."

"Do you know the sitter?"

"Sure, it's Margo Stewart. She lives in the house on the other side of Jessica's."

"Thank you very much for the coffee — and for your help," Sister Agatha said, swallowing hard and trying to get that awful taste out of her mouth.

"Sister, that wasn't coffee! That was my special mix — two parts coffee-flavored protein drink and one glug of tequila."

It took all of her strength not to gag. Somehow she forced herself to smile and continue walking to the motorcycle. As soon as she was sure Esther wasn't watching, she reached into a saddlebag and pulled out a bottle of water. The vile taste remained in her mouth even after a long drink. "Next time I assume something in a coffee cup is just coffee, Pax, bite me."

The dog looked up and gave her a panting grin.

At Mrs. Stewart's, Sister Agatha knocked, not seeing a doorbell. Although she could hear someone inside, no one answered. She knocked again. Then, instead of footsteps, she heard a creaking noise following by a heavy thunk. The sounds were as rhythmic as they were ominous. Pax's ears pricked up and he stood.

"No, sit and stay, Pax," Sister Agatha said, but remained alert. Taking a firm hold on his collar, she waited.

A heartbeat later, the door opened and a woman in a wheelchair holding a long, hooked wooden staff appeared. "Hello, Sister," she said pleasantly. "What can I do for you?"

As she explained why she'd come, Sister Agatha's gaze strayed to the long cane, which reminded her of a shepherd's hook from children's Bible stories.

Following her line of vision, the woman smiled. "I've got two cats who refuse to move aside and make room for my wheelchair, so I push them out of the way gently with this. I use the hook at the other end for pulling things closer so I can reach them." She laid the cane across her lap, then moved her wheelchair back and gestured for her to come in. "If your dog will behave, he's welcome, too. But remember my cats. There'll be no chasing."

"Pax'll stay right by my side, don't worry." Sister Agatha followed her into a small, simply furnished living. The leather sofa had been repaired in several places, but it had been done with care. At each end were two angel dolls — one was a bear with wings, the other one a hippo with similar flight gear.

"I bought those for Natalie, but she only plays with Gracie, a wrinkly-faced rag doll with wings. She loves it. So much for taste," Mrs. Stewart said with a shaky smile. "Natalie stays with me on weekdays until her mom gets home. Jessica works at Grayson Construction all day then a few hours at night at the library. Jessica needed help so we worked out an informal arrangement that works well for both of us. I babysit and she fixes me dinner on weekends."

"Has anyone been bothering her lately?"

"People come up to her and Natalie all the time, but Jessica can handle herself. She's very independent and a bit of a loner, too, which is odd because she's young and very pretty. But the few times I've been at her house I've noticed how jumpy she gets whenever someone comes to her door. I may be wrong about this, but I don't think anyone's that nervous without a specific reason."

"Think back. Did you ever see anything out of the ordinary going on over there? I don't mean something blatant like a man with a crowbar lurking by the windows. I'm thinking of something that might have struck you as odd at the time, but didn't seem worth mentioning to anyone. Since there's no hedge between your home and Jessica's, you have an unobstructed view."

Mrs. Stewart mulled it over for a few minutes, then nodded. "I'd forgotten all about it until now. It happened the night we had that bad rainstorm. I was out on my porch pushing the sandbags into place. My porch floods easily because the water in front drains toward the porch when the rain really comes down. That night, as I was working, I saw a pickup pull into Jessica's driveway. Although it was pouring rain, she came out to talk to the driver, who'd started to get out. Less than a minute later the pickup drove away and Jessica ran back inside the house."

"Did you get a look at the driver?"

"No, no way. The downpour was as thick as soup by then."

"Did you notice the color of the pickup?"

"A light color," she said, her eyebrows knitting together. "Light gray, I think. But it was dark by then and Jessica's porch light isn't very bright."

Sister Agatha weighed what she'd learned, then added, "Had you ever seen that pickup there before?"

"No, but it could have been a mail carrier. Our post office contracts mail delivery out, so our carriers use their own cars or pickups sometimes."

"Thanks. I appreciate the help."

Sister Agatha headed to the post office next and, after checking, found Jessica's neighborhood mail carrier out in the back loading his truck. She recognized him right away as the monastery's mailman.

"Hey, Jerry, how are you?" she asked, noting that his truck was light blue.

"Fine, Sister. What brings you here?"

"I'm trying to figure out something," she said, and explained about the pickup at Jessica's. Giving him the address, she added, "Did you make a delivery there that night?"

"Sister, I make a lot of deliveries. I have no idea if I was there that night or not. But I do remember I was backlogged that day because my regular vehicle broke down around noon. My wife had our truck, so I had to borrow my son's SUV. I didn't get through until very late because of the weather."

Disappointed by his vague answer, she added, "Have you ever seen anyone or anything that seemed out of place in that neighborhood?"

"Not really," he said. "I spoke to Joe Rodriguez, the Parcel Express guy who works that neighborhood. Jessica does a lot of catalog shopping so Joe goes by almost every week. We had a few beers at The Hog last night and we got to talking about what happened to Jessica Tannen. We both tried to remember if we'd seen anyone bugging her, but we struck out. That's a quiet neighborhood with several nosy, retired ladies who seem to hang out by their windows. If anyone had been skulking around, one of those old gals would have a deputy there in zero flat."

"Thanks, Jerry. If you happen to remember anything else, just drop me a note in the turn when you go by the monastery."

After saying good-bye, Sister Agatha headed to the sheriff's station with Pax. If Sheriff Green was back, she had a few questions for him. She also wanted to follow up on the phony nun and the red sedan she kept seeing.

Underway, Sister Agatha thought of the sisters back at the monastery. They'd be going crazy by now trying to find a way to concentrate on their prayers despite the noise that surrounded them. Instead of finding the comfort and promise of God's love in the Divine Office, they were bound to be frustrated by the distractions and their inability to focus on their duty. But the roof had to be fixed. Just as she was about to pronounce it a hopeless situation, she had a burst of sheer inspiration. There was one more donation she needed to get for the monastery and this one would have to come from the county sheriff's department.

9

Sister Agatha walked into the police station a short while later with Pax at her side. Spotting her, Tom Green came out of his office and invited her to take a seat in his office. "I heard about the incident. A deputy was dispatched to the monastery and interviewed every one of the roofers about that intruder of yours, but they weren't any help. Sister Bernarda spoke to the cloistered nuns, but none of them got a look at the bogus nun's face, either. You also didn't see a face, right?"

"No, but I'm pretty certain, by the way the person moved, that it was a man. Did the officer check for fingerprints?"

"On the doors in the chapel and St. Francis's pantry, yes, but what he got was too smudged to be of much use," he said. "According to their foreman, all of the roofing crew was accounted for at the time you saw the nun. But we've asked the workmen to keep an eye out for anyone approaching the grounds who's not part of their crew."

"Thank God the intruder didn't harm anyone."

"I personally think that this incident is related to your guest," Tom said. "I had a reporter from one of the tabloids on my back earlier today. The fool actually started following me. I threatened to throw his sorry butt in jail if he ever pulled that again."

"Tabloids? They're following the story?"

"At least two of them are here from out of town. They want to interview Natalie, so stay sharp."

"Thanks for the heads-up. I'll try to find out if there's any possibility that the phony nun might have seen or heard Natalie. Maybe it was one of those reporters."

"Maybe, but anyone trying to find Natalie would eventually consider the monastery, particularly since her uncle's your chaplain." Tom crossed his arms across his chest. "Please ask the sisters to be extra careful now."

"Have you made any progress on the case?"

Sheriff Green leaned back in his chair. "There are no new leads, not even an address on the ex-husband, Henry Tannen. Can't even get his fingerprints, though he apparently served some prison time in Colorado after the divorce. Some red tape glitch. Nothing from locals, either, about the rest of the family. Truth is, people are reluctant to talk about Jessica because of Natalie."

"I don't get it. What do you mean?"

"I'm guessing some of the true believers are afraid Natalie will sic the angel on them if they speak badly of Jessica," he said. "Or maybe it's simpler — they just don't want to upset anyone who has contact with the supernatural."

"That makes sense — in a crazy kind of way."

"I'm also looking into the possibility that someone wanted to take Natalie out of the picture completely. There are people around who think she's channeling something nasty."

"That, I can categorically say, is baloney."

"So does Father Mahoney, and that's kept the lid on things somewhat."

"I've been trying to tackle things from another angle. I want to find out what made Jessica take Natalie out in that downpour. Did you find anything at all in the car that might help explain it?"

"Jessica kept that car spotless. We didn't find as much as a candy wrapper."

"I *may* have found a connection to her sudden departure." She told him about the pickup Margo Stewart had seen in Jessica's driveway earlier. "Did you know about all that?"

"No," he said, leaning forward. "What else did the neighbor say?"

"That's all I got from her," she said, then told Tom about her conversation with the mail carrier.

"People always open up to you and remember things they never told us," he grumbled. "It's the nun thing. You're not threatening to them," he said. "But come to think of it, Natalie should have known about her mother's stepping outside during the rain that night and she didn't mention it to us here. Has she said anything to you about that?"

"No, but I haven't seen her since visiting Mrs. Stewart. I'll talk to Natalie when I get back. My guess is that she forgot."

"Press her. This could be critical. And make sure you keep me current on whatever you find out."

"You've got it," Sister Agatha said, then added, "There's one more thing I need to talk to you about." She told him about the beat-up red sedan.

"Officers are already checking in the area

165

of the monastery, and deputies are on the watch for a vehicle matching the description. Let's see what pops up. Meanwhile, if you see it again, call me — immediately."

"It doesn't stick around, Tom. It's there, it disappears, then appears out of nowhere again when I least expect it."

"That's the mark of a really good tail. Just call me next time you spot it. And remember to let me know right away if you hear from the mail carrier. We got zero from him the other day."

"I'll be happy to help, but now I need to ask you a favor." There had never been a better time. It was almost providential. "The monastery needs you to make a donation — well, it's more like a loan."

As Sister Agatha told him about her idea, she knew she wouldn't be turned down. The sisters and Reverend Mother would be getting a much deserved blessing by the end of the day.

Sister Agatha left for the monastery in high spirits. She was coming bearing gifts and couldn't wait to approach Reverend Mother. Of course, it could have been argued that she should have asked Reverend Mother *before* asking Tom, but once the idea had come to her, she'd wanted to act on it right away.

As she walked into the parlor, Sister Bernarda saw what she had dangling from her arm and laughed. "Ear protectors — the kind used on a firing range? Are you sure you brought that donation to the right place?"

Sister Agatha looked at her as a new burst of hammering rocked the air. "Can you think of a better place for these?" she shouted.

"And Reverend Mother approved?"

"Well, not yet, actually," Sister Agatha said, less sure now. "So I'm going to leave them here and go speak with her first. Of course, the portresses won't be able to wear them at all since we need to know when someone comes to the door, but these would be a huge blessing for the cloistered sisters."

Sister Bernarda nodded slowly. "They would at that. Sister Eugenia said she's had a run on aspirins."

"I'll go talk to Reverend Mother now."

"I think the issue of the ear protectors will have to wait. Reverend Mother left word that she wanted to talk to you as soon you got back."

Sister Agatha felt her stomach tighten.

"What's up?"

"I'm not sure, but the chancellor is still here, though he spoke to Natalie quite a while ago."

"Does he know about our intruder?"

"I have no idea. It's not my place to ask — nor yours." Her Marine drill instructor's voice was now at its best. "Your duty is to obey."

"I'm on my way," she said, handing Sister Bernarda the ear protectors.

Sister Agatha walked down the corridor and rapped lightly on Reverend Mother's open door.

"Sit down, child," Reverend Mother said after the customary greeting. "This is Father John Roberts, chancellor of our diocese. He has some questions for you about Natalie."

"I'll be happy to answer them, if I can," she said. Grasping the rosary's crucifix hanging from her cincture for courage, she looked directly at the priest.

"I spoke to Natalie for about fifteen minutes earlier today and she continues to insist that she sees an angel. You've been around the girl. What's your opinion?"

"I suspect, Father, her keen interest in angels began as a game. The child prayed for an angel to come and be her friend because she was lonely. Pretty soon, if Natalie pretended hard enough, she could visualize the angel, and in time her creation became real to her."

"Is she unstable?" Father asked.

"I'm no psychologist, but I doubt it. I think what we're dealing with is a lonely little girl — nothing more. Natalie's father abandoned them. She's never even seen him. Her mother works long hours. I think Natalie wanted a friend who would never go away."

As the noise on the roof began again, they all cringed. Father Roberts went to the window, verified that it was shut, then returned to his chair and continued in a louder voice.

"According to witnesses to the first incident, she shouted at the car, telling it to stop, and it did. Natalie insists it wasn't her doing, that the angel did it. Then there was that fire at a friends' house she predicted," he added. "Natalie says that her angel told her it was going to happen."

"It's still all just circumstantial evidence fueled by a truckload of gossip and media hype," she said, offering the other explanations she'd heard.

"So, in your opinion, should the church step in and debunk these incidents?"

Sister Agatha considered the question for

a while before answering. "This is a tricky situation, Father. No one else outside of Natalie can see this angel and none of the incidents can be said to be genuine miracles because each instance also lends itself to another, rational explanation. Natalie's not really the problem. She's just the victim of overblown media attention and gossip."

"Have you ever seen her go into a trance or an ecstacy?"

"No, but occasionally her gaze will become focused and she'll stare at something no one else can see. She acts as if she's really concentrating and trying to listen carefully but that's scarcely evidence in itself."

"When I questioned Natalie, she wasn't very talkative. I think she was afraid, so I'm going to try a different strategy this time. I'd like you to stay with us. Maybe she'll relax and speak more freely with you present."

The hammering continued at a furious intensity that seemed to rock the walls around them. It was coming from two different directions now, trapping them between thunderous walls of sound.

"I need answers to a few more questions," he said, handing Sister Agatha a piece of paper. "Perhaps if you ask, and Reverend Mother and I remain in the background, we'll have better results."

Sister Agatha read them over and took a deep breath. "I think you're overestimating the rapport I have with Natalie. You'd be better off asking Sister Ignatius to come in with her."

The chancellor looked at Reverend Mother, who shook her head. "Sister Ignatius won't be much help with something like this. She'll feel uncomfortable, and that feeling will communicate itself to the girl. Sister Agatha was a journalist before she came to us. She'll know how to phrase the questions in a way that won't upset Natalie. I believe she'll get the answers you need." Reverend Mother looked back at Sister Agatha. "Will you try, child?"

"I'll do my best, Mother," Sister Agatha answered.

"Then bring Natalie to us."

Sister Agatha walked through the monastery, glad that she hadn't had to answer questions about their intruder in front of the chancellor. Since no one had brought up the subject, she wasn't sure if Reverend Mother had even told him about it. Just in case, she made a mental note to be careful not to say anything herself.

Sister Agatha found Natalie removing flakes of wood from a big block with a special carving knife. She was wearing protective gloves, a wise decision by Sister Ignatius.

"What are you doing?" Sister Agatha asked, intrigued.

"I'm trying to carve a mold in this balsa. By pressing the clay into this, and then lifting it out carefully, Sister Ignatius will be able to make the Christmas angel figures quickly, and she'll have more to sell at the bazaar."

"That's a wonderful idea," Sister Agatha said, then glanced at Sister Ignatius. "But let Sister Ignatius put that away for you right now. You and I are needed in Reverend Mother's office."

Natalie placed the knife down and looked at Sister Agatha. "You're going to help me with Chancellor Roberts," she said. "Samara told me you would."

Sister Agatha didn't comment.

After washing her hands in the small sink in the corner, Natalie gave Sister Agatha a tentative smile. "I'm ready, but I sure wish Father Roberts would believe me. I've told him all I know. Samara keeps me company, but it's not as if we're always talking to each other. Most of the time she's just there — not saying anything."

"Then that's exactly what you should tell him."

"I did last time, but he's never seen an angel, so they think for sure I'm making it all up. They probably want to send me to one of those head doctors."

"Has your angel given you any advice about how to convince them she's real?"

Natalie shook her head. "I asked Samara for a lock of her hair. It's down to her waist and it's very pale yellow — almost white. But she said that if I want blond hair, I should buy a wig."

Sister Agatha burst out laughing, and Natalie joined in.

As they drew closer to the chapel, the scraping of tools and the pulling of nails grew in intensity — a cacophony of discordant sounds that seemed to rip through her skin and resonate against the marrow of her bones. She made a mental note right then to ask Reverend Mother about the use of the ear protectors as soon as possible.

"Samara just told me to tell you that there's danger coming. You should prepare," Natalie said during a lull in the racket overhead. Natalie looked to her side, then finally back at Sister Agatha. "She said it'll come in silence and you won't see it until it's too late. Samara says that you should remain on your guard because Satan loves the unsuspecting soul."

Sister Agatha's skin prickled. The girl had a great delivery — very convincing. "Well, if it comes in silence, it won't be anywhere near this monastery while the roof is being replaced."

When they arrived at Reverend Mother's office, Natalie was directed to one of the chairs, and Sister Agatha to the seat next to her. Father Roberts stood at the far side of the room, and Reverend Mother remained behind her desk.

"Natalie, you know that Sister Agatha's your friend and would never do anything to hurt you. That's why we asked her to be here while you tell her — and us — everything else you can about your angel," the chancellor said. "We don't want you to be afraid."

"I've already told you all I know. *Why* don't you believe me?"

"It's not that, Natalie," Sister Agatha said. "The problem is that we don't really understand it. It's kind of like when you're at school and the teacher has to explain about a math problem several times before everyone in the class gets it."

"Yeah, okay," Natalie said with a nod.

"How did the angel first let you know she

was there?" Sister Agatha asked her.

Natalie shrugged. "She just came."

"When?"

"A few months ago, I guess. Mom had just started to work her second job and was always too tired to play. I prayed like they taught us in catechism class, but nothing happened. Then one day Samara was just there."

"How did you know she was an angel? You mentioned she didn't have wings."

"What else could she have been? She shimmers, and when I look at her, it's like looking at the sun, only the light that comes from her doesn't hurt your eyes. She's beautiful," Natalie said.

"When did she begin talking to you?"

"I was talking to Louann Madison one day at lunch, and she invited me to a sleep-over at her house. But Samara told me not to go. It surprised me 'cause she'd never spoken to me before. I did what she wanted, but later I asked Samara about it. She told me about the fire and also said I shouldn't tell anyone at school about her or her warning. But I had to — Louann was my friend. So I told her to watch out for a fire, and I told Louann all about my angel," she said softly. "But Samara was right. It just made things worse, and it didn't stop the fire, either."

"So what did you do then?"

"I guess I should have stopped talking about Samara. No one believed she was real even after that car stopped because of her. They just thought I was crazy. I really wanted everyone to believe me so they'd like me," she said, and exhaled softly.

"But I messed up bad because the more I talked about her, the worse things got. Strangers started coming up to me wanting to know what was going to happen to them, or asking me to get my angel to help them. Samara stayed out of it — she wouldn't even talk to me. Then the TV people came and did their story. After that people thought that my guardian angel would do whatever I asked her, but that isn't the way things work."

Natalie sighed softly. "All I wanted was to have more friends, but after that everyone started avoiding me. Even Louann's mom was afraid. She told Louann not to hang out with me anymore."

"You must have been very sad and lonely," Sister Agatha said with genuine sympathy.

"I was, until Samara started talking to me again. But she didn't say what was going to happen anymore, or fix things for me."

"When your angel talks to you, do you hear her like you're hearing me now?"

"No, it's not like that. I hear the words in my head."

"Is she here now?" Sister Agatha asked.

"Yeah. She's standing just to the right of Father, on *his* left."

Father Roberts's eyes widened slightly and he turned to look. Instantly aware of the lapse, he gathered his composure quickly then cleared his throat. "Well, I think we have enough for now. Thanks for talking to us again, Natalie," Father Roberts said.

Sister Agatha smiled at Natalie. "I bet that all this has made you hungry. How about a snack?" she asked.

"If you have a cookie in mind, I'm in," Natalie said.

Reverend Mother looked at Sister Agatha. "We'll need you to come back as soon as Natalie is settled, child."

"Yes, Mother," Sister Agatha said, then focused on Natalie. As they walked down the corridor they saw Sister Maria Victoria coming toward them carrying a large quilt.

"The quilt is done," Sister Maria Victoria said, taking advantage of the rare quiet moment. "I was on my way to the scriptorium so I could give it to Sister de Lourdes. She's going to take a photo of it so you and Sister

Bernarda can put it up on our Web site. I hope it brings us a good price, but I know it won't be even close to what Reverend Mother needs to pay for this roof," she said quietly.

Sister Maria Victoria held it up for them to see. The quilt had the outline of the Blessed Mother in shades of light blue against an intricately quilted background of eggshell and white.

"It's exquisite, Sister," Sister Agatha said. "I'm sure it'll do well for us."

As they walked away, Sister Agatha glanced at Natalie. "I know you already talked to the sheriff about the night of the accident, but I have a question I'd like to ask you about that. Do you mind?"

Natalie shook her head.

"Did your mother go outside in the rain just before you went for a drive with her?"

She thought about it for a moment, then nodded. "Mom was all wet when she came to get me, so I guess so. But I didn't see her outside. I was in my room playing."

Sister Agatha nodded. "Someone came up to your house that night before you left. That's why your mom first went outside. Do you have any idea who it might have been?" She was hoping to trigger Natalie's memory. "The person was driving a pickup."

"Like the one that hit us?" she asked, her voice rising slightly.

"Not necessarily. Lots of people have pick-ups."

"Mom didn't say anything about it." She gave Sister Agatha an earnest look. "Let's wait until we can talk to Mom and then I'll ask her. Will I be able to see her soon?"

"I'm not sure. Try to be patient, okay?"

"Okaaay," she answered drawing out the word with mock weariness.

They were almost at the crafts room when Sister Maria Victoria caught up to them. "The photo came out lovely. Say a prayer that lots of people bid on our quilt," she said.

"We all will, Sister," Sister Agatha said.

As she moved away, Natalie looked at Sister Agatha. "Is the monastery broke? Mom and I get that way sometimes."

"We have some money problems right now that we're trying to work through," Sister Agatha said.

Natalie stopped in midstride and looked to something only she could see on her right. "Samara says that you and the sisters should stop worrying. She says that the monastery has its own angel who works for all of you. I'm supposed to remind you of the story of Jacob and Esau that tells how Jacob scared himself silly by imagining the worst."

Sister Ignatius, who'd come out into the hall, heard Natalie plainly. She stared at the girl with widened eyes, then gave Sister Agatha a bewildered look.

Afraid that Sister Ignatius would read too much into what Natalie had said, especially after today's intruder, she waited for Natalie to go into the room, then whispered, "Every child knows the story of Jacob and Esau, Your Charity."

Sister Ignatius gave her a sad smile. "Helen Keller was once asked if there was anything worse than being blind. She replied that there was — a person with sight and no vision."

When Sister Agatha returned to Reverend Mother's office, she told her and the chancellor what had just happened in the hall.

"Jacob believed that Esau was coming to kill him. But what he feared most never happened," Reverend Mother said.

"It's an appropriate story and lesson, particularly in light of the financial problems facing most New Mexican monasteries," Father Roberts said.

"But surely an eight-year-old couldn't

have extracted that lesson from the story all on her own," Reverend Mother said.

"She may have been taught it," Sister Agatha said.

"Just the point I was about to make," the chancellor said.

Reverend Mother nodded slowly. "So what will you recommend to the bishop?" she asked the chancellor.

"That the church stay out of this matter. There are no miracles to substantiate, or messages for mankind. I don't think it'll ever be possible for us to know whether or not Natalie is really seeing an angel. But I will recommend that Father Mahoney point out to his parishioners that most of the claims have been enhanced and exaggerated by gossip, not from anything that his niece said or did."

After the meeting ended, Sister Agatha accompanied Father Roberts outside. She was standing on the front step watching him drive away when Pax came up and pushed against her the way he usually did when he wanted to be petted.

Even though she'd already placed her hand on the dog's head, Pax pushed her again. Sister Agatha almost lost her balance and had to take a few quick steps to the side in order to recover. "Will you cut that out?" she demanded, annoyed.

Not daunted in the least by her tone of voice, the dog licked her hand, then ran off to chase a piece of roofing felt that had been caught by the breeze. He barked back at her, trying to get her to play chase.

Suddenly Sister Agatha heard a noise up on the roof. She turned her head to look up just as a large piece of rotting lumber fell down. It crashed to the ground and broke into two jagged pieces on the spot where she'd been standing before Pax had pushed her aside.

Her heart beating overtime and her body trembling, she pressed back against the wall. The horrifying certainty that she'd barely escaped death drained the warmth from her body, leaving only fear and an unbearable cold in its wake.

10

"Hey, anyone down there?" a workman peered over the edge. "Sister? You okay?" the excited man yelled.

Sister Agatha managed only a nod. Shaking, she stared at the jagged piece of water-soaked timber. Large, rusty nails the size of pencils were sticking out of it like slender daggers. If the dog hadn't pushed her aside when he did, she would have been on her way to the hospital — or worse — by now.

Sister Bernarda came rushing out from the entry and put her arm around her. "Are you okay? I heard the crash and looked out the window. You could have been killed!"

Del Martinez, the owner of the roofing company, and his foreman, Justin Clark, came rushing around the corner of the building. "Who let this fall over here?" Del demanded, looking up at the men who'd gathered on the roof above the debris.

"Don't look at us, boss," said the same

lanky, dark-haired man who'd peered over the edge first. "We were all working at the north end of the roof until we heard the noise."

"You were the only one in this section, *jefe*," another member of the crew said, using the Spanish word for *boss* and looking directly at Del.

Del turned on him, his eyes sparking with anger. "Exactly what are you implying, Ramon?"

"Nothing, *jefe*. I was just answering your question."

"I'll get to the bottom of this," Justin said, moving toward one of the ladders.

Del looked back at Sister Agatha. "I'm very sorry about this, Sister. All the debris was supposed to be thrown off the east side, closer to where the truck's parked. This must have slid off the crown of the roof. But between that nun who ran off and the sheriff's deputy bugging my men, work just hasn't been in sync today. And now everyone's hurrying so they can go home for the day."

"Then get it together," Sister Bernarda snapped. "This should have never happened."

"You're right," Del admitted. "I'll have a talk with my crew. Nothing like this will happen again."

As Del climbed up the ladder to join his foreman and the men, Sister Agatha went back inside with Sister Bernarda.

"I'm all right," Sister Agatha said, finally finding her voice. "It scared me witless, but everything's all right now, thank God. All that's left is for me to stop shaking like a leaf."

At that moment, Natalie and Sister de Lourdes walked into the parlor and that was when she suddenly remembered the angel's warning. Sister Agatha met the little girl's gaze, but no guile shone there, just concern.

"What happened?" Natalie asked, sensing something wrong.

"Some old roofing material fell from the roof," Sister Agatha said, her voice quiet and calm for Natalie's benefit. "Sister de Lourdes, will you stay with Natalie for a while longer? Since the workmen are right outside, we need to be extra careful and make sure no one sees or hears a young girl. Sister Bernarda is taking care of the phone and the door so you won't have to worry about portress duties. But I'd like to go to my cell for a few minutes."

"Of course," Sister de Lourdes answered.

As soon as she started walking down the hall, Pax came bounding up to her from inside the enclosure, cookie crumbs all around his snout. Sister Agatha bent down and hugged the dog tightly. "Thanks, old guy," she whispered, and smiled as the animal tried to lick her face. "I'm glad you're demanding when you want to be petted. I owe you big time."

Once alone in her room, she took the pills Sister Eugenia had left for her, then dropped to her knees before the small statue of Mary on her nightstand. Mentally shutting out the noise from above, she said a heartfelt prayer of thanks. As her thoughts grew still, she heard the words of the angel's warning clearly in her mind: "It'll come in silence when you least expect it." The words made sense now. Coincidence? And what about Pax's timely push? She just wasn't sure what to think anymore.

Sister Agatha spent twenty minutes in silent meditation. It wasn't that she didn't want to believe Natalie and her stories about her angel. It was just that there was no clear evidence to support the girl's claims, and experience told her that there was danger in believing something just because it held the promise of comfort. Maybe she didn't have any vision, but good journalists were known for their dedicated search for truth, and there was something to be said for that, as well.

After Vespers, Sister Agatha went by the parlor, picked up one set of ear protectors, then walked to Reverend Mother's office. The abbess was at her desk, going through tall stacks of paperwork.

After the customary greeting, Sister Agatha said, "Mother, I need to talk to you for a moment. Is this a bad time?"

"No, child. To tell you the truth, I'm not getting a lot done." Reverend Mother rubbed her temples as a new round of hammering began: "You'll have to speak up. I do believe my hearing is going. But at least the roofers will be gone shortly. They wanted to finish the worst section up there before calling it a day, just to make sure there wouldn't be any more accidents."

"About all this racket, Mother," Sister Agatha said. "I've had an idea." She held out the ear protectors.

"Earmuffs?" Reverend Mother smiled.

"No, much better than that. These are ear protectors. They're used by the police when they're shooting. They deaden sound enormously." She placed the pair on herself, smiled, then took them off and handed them to Mother. "Try them, Mother."

Reverend Mother put them on. After a

moment, she smiled. "I *love* them," she said, and took them off carefully.

"They'd be out of the question for the externs when we're working the parlor, but think of the relief it would give the cloistered sisters."

"I suppose we can all share this one, taking turns," Reverend Mother said slowly.

"There's no need. I borrowed a pair for each of us."

Reverend Mother looked at her telephone, then sighed wistfully. "I have to be able to hear the phone so I can answer it, so I wouldn't be able to use it during the day, and at night the roofers are gone."

"We could transfer all your calls to the parlor. Then whichever one of us is on duty can come find you if you get a call," Sister Agatha suggested.

Reverend Mother's smile was one of unadulterated joy. "I think that would be perfect," she said, then suddenly paused. "But it's not dignified," she added hesitantly. "What if we get another visit from the chancellor?"

"We'll give you advance notice before escorting him here," Sister Agatha assured. "Mother, the sisters and you desperately need some peace and quiet. Think of being able to pray without distractions again! I don't think Our Lord would disapprove of ear protectors. Remember the reading in Office today. 'The Lord sees not as man sees, for man looks on the outward appearance, but the Lord looks on the heart.' "

Reverend Mother smiled, then nodded. "Give them out to the sisters." She cleared her throat. "But first we need to talk about our intruder."

"I got the impression the chancellor wasn't told. Am I right?"

"You are. I saw no reason to bother him with that. But I need to know everything that you saw or heard. Sister Bernarda gave me some of the details before and after the sheriff's man left, but now it's time to hear from you."

Sister Agatha nodded, and told Reverend Mother everything she knew, including Sheriff Green's reactions, and his offer to provide them with some protection.

Reverend Mother considered it at length. "Do you think there's a connection between this intruder and that piece of roofing material that narrowly missed falling on you?"

Sister Agatha shook her head. "I'm sure that was just an accident, Mother, a result of carelessness," she added, hoping she was right. "But the intruder was looking for something or someone. Natalie, I think."

"Sister Bernarda said that the stolen habit hadn't been in the laundry room until after lunch. She guessed that the intruder must have come in and taken it from there. Thankfully, that didn't give him much time to wander around."

"Since he took the chance of coming to the main building *after* I spotted him, my guess is I caught him a very short time after he began his masquerade. He ran to the main building hoping to spot Natalie, but got nothing for his trouble except an angry nun chasing him — me."

"From now on I want the sisters alert. I'll be bringing this up at recreation," Reverend Mother said. "Now go share our blessed earmuffs."

Sister Agatha began to distribute the ear protectors a short while later. They came in two colors — bright orange and vivid red — and both colors stood out like beacons against their dark veils. But not one sister met the gift with anything less than unbounded relief.

Sister Clothilde's eyes lit up when she received her pair. She'd been working on the cookie dough with a pained expression on her face, but the second she put on the ear protectors, Sister Agatha was rewarded with a blissful smile.

Sister Maria Victoria had been sweeping the floor in the refectory and cringing each time a nail gun fired or a saw started screeching. When she placed the ear protectors on, her eyes danced and a huge grin lit up her face. She pointed to her rosary and then back to Sister Agatha, indicating she'd be saying a rosary for her soon.

"Everyone's got their ear protectors," Sister Agatha told Sister Bernarda later. "I can say without reservation that they were a hit!"

"I saw Sister Eugenia and Sister Maria Victoria going down the hall, Sister Gertrude behind them, all wearing ear protectors. We now look like a monastery of militant nuns," she said, then smiled. "You did a good thing today, Sister Agatha."

During the nuns' recreation hour Sister Agatha stayed with Natalie in the parlor area.

"Sister, can I talk to you?" Natalie asked, her mouse slippers squeaking as she approached. Hearing them, Pax sat up, stared at them, then lay back down.

"Don't let Pax get near your slippers," she said, setting down the veil she was mending. "He'll chew them up for sure."

Natalie laughed and sat next to the dog, putting her arm around him, then looked

191

up at Sister Agatha. "I really need to see my mom. When can I go visit her?"

Sister Agatha hesitated, unsure of what to say. She was absolutely certain that the phony nun had been searching for Natalie. Now more than ever they had to make sure she remained protected.

"I know she's in the hospital," Natalie said. "Uncle Rick said that she's in a deep sleep and won't hear me. But Samara said that Mom will, so I want to go talk to her. She needs me. And I miss her." Her bottom lip trembled, and she wiped an errant tear from her cheek quickly.

No one without a heart of steel could have ignored the cry of a child who needed her mother. Sister Agatha felt her chest tighten. "Natalie, I promise that I'll do my very best to get permission to take you there. But give me some time to try and make your case. I'm going to have to convince people who'll think it's a bad idea right now. And they could be right."

"I know everyone's afraid that the person who hit us on the road will come after me, but I *have* to see Mom. And I know Mom would approve. She told me that nothing good ever gets done without courage."

"She's right," Sister Agatha admitted. "What were you talking about when your mother said that?" she asked, picking up on it immediately.

"She didn't like her boss, Mr. Carlisle, and she was upset with him. She's very good at her job. She said so herself. But Mr. Carlisle always wants to do things *his* way. They argued a lot. He kept calling her at home, and Mom really hated that."

"What was it that Mr. Carlisle wanted her to do?"

"I don't know. Something to do with work," she said. After a pause, she added, "Sister, you *have* to convince everyone to let me go see my mom. I've just *got* to see her!"

"I'll try my best," she said, meaning it. If there was a way, she'd find it.

The following morning, Sister Agatha returned to the parlor after Mass. Sister de Lourdes had taken Natalie to the kitchen, with Reverend Mother's permission, so she could help Sister Clothilde bake cookies. The new oven had already been delivered and hooked up, under the watchful eyes of Sister Bernarda.

Natalie was a natural inside cloister. She spoke only when necessary, keeping the silence as diligently as any of the nuns. Of course, the ear protectors were a constant reminder of the need for quiet.

Sister Agatha picked up the ringing phone and heard a familiar voice.

"It's Tom," Sheriff Green said. "Have you learned anything useful from Natalie?"

She told him everything she'd found out. "You might want to check and see if Jessica's boss, Carlisle, drives a pickup, and if so, what color it is."

"I'm sure one of my deputies already covered that, but I'll look into it myself. Then I'm going to do a background check on the man. I questioned everyone in the construction office who worked with Jessica, but I didn't get much. Jessica wasn't one to get together with the girls after work."

"Didn't you tell me once that Jessica was a bookkeeper? If that's so, that opens the door to a lot of possibilities."

"No, not a bookkeeper. Jessica worked as an accounts receivable and payable clerk," Tom answered. "And Carlisle told me that if there had been any irregularities he or his boss would have found them. Carlisle is the head bookkeeper at the local office, but all their books are passed on to an accountant at company headquarters in Albuquerque. I'll look into all that a little more when I talk to the people in Albuquerque."

"Let me know if anything useful turns up."

"Sure, but in the meantime keep pressing Natalie. She doesn't remember her father apparently, but see if she can tell you who her mom's last boyfriend was, or how long it has been since Jessica had one."

"I'll try, but she's having a rough time of it, Tom. She misses her mom terribly. If we could figure out a way to get her in to see Jessica, it would definitely help me earn her trust."

"That's out of the question," he said after a long pause.

"Tom, we have workmen all around us and a phony nun nosing around, but we've still managed to keep her hidden and safe. Surely there's a way to sneak her into the hospital."

"This isn't the time to be taking unnecessary risks."

"It's not unnecessary. Natalie needs to see her mother, Tom. Come up with a way."

"I'll try to think of something."

Sister Agatha hung up and used the clapper, a traditional wooden device reminiscent of castanets, to call Sister Bernarda to take her place. As soon as she arrived, Sister Agatha went to find Natalie.

Moments later Sister Agatha found Sister de Lourdes watching over Natalie while she played tug-of-war with Pax. Sister Gertrude sat in her wheelchair across the room, mending some habits.

Sister Agatha waited, watching Pax bring out a side of Natalie she hadn't seen — a girl who smiled and laughed like any other kid her age. When Pax finally lay down, tired, Sister Agatha signalled Sister de Lourdes, and took Natalie aside.

"Will you come sit with me for a bit?" Sister Agatha asked.

"Sure. Did Sheriff Green say I could go see Mom?"

"I'm still working on getting the sheriff's permission, but I'm hoping he'll say yes soon. Okay?" Seeing Natalie nod, she continued. "But if we want the sheriff to help us, we're going to have to help him catch the bad guy who caused the accident. Will you answer a few more questions about your mom for me?"

She nodded. "I'll try."

"Has your mom ever had a special friend, someone who would visit every once in a while and stay to talk or maybe have dinner?"

Natalie thought about it for a while. "Mom works a lot, so we don't have people come over. She says that we're each other's best friends."

"Is she friendly with the parents of your friends at school?"

"She used to be, but she's mad at most of them now because of the way they act around me — they either want something or they won't talk to me at all."

"Is there any one person she's particularly upset with?"

Natalie considered it for several long moments. "Mrs. Pacheco, who teaches life science. She and her husband were there one day when Mom picked me up. Mrs. Pacheco wanted Mom to let me go with them so I could visit her son. Mom tried to explain that I couldn't do anything for him, and I told them that, too, but Mrs. Pacheco just wanted me to talk to him about my angel. She said it would be like a visit from heaven.

"Mom said that Mrs. Pacheco should call Uncle Rick instead. That what her son needed was God's help, not mine. Then Mrs. Pacheco got mad and we left."

"That was the end of it?"

She shook her head. "The next day at lunch Mrs. Pacheco said that she needed to show me something and took me to the teachers' parking lot. Her son was in the car. He was a lot older than me, and really sick, and I didn't know what to do. They wanted me to touch him and I did, but I

197

don't think it helped. He was still sick. Samara told me that he was going to die soon, but I didn't tell them that. That afternoon the principal found out and Mrs. Pacheco never came back. Now Mrs. Winters is our teacher."

Sister Agatha nodded but said nothing. The heaviest burden placed on Natalie came from people's expectations. It hurt her deeply to think of the weight those young shoulders were expected to bear.

"Sister, I really have to go see my mom soon. Samara said that Mom needs to hear me tell her that I love her and that I'm waiting for her to get better. Samara's already said it would be fine and I'd be safe, but nobody believes me," Natalie said, crying tears of frustration. "It's just not fair! Uncle Rick, Mom, and the sisters always say that we need to have faith and that God can do anything. So why don't they believe me when I tell them about Samara?"

Sister Agatha searched her heart for an answer. "It's just hard to believe in the extraordinary — particularly when it happens in the midst of very ordinary lives."

11

Sister Agatha sat across from Tom Green's desk at the sheriff's office. The door behind her was closed and Pax was outside with other officers.

She'd told him the few bits of information she'd been able to learn from Natalie, and now watched her old friend consider his options. In the last few years, with the additional weight of his responsibilities, he'd become more reserved and cautious. Tom liked things nice and neat — black or white — which was why law enforcement suited him. But this case was filled with too many intangibles and those clearly made him uncomfortable.

"What do *you* make of the angel?" he asked.

"I believe in angels, but I'm not really sure that what Natalie sees isn't just a product of her own imagination."

He gave her a long hard look. "You don't

like this angel thing at all, do you? Reality and fantasy don't mix — one destroys the other — and that's what makes you uncomfortable."

"I don't know what you mean."

"Come on. It's me, Tom Green. I *know* you. You went into the monastery because you fell in love with the ideal man. As long as He's not tangible, you're safe. I'd bet the farm that the last thing you want is to actually *see* an angel."

Although there was some truth to what Tom was saying, the bottom line was that he had no idea what a calling really was.

"I felt compelled, for lack of a better word, to go into the religious life. Despite what you think, God is as real to me as the beat of my own heart," she said. "But what I fell in love with is the gentleness that shimmers through every answered prayer. When there was no one else I could turn to, He gave me peace. The apostle John said it best, 'We love Him because He first loved us.' "

Sister Agatha shook her head in exasperation. "This is a tough thing to talk about in a way that makes sense to someone else. It's like asking you to explain why you love your wife or your kids. You can list all the things that draw you to them till you're blue in the face, but that still doesn't explain it. Love is much more than just that."

"Maybe I don't understand what drives anyone to the religious life, but I'm not wrong about this — something about this angel thing really bothers you."

"I'm not sure what to make of it. But you're right about one thing. I don't want to see Natalie's angel. A part of that is due to plain, old-fashioned fear. But there's more to it than that. Not seeing the spiritual means that I live by the words, 'the substance of things hoped for and the evidence of things not seen.' That gives wings to my faith. It challenges me to continually reach upwards and be better. If you *see,* you don't need faith, and faith is the only sure gift I bring Him daily along with my love."

He remained silent for a moment, then said slowly, "I've heard of children seeing angels when they're facing death. Maybe that's the case now with Natalie," he muttered. "I'll ask around about the deal with Mr. and Mrs. Pacheco," he added in a stronger voice. "Judging from what Natalie told you, they may have a monumental grudge against Jessica."

"Do you know what happened to their son?"

"If they're the same Pachecos I know about, their son just died from leukemia."

"Those poor people must be going through their own version of hell. It may be easier for them to talk to a nun right now than to you. You can always send a deputy later if you need to make it official," she said.

"If you pick up a lot of hostility or evasiveness, give me a call," he said, giving her their address.

Sister Agatha and Pax got underway a few minutes later. The Pachecos lived just west of the river. Although she knew some of the families in the area, she couldn't remember ever having met them.

As she drew closer to the address, Sister Agatha was forced to drive up an unpaved, graveled road thick with dust despite the recent rain. Even Pax ducked down after several sneezing fits. When they arrived about five minutes later, Sister Agatha glanced down at her dark habit and saw that it was coated with dust. Brushing it off the best she could, she placed Pax at stay beside the bike and walked toward the wooden porch of the long, narrow mobile home.

Before she reached the steps, a heavy, middle-aged woman wearing black pants and a loose-fitting black cotton shirt walked outside to the porch. "Can I help you, Sister?"

Sister Agatha introduced herself. "I heard about your recent loss and wanted to assure you that the sisters will be praying for the soul —"

The woman held up her hand. "*Now* the Church wants to help? They had their chance. Father Mahoney could have insisted Natalie be allowed to come and spend a few moments talking to my son. Instead, I had to put my job on the line sneaking her out to the school parking lot. And all that, for what? So she could see Peter for all of thirty seconds? God gave Natalie the ability to speak with angels so she could help others, but the priests want to keep her hidden away. It's all about control."

Understanding that the root of her anger was pain, Sister Agatha was filled with compassion. "I am so very sorry for your loss, but believe me, there was nothing Natalie could have done for your son."

"You're wrong, and so was Father Mahoney. My son *did* get better after he saw Natalie. He stopped being afraid of dying, and for a little while before he passed away I think he saw angels, too." Mrs. Pacheco's voice broke and she swallowed, wiping her tears away quickly. "If Natalie could have stayed a bit longer, maybe . . ." She shook her head. "I don't know why you came, Sister, but you better leave. There's nothing we want from you *or* the church."

"No matter what else happened, Natalie did help you. Now her mother's in a coma because someone ran them off the road. This is *your* chance to help Natalie. Won't you answer just a few questions?"

Mrs. Pacheco took a long shuddering breath. "All I know about that accident is what I read in the papers. What else can I possibly tell you?"

"When was the last time you spoke to Jessica? And can you think of anyone else at school who wanted Natalie's help?"

"The last time I spoke to Jessica was the day she refused to let Natalie come to my home and talk to Peter. But there *was* someone else hanging around school the day Natalie saw my boy in the parking lot. I had duty outside later that afternoon while the busses were there, and I saw him watching the children waiting for their rides. When Natalie came outside to sit on one of the benches, he started walking toward her. Then Jessica pulled up and called Natalie. The guy did a quick about-turn and that was the last time I saw him. I was called into the office by the principal just after that. I forgot all about it until now."

"Did you recognize the person?"

"I thought it was Joey Rubio, my next-door neighbor. He works for Del Martinez's roofing company. I can't swear it was him, though. I was standing in the bus loading zone and he never looked in my direction."

"Did you go to the Tannen house to try and see Natalie the night of the accident?" Sister Agatha watched the other woman's expression closely.

Tears filled her eyes and Mrs. Pacheco shook her head. After a long pause, she answered, "The night of that downpour my family and I gathered here for a prayer vigil. A priest was here, too."

"Father Mahoney?"

"No, I don't want anything to do with that man. We asked Father Ramirez to come over from the Corrales parish."

Sister Agatha felt the woman's pain and anger and wished there was something she could say to ease that awful burden. As she stood there, Mrs. Pacheco drew back into herself as if trying to escape the grief that lay like a weight over her shattered heart.

Out of respect, Sister Agatha waited a bit before speaking. "Why do you think Joey might have wanted to see Natalie?" she asked at long last.

"Joey won custody of his daughter after his divorce, but his ex took the girl and ran. Joey's been looking for his daughter ever since. He was probably hoping Natalie and her angel could tell him where they are. But, remember, I'm not sure that was Joey."

It saddened her to think of all the people who were looking exclusively to Natalie, not realizing or understanding that they, too, had the power to pray and ask for God's help on their own. But one thing was becoming very clear — Natalie would never know a normal childhood in this community.

"Sister Agatha, Natalie *has* received a special grace. That's why she's able to see that angel. She's God's gift to us."

"No one has been able to prove the existence of that angel."

"Nor disprove it. Why doesn't Father Mahoney take Natalie to the hospital and let her help her own mother, for God's sake? She should be allowed to try at least." Mrs. Pacheco backed into her home, tears in her eyes, and closed the door.

With a heavy heart, Sister Agatha walked back to the Harley and signalled Pax to get into the sidecar. She'd go to the Rubio home next. He was probably at work, but maybe someone else was there.

Sister Agatha drove down the lane to the next house. The residences stood on one-acre lots that also held old sheds, corrals, and inoperative or additional vehicles. As Sister Agatha drove up the graveled road to the Rubio home, she noticed an elderly woman tending a small garden near a dilapidated stucco building that looked like a workshop. She pulled a long hose, watering each plant patiently. Sister Agatha looked around and, not seeing any other animals, gave Pax the command to accompany her.

"Good morning," Sister Agatha greeted the woman, and introduced herself.

"*Buenos dias, Hermana.* I'm Carmen Rubio. What can I do for you?" She crouched down and picked a large green caterpillar off a plant, then tossed it to the ground, squashing it with her heel.

"I need to talk to Joey. Is he here?"

"No, he's probably still at the monastery. Unless it rains they're going to be working on that roof of yours every day until it's done. Didn't you see him over there?"

"I didn't even know that he was part of the crew," she said.

Sister Agatha knew that Joey wasn't the person who'd disguised himself as a nun because the other workers would have noticed his absence. But that didn't mean he wasn't the person who'd run Jessica and Natalie off the road. The two incidents didn't have to be related.

"How's the search for Joey's little girl going?" Sister Agatha asked, deciding to check out the possibility that he'd been the man Mrs. Pacheco had seen.

The woman's face clouded with grief. "*Mi nieta,* my granddaughter, will grow up never knowing how much her father misses her. She'll just believe that we didn't care, if I know her mother. But someday we'll find her. We'll never give up hope."

"Has Joey considered hiring a private detective?"

"He did once, but it cost a lot of money and the man never found my granddaughter. He said he was getting close, but I think he was lying. Once we ran out of money, the detective threw up his hands and stopped doing anything at all. When we heard on TV about Natalie, Joey said he wanted to talk to her. But Natalie's gone now, hiding with the police."

"Did Joey ever actually talk to Natalie or Jessica?"

"He wanted to — was thinking about it, you know? But all the men in this family like to think a long time before doing anything."

"So Joey never got the chance to find out if she could help him or not?"

The woman shrugged. "Not as far as I know, but these days my grandson doesn't tell me anything."

"Did Joey ever go to Natalie's school to try and find her?" Sister Agatha asked. "Other people did."

Carmen stopped and looked at her long and hard. "And what if he did? What are you really asking, Sister? Are you thinking that he wanted to see her so badly he caused that accident? I know you work with the police sometimes."

"I don't know what happened that night, so I'm trying to put the pieces together. That's all."

Carmen shook her head. "You're looking for someone to blame. Don't try to fool me. Do you know the saying, *'Mas sabe el diablo por viejo que por diablo'*?"

Sister Agatha nodded. "The devil is wiser because of his age than because he's the devil."

"My grandson is a good man. He wants to find his daughter, but not by endangering someone else's. *Usted comprende?*"

"Yes, I do. Thanks," Sister Agatha said,

and turned to walk back to the Harley with Pax.

"Sister," Carmen called out before she'd gone more than a few steps. "If you care about that little girl, you should convince Father Mahoney to let people find out for themselves what she can or can't do. Everyone's curious and the more they talk about Natalie, the more the story will grow. Pretty soon they'll claim she parted the Rio Grande, and ten people will step up and swear they saw her do it. *Es verdad.*"

"Yes, there's truth to that," Sister Agatha said. She was quickly coming to the same conclusion herself.

12

Sister Agatha entered the parlor, Pax at her side, hours later, and glanced at the new Parcel Express delivery man, who was speaking to Sister Bernarda. The man was about her height but thin and weary-looking, as if he'd just worked a double shift.

"This is one of our other externs," Sister Bernarda said, and introduced them. "Sister Agatha, this is Andrew."

Sister Agatha shook his hand. "It's a pleasure to meet you, Andrew. You look tired — they must keep you running. Are you new to the route or to the company?"

"Both, pretty much, and, yes, I've been very busy. But I've got to say, I'm glad I had the chance to make a delivery here. I've never seen a real monastery up close before. It looks so peaceful. Is it true that the other nuns never come outside?"

Sister Agatha nodded. "They've taken a vow of enclosure."

"What do they do all day? Read the Bible?"

She smiled. That was invariably the first question people asked. "That, too. And they pray and work. We have to support ourselves."

"That's something we all have in common, don't we?" Andrew said.

Hearing the bell for Vespers, Sister Bernarda and Sister Agatha looked at each other. "It's time for us to close the parlor doors, Andrew," Sister Agatha said.

Andrew looked at his watch. "It's five thirty and I still have another delivery to make. I better run, too." Andrew nodded at both of them, then hurried outside to his truck.

Sister Bernarda knocked and opened the door to Natalie's quarters. "Are you ready to go to Vespers?" she asked.

The child looked up in surprise, then took off her earphones. They belonged to a radio Sister de Lourdes had found for the girl among their donations. "I'm sorry, Sister. I couldn't hear you with the music going."

"I don't see how you stand it, listening to that noise all day," Sister Bernarda said.

"Music helps me think. There are times when I need to figure out something for myself and it helps not to listen to anyone else then."

Natalie's guileless expression told Sister Agatha that the girl wasn't trying to be rude, but it still sent a message. She made a mental note to ask Natalie what was troubling her as soon as Vespers was over. For now, they had to get going.

As Natalie put away the radio, Sister Agatha nodded to Sister Bernarda. "Go ahead. We'll follow."

"Sit on the south side of the chapel. Mr. Martinez made sure that the area above the tabernacle was finished first because he doesn't want any more problems. And neither does Reverend Mother, which is why the public side of the chapel will remain closed for now."

Sister Agatha knew that the possibility their intruder might return was still worrying Mother. Natalie hadn't been told about the phony nun, just warned to keep her voice low and stay away from windows despite the heavy curtains while the workmen were around.

Several minutes later Sister Agatha led Natalie to the chapel. The girl seemed more subdued than usual and that worried her. Yet as all the nuns began to chant the Divine Office, a sense of peace enveloped

Sister Agatha.

Sister Agatha glanced down at Natalie, hoping that the serenity and blessedness of their chapel would soothe her broken spirit. It didn't take a mind reader to know that the girl had never stopped worrying about her mother. There was no peace in Natalie's expression.

Sister Agatha brought her thoughts back to the Office, and as the two-tone chant rose high into the air, their voices joined symbolically with the choir of angels who praised God unceasingly.

After Vespers, Sister Agatha escorted Natalie to her room. Pax, who'd been waiting outside of chapel for them, came along. "It won't take me more than a minute or so to bring us both some dinner, so just wait for me here. Sister Bernarda and Sister de Lourdes are busy helping Sister Clothilde because she's behind on her baking, despite the new oven. Tomorrow we'll need to deliver our first shipment of cookies to Smitty's grocery, which is why most of us will be working in the kitchen tonight, even after the Great Silence."

"Don't get dinner for me, okay? I'm not hungry. Uncle Rick brought me a hamburger and fries earlier," Natalie said. "All I really want is to go see my mom. Will you take me?"

"I spoke to the sheriff about that, and we're trying to find a safe way to get you there. We'll make it happen, but I need a little more time, okay?"

Natalie shoulders drooped. "Can I go to bed early tonight? I'd like to listen to music, then go to sleep."

"Are you sure you wouldn't want me to bring you a sandwich at least? How about peanut butter and jelly?"

"No, thanks. I'm still full. I just want to go to bed."

"Okay. I'll go get myself a bowl of soup, then come back."

Natalie crawled into her cot, placed her headphones on, then closed her eyes. Once she'd settled in, Sister Agatha turned off the lights. "Good night," she said, then realized Natalie couldn't hear her.

Sister Agatha went to the kitchen to get a quick dinner for herself, but as she stepped through the double doors of the refectory the thick and pungent smell of burnt food seemed to come at her from all sides. Rushing to the kitchen, she saw Sister Maria Victoria and Sister Clothilde pulling three trays of blackened lumps from the oven. Other sisters, alerted by the unmistakable scent, rushed in all together, and as they crowded into the room, a huge bowl of batter went crashing to the floor. Reverend Mother tried to step back and slipped, but Sister Bernarda caught her before she fell. However, in all the confusion, a second batch of cookies burned to a crisp.

Forty minutes passed before everything had been cleaned up and the baking order had been restored. Sister Agatha returned to the parlor and peeked into Natalie's room. Although it was dark, she could see the girl's outline in the bed under the covers. Then, just as she sat down, the bell for Compline rang. Remaining where she was, she opened her breviary to pray. If Natalie woke up again tonight, she'd take the opportunity to have a talk with her. For now, the girl was sound asleep.

As she read from the breviary, Sister Agatha suddenly realized that she hadn't seen Pax in the room with Natalie. Maybe it had just been too dark. Deciding to take another look, she reached for the penlight in the bottom drawer of the parlor desk, and switched it on. The muted glow it gave off would be more than enough.

Moving with practiced silence, Sister Agatha opened the door and looked around. The dog wasn't on the floor or under the cot. Wondering if Natalie had decided to share her bed with him, she studied the lump on the cot. There was no breathing movement at all.

Sister Agatha stepped over to the cot and lifted up the sheet. Instead of Natalie and Pax, the child's clothes and her fancy doll, Regina, were arranged there in a humanlike form.

She'd fallen for the oldest trick in the book. Natalie and Pax were both gone. Her heart hammering at her throat, she turned on the lights. Sister Agatha frantically searched for a note and found one on the floor by the dresser, where it had probably been thrown when she'd lifted off the sheet. It was written on paper taken from one of the monastery's memo pads. Sister Agatha read it.

There's someplace Samara wants me to be tonight. Pax is coming with me. Don't worry. We'll be back soon.

Galvanized by fear, Sister Agatha ran to the phone. There was no time to lose. She had to call Sheriff Green and then let Reverend Mother know. After explaining to the desk sergeant what had happened and asking her to relay everything to Tom, Sister Agatha ran to Reverend Mother's office.

The words tumbled out of her in a rush

as she told the abbess, then added, "This is my fault. I should have seen this coming and never left Natalie alone."

Reverend Mother's face turned pale, but she remained outwardly calm. "This was not your fault. All our doors open from the inside. Our locks are meant to keep the world out, not to keep us in. You trusted her, that's all. Pax will guard her as best he can, but you need to go and find her as quickly as possible."

"She's talked quite a bit about going to see her mom. She's probably headed to the Far West Medical Center. The shortest route is down our road to the highway, then straight into town. I'll check it out." She turned to leave, then stopped and turned her head. "We should call Father Mahoney, too."

"I'll take care of that, child. You go search. I'll wake all the sisters who aren't already working in the kitchen and we'll start a prayer vigil immediately. No help is more powerful than His."

Sister Agatha hurried to the parlor, grabbed a jacket and the big flashlight, then said good-bye. It was a clear night, but the temperature was dropping quickly. For a brief moment she considered taking the Antichrysler. The monastery's old station wagon would be warmer. But in cold weather it also had a tendency not to start up, and sometimes it needed to be coaxed to continue running.

She didn't have time for that now. Moments later, she got underway on the Harley. Pax would do his best to protect Natalie, but the thought of the girl wandering about in the dark still terrified her.

Angry with herself, and knowing how vulnerable Natalie had become by leaving the relative safety of the monastery, Sister Agatha vowed not to return home without Natalie Tannen.

Reaching Bernalillo, Sister Agatha directed her search onto the shoulders of the road ahead. The ground was too hard to leave a trail, but she stayed alert for even a shadow of movement. The road contained some very old residences and a few small businesses. There was no sidewalk, just a low chain-link fence on both sides running nearly to the road. There were streetlights at the end of each block, but tall trees made the area dark and lonely looking, and only a few porch lights were on.

It wasn't until she drove past the old graveyard at the south end of Bernalillo that she spotted a small figure moving directly ahead. Sister Agatha pressed the Harley for more speed, and a heartbeat later she heard Pax bark. He'd recognized the distinctive Harley engine instantly. As she pulled up, Pax was sitting on the right side of the road, tail wagging, happy to see her.

Natalie tried to hide behind a young elm, but Sister Agatha had already seen her. After giving Pax the command to jump into the sidecar, she turned off the engine.

"I know you're standing behind the tree, Natalie, so you might as well come out," Sister Agatha said gently, taking off her helmet.

Natalie stepped away from the tree, but didn't move toward the motorcycle. "You can't make me go back. Samara never lies and she said Mom needs me. Mom has to fight right now or she may never come back. Call the hospital. They'll tell you."

The intensity and emotion behind her words made Sister Agatha believe her. "I understand that you really want to see your mom but, Natalie, do you have any idea of how dangerous it is for you out here?"

"I was careful," she said, "and I had Pax to protect me. Sister, unless you take me to see my Mom, I'll just run away again."

Looking at Natalie and hearing the desperation in her voice, Sister Agatha didn't doubt it for a minute. "Okay. I'm going to talk to the sheriff. But first you have to come and sit in the sidecar with Pax while I let everyone know you're safe." She handed Natalie the spare helmet.

As she spoke to Tom and assured him that Natalie was fine, Sister Agatha caught a glimpse of something like a mist or maybe smoke directly behind Natalie. The second she turned her head to look at it squarely, it was gone. Sister Agatha rubbed her eyes, wondering if allergies were fogging her vision.

"You saw Samara, too, didn't you?" Natalie said with a smile.

Natalie's question unnerved her. "I saw a mist . . . no, smoke. I don't know."

Natalie looked disappointed, but then her face became set, determination shining in her eyes. "We have to go *now,* Sister."

Realizing that Tom was still on the line, she nodded to Natalie and turned her attention back to him. "Natalie needs to see her mother tonight, Tom. If I take her back to the monastery, she'll find a way to get out again. I think we should arrange for that visit right now. Preempting another attempt is the best way to protect her."

"I'll call the hospital right away and see

221

how Jessica's doing," Tom answered. "Hang on."

Sister Agatha glanced at Natalie. "We're trying to work things out now."

"Mom's in trouble, Sister. I'm just supposed to talk to her, but maybe I can make her get better, too. Lots of people seem to think I can do that."

"What if you try and she doesn't get better? How will you feel then?"

"Disappointed. But I'll know for sure then. And Samara says what's most important now is that Mom hears my voice. I can do that at least."

"Okay," Tom said, coming back on the line. "The head nurse in ICU says that signs are there that suggest Jessica is trying to come out of the coma. But so far she hasn't regained consciousness, and the longer she stays in that state, the more uncertain the prognosis. She's also battling a secondary infection, so they have reason to be concerned."

"We're going to the hospital," Sister Agatha said flatly.

"Okay, then here's the deal," Tom said. "I'll meet you there, and we'll go in through the side door. No stops along the way to ICU, and Natalie can only stay for a few minutes. Clear?"

"We'll be there."

13

Sister Agatha followed Tom's directions, and as she pulled up to the side entrance, she found him seated on the steps, waiting as inconspicuously as possible.

"Hurry up," he urged, coming out of the shadows to meet them. "Leave Pax in the sidecar and let's get going."

Urging Natalie to walk quickly, Sister Agatha stayed on her right while Tom remained a step ahead. Once inside, they went down a long, dark hallway that smelled of disinfectant. The lights were muted and the hospital was quiet now that visiting hours were over. As they hurried into the elevator and the doors slid shut, Sister Agatha caught a glimpse of a man wearing a blue Dallas Cowboys baseball cap standing by the soft drink machine. He seemed to be the only person around not wearing white.

The moment they reached the second floor, they continued down the corridor at a brisk pace and on through twin doors to a ward marked ICU. A tall, redheaded nurse came out from behind the nurses' station.

"Mrs. Johnson," Tom greeted her.

The nurse supervisor, according to her photo ID, crouched down in front of Natalie. "This is a very special favor, Natalie. We normally don't allow anyone under the age of thirteen to come into this area — and never after hours. The only reason I'm allowing you to go in there is because your mom is fighting to wake up and, like you, I'm hoping that somehow she'll hear your voice and that'll help her find her way back. But don't worry if we don't see any changes right away. Your mom will need lots of time to get well again."

Natalie nodded, then glanced back at Sister Agatha. "Will you come with me?"

Sister Agatha nodded, suddenly very afraid for Natalie. If a miracle occurred tonight and it turned out that Natalie had the gift of healing, then the girl's childhood — what was left of it — would vanish in that one instant. But if nothing changed, Natalie would have to face the fact that neither she nor her angel had been able to help the person she loved most in the world.

Sister Agatha nodded to the uniformed deputy stationed by the door. He was short, broad, and built like a tree trunk with arms. More importantly for Jessica's sake, he had the cop look — that unblinking gaze that went through you somehow and said "back off" without the need for words.

Sister Agatha walked behind Natalie as they passed other patients, and those awake and able to do so followed the girl with their eyes. Sister Agatha saw the spectrum of emotions Natalie inspired on their faces — acceptance, hope, fear, and even desperation.

She was suddenly reminded of how precious and how fragile the gift of health was. Here, Sister Agatha was once again face-to-face with mortality, and she had to resist the impulse to run away from this place that echoed with the pain of too many endings and lost second chances.

Mingled with the scent of antiseptics that filled the room were other odors — those of despair, and death. Sister Agatha knew it by heart. It had been indelibly etched into her memory during the long days and nights she'd sat by Kevin's bedside, watching him slip away from this life. Her only comfort back then had come from the worn rosary she'd owned since her first communion.

Natalie went to her mother's bedside, then took her hand and rested her head against

Jessica's side for a long time. After a while she rose on tiptoes and began whispering something in her mother's ear. Her words were lost amidst the beeps and hums of the machines and the wheeze of respirators scattered around the unit.

Minutes passed slowly. When Tom signalled her, Sister Agatha placed a hand on Natalie's shoulder. "Natalie, it's time."

Natalie hugged her mother then, and as she did, Sister Agatha saw movement behind Jessica's closed eyelids. Signalling Mrs. Johnson, who came over immediately, Sister Agatha pointed down.

"Jessica's fighting it," the nurse agreed, "but she's got a ways to go."

Natalie let go of her mother, then looked at Sister Agatha. "Mom heard me," she said with such conviction that none of them refuted it.

As Natalie turned to walk out of the ward some of the other patients reached out to her with their hands, or called to her softly. Natalie stopped by their beds and spoke to each, talking about her angel and telling them not to be afraid. Mrs. Johnson didn't try to stop her, but remained close by, watching.

"That girl's got a real gift," Mrs. Johnson said to Sister Agatha in a whisper-soft voice.

"Not for healing. Her mom's still in a coma," Sister Agatha replied quickly, relieved for Natalie's sake, yet disappointed for Jessica.

"Sometimes the best gift is the ability to bring hope. A few of the patients who reached out to her tonight have been so consumed by their own pain, they haven't cared about anything or anyone for some time. But look at the way they respond to her," the nurse said, watching Natalie as she held the hand of an elderly woman.

When they stepped back out into the hall, Tom was waiting. Anxious to leave, he led them quickly back down the hall. As they reached the elevator, Sister Agatha caught a glimpse of the same man she'd seen downstairs wearing the cap. Once again he was in the shadows, this time near a visitor's waiting area at the end of the hall. As she turned to point him out to Tom, the man disappeared into the stairwell.

Uneasy, Sister Agatha pressed the elevator button so the doors would slide shut, and then told Tom, choosing her words carefully so as not to alarm Natalie.

"I'll handle it. But now you and Natalie have to go home." He paused. "I'll have a deputy follow you from a distance, just to be safe."

"Bad idea. The more attention you call to us, the worse off we'll be. I'll have Natalie duck down in the sidecar on the way back so no one sees her. And don't worry. If I even think for a moment that someone's following us, I'll head straight for the station."

"Okay, then get going. I'll track down the man you saw," he said as the elevator doors opened.

Sister Agatha led her charge back outside quickly to where Pax was waiting. As Natalie climbed into the sidecar, Sister Agatha handed her the helmet. "Now scrunch down like a turtle in its shell, because we don't want anyone to see you, and hang on."

Sister Agatha sped away from the hospital, staying on the main street. If she did pick up a tail, she'd have more maneuvering options. At first, she glanced back in her rearview mirror every few seconds. But after ten minutes, she relaxed. No one was behind her.

As they passed The Hog, the biker bar at the north end of town, she saw someone waving at her. When she waved back but didn't slow down, the man let out a shrill whistle that managed to pierce even the deep rumble of the Harley. Pax jumped up instantly.

"Natalie, stay down," Sister Agatha said quickly as she continued north. "A lot of people wave when they see me and Pax on the motorcycle. But we don't want anyone to know I've got an extra passenger tonight."

As she continued down the dark highway north of Bernalillo, she caught a glimpse of twin headlights in the rearview mirror. A car was quickly gaining on them.

Her heart began to hammer, and she reached toward the sidecar, handing Natalie the phone. "Press the number one," she shouted so Natalie could hear. "Tell Sheriff Green someone's following us."

Sister Agatha turned down a farm road that she knew well, and the car behind them followed. She'd selected this route on purpose. The dirt road circled around, allowing her to reverse course without risking a confrontation with whoever was following. Reaching the highway again in two minutes, she pressed the bike for more speed. Her next stop would be the police station.

The headlights loomed behind them, so close that Sister Agatha couldn't look in the rearview mirror without being blinded. As she slowed momentarily for a familiar bump in the pavement, the car behind them suddenly accelerated and pulled up right alongside her.

Clinging to the handlebars in a death grip, Sister Agatha turned her head to look at the driver. It was Chuck Moody — a young, local man she'd testified against in court two years ago on a hit-and-run charge. He'd been sent to prison, last she'd heard.

Moody waved at her and grinned widely. "Sister, it's me, Chuck! Pull over!" he yelled out.

Before she could answer, he backed off, allowing her to continue and ducking back into the lane behind her motorcycle. Seconds later, red and blue flashing lights appeared just ahead of her on the road. A police cruiser was blocking her lane and another unit was coming up rapidly from behind them. Moody slowed and moved over to the side of the road.

"Natalie, stay down!" Sister Agatha yelled without turning her head, then pulled over to the shoulder and parked.

Moody, who'd parked some distance behind her, got out of his car with his hands up in the air. "Whoa! What's going on here?" Chuck's straw-colored hair was already starting to thin though he couldn't be more than twenty-three, and he had the reddish beginnings of a beard. "I was just trying to get Sister Agatha's attention so I could talk to her."

The deputy who'd pulled Moody over patted him down for weapons, then nodded to Tom. "He's clean."

"What did you want to talk to Sister Agatha about?" Tom demanded, walking up to Moody and shining his flashlight in the young man's eyes.

"Okay, okay. Chill out. I'll tell you. During the trial, when she testified against me, I said a lot of crap I shouldn't have. But I've changed now — yeah really," he said seeing the skeptical look on Tom's face. "As corny as it sounds, I've been wanting to ask her to forgive me for what I said. I was hoping we could mend some fences here."

He looked directly at Sister Agatha, who'd approached cautiously. "You helped me more than you know, Sister. I haven't had a drink in over a year, and I'm finally getting my act together. I've got a job at the paper doing the editor's legwork — you know, research, getting copies of county records, stuff like that. It doesn't pay much, but I'm hoping for the chance to start writing copy in a few more months."

Chuck looked at Sister Agatha with pleading eyes. "I just wanted to let you know you did a good thing. I've seen you around a few times, but my boss kept calling me away to do this or do that. Cell phones can be a curse."

Seeing the dark red beat-up sedan he drove, Sister Agatha glared at him. "Chuck, you scared me half out of my wits! If I'd have known it was you all this time . . ."

"I really *am* sorry, Sister Agatha. But, listen, one of the things I wanted to tell you is that you can use my employee's discount to place an ad in the paper. That way you can advertise the monastery's cookies. I've heard the sisters are going into business now."

"My mistake, Tom," Sister Agatha said with a sigh. "Let him go."

"Not quite yet," Tom answered. "Mr. Moody, tell me where you were the night of the storm."

"Easy. I was working with Janice Bose, my editor at the *Chronicle,* until nearly two in the morning. The wind blew a cottonwood branch through the office window. We spent hours shutting down and moving the computers, cleaning up the mess, and getting the system up again in the next room. The security guard helped us block out the rain with a sheet of plywood, but it was an all-nighter, Sheriff. You can check it out with Janice," he said.

"I know Janice. I'll check your story."

"Sister Agatha," Chuck said, turning to look at her, "I learned one big lesson in prison — I *never* want to go back again. If there's anything I can do for you to make up for all the trouble I caused before, just let me know. From now on, I'm one of the good guys."

"Thanks, Chuck. I'll keep it in mind." After shaking his hand, she glanced at Tom. "I've got to get back to the monastery. Everyone will be worried because I've been gone so long."

"Go. Chuck and I are going to have a little talk about reckless driving."

Sister Agatha hurried over to the Harley. Right now all she wanted to do was get Natalie home — safe.

Ten minutes later Sister Agatha stopped the Harley in front of the monastery gates and switched off the engine. "We'll push the bike from here," she said softly. "We don't want to wake the sisters — if any of them actually managed to fall asleep."

Natalie nodded, still downcast, but helped Sister Agatha push the motorcycle through the entrance and over to the parking area.

Pax beside them, they closed the gates and Sister Agatha locked up, noting that the girl hadn't said a word since they'd left the hospital.

"Natalie, don't be sad. You did a wonderful thing tonight. You may not realize it but you brought hope back into the lives of some of the patients in that ICU ward."

"But I didn't *do* anything," she said.

"Yes, you did. When you told those people about your angel, you reminded them that there's more to life than what you can see and touch. And by doing that, you healed their spirits. We all need to believe in something."

"But that's not enough. I wanted Mom to get up and walk out with me."

"The fact that it didn't happen may be a blessing in disguise, Natalie. When word gets around — and it will — that you can't heal people, that will make things easier for you. People won't be bothering you as much."

When they entered the parlor, Sister Bernarda was waiting.

"Several sisters are still in the chapel praying. Let me go tell everyone you and Natalie are back safely."

"Thank you," Sister Agatha said. "While you're doing that, I'll get Natalie into bed."

After making the girl promise that she'd never run away again, Sister Agatha turned off the lights and shut the door.

"I'll stay with her now," Sister Bernarda whispered, having returned.

Before Sister Agatha could answer, Reverend Mother came up to the grate. "Children, I've just received some exciting news. Jessica Tannen has regained consciousness. She's still in serious condition and her memory is fuzzy, the way it can be with a mild stroke, but she's finally opened her eyes and is apparently aware of her surroundings. Father Mahoney, who's at the hospital now, called to give me the news."

A sense of foreboding filled her. "Did he know that Natalie was there earlier?" Sister Agatha asked.

"Yes, and he wasn't very happy when he heard," she said. "But he's sure that Natalie won't be credited with a miracle. Her mother is still very confused and is having trouble processing any kind of information. And one of the patients Natalie touched passed away not long after she left. Under those unhappy circumstances, I don't think anyone's going to credit her with the gift of healing." Reverend Mother exhaled softly. "Get some sleep, children. Matins will ring soon enough."

The abbess moved away with scarcely a sound and Sister Agatha peeked in one last time to check on Natalie. The girl was sound asleep, Pax on the floor beside her. Envying the young for their ability to fall instantly asleep, Sister Agatha left Sister Bernarda in charge, and went to her cell.

The next morning, following the Divine Office, Sister Agatha escorted Natalie to the crafts room. The girl had already been given the good news about her mother and was in bright spirits. "Will you be all right with Sister Ignatius? I need to go back to town and spend a few hours there."

"Sure, Sister Agatha. Will you be stopping by to see my mom?"

"If I get a chance."

"If you do, tell her I miss her, okay?"

"I will, but she may be asleep — regular sleep — when I get there. Her body is still trying to recover and she needs lots of rest."

"Samara was right, you know. Mom needed me to tell her that it wasn't time for her to go to heaven."

"You wished with all your heart that she'd get well and your prayer went straight to God. You received a blessing, so be sure to say thank you."

"I will, but how come God doesn't always hear me when I pray?" Natalie asked softly. "Ever since I can remember I've been praying really hard that my dad would come back to us, but nothing ever happens. He wouldn't have to live with us, either. All I want is to meet him for real."

"I'll tell you something I learned a long time ago. You have to trust God all the way, Natalie — when he says yes and when he says no."

Natalie nodded, but didn't answer.

"I mentioned this once before, but think about it real hard. Did your mom ever talk to you about your dad?" Sister Agatha knew that she was probably grasping at straws, but she had to ask.

Natalie shook her head this time. "When I ask about him Mom gets really upset and tells me that God is my father. That's why I used to make up stories about my dad whenever my friends talked about their dads. I told Marcie and Louann that he was an undercover cop and couldn't come to see us because then the bad guys would know where we live. But Marcie's mom told her that my dad was no good, had even been in jail, and that I'd made up the whole thing. Then Marcie told everyone else at school. I never talked about him anymore after that — except to Samara."

Sister Agatha wondered what Henry Tannen had done that had led to his incarceration, and decided to ask Tom about that sometime soon.

Seeing them at the doorway of the crafts room, Sister Ignatius smiled and held out a ceramic angel. "Sister Agatha, look what Natalie made for our Christmas bazaar. It just came out of the oven a while ago, but it's cool enough to handle," she added, gesturing to the ancient oven in the corner. These days it only handled the higher temperatures well, which was why Sister Clothilde hadn't even attempted to bake cookies in it. "Good thing these special polymer clays don't require a kiln. The electricity bill alone would have made it impossible for us to do any ceramics."

Sister Agatha turned the sculpture around in her hands, looking at the blues and soft lavenders she'd used for the angel's robes and the shimmery soft cream color that tinted the wings. "It's beautiful, Natalie!"

"Thank you, Sister Agatha." Natalie walked toward the table, then stopped and turned to look at Sister Agatha. "Samara says to tell you that you don't need to worry about the down payment for the roof. The money will come in."

Sister Agatha and Sister Ignatius exchanged a quick glance. Natalie hadn't been told that the down payment had been a problem, though she might have guessed from their active campaign to raise money.

The girl took a seat and begun working with the clay as if nothing out of the ordinary had just happened. "Oh, and Sister Agatha, you promised you'd go get Gracie. Since you're going to town, will you stop by my house and bring her to me today? She's on my bed."

"I'll try, Natalie."

Sister Agatha walked to the kitchen next to see if the shipment of cookies was ready to be taken to Smitty's. Seeing her arrive, Sister Clothilde led her to the provisory. Ten large boxes had been packed, labeled, and stacked.

"That's a lot bigger load than I'd envisioned. Even with the car, I think I'll have to leave Pax behind." As Sister Agatha picked up one of the boxes, Sister Gertrude and Sister Maria Victoria appeared almost instantly to help, each taking another container. They walked across the corridor and stopped in front of the grate. That was as far as the cloistered sisters could go.

"Set these boxes down, go get the others, and I'll take them all from here, Sisters. Thank you so much," Sister Agatha added.

Sister Bernarda and Sister de Lourdes

helped her load the boxes into the Antichrysler.

As Sister de Lourdes went back inside, Sister Bernarda gave Sister Agatha a hesitant look. "Do you think people will spend their hard-earned money to buy our Cloister Cluster Cookies?"

Sister Agatha nodded. "They're an inexpensive indulgence, and everyone has to eat. I think they'll do well."

"A big win would certainly boost morale after all the long hours and hard work the sisters put in," Sister Bernarda said.

"Maybe Natalie's angel will come through for us," Sister Agatha said with a half smile, then told Sister Bernarda about the prediction made in the crafts room.

"Whether or not you choose to believe in Natalie's angel, the fact remains that Natalie's predictions have been pretty accurate so far," Sister Bernarda said.

"Which brings up another point. If the angel is the product of her imagination, then it's very possible that Natalie has a gift for foretelling events."

"Interesting point," Sister Bernarda said slowly.

"Just speculation." Sister Agatha switched on the ignition, and after two attempts the engine finally caught. Nodding to Sister

Bernarda, who gave her a thumbs-up, she set off for town.

14

Sister Agatha said a prayer of thanksgiving when she finally arrived at Smitty's Grocery. At least three times on her way into town, she'd been certain that the Antichrysler was wheezing its last breath.

"Good morning, Sister!" Smitty greeted her with a wave as she backed into a parking slot. "I see you've got my shipment."

As Smitty carried in the carton to stock his shelves, Sister Agatha walked to the front of the store. Beneath the window was a coffee counter and several small tables for patrons. Sheriff Green was seated by himself, sipping coffee from a big foam cup.

As she approached, Sister Agatha saw the growth of stubble on his chin that told her he hadn't been home since yesterday. "Tom, you look awful," she said.

"Gee, such flattery. I'll try not to let it go to my head."

"What's going on? You look like you've

been up all night."

"Haven't you heard?" Seeing her puzzled expression, he added, "Someone tried to kidnap Jessica Tannen last night long after Natalie left."

"Is Jessica all right?"

"Yes, the perp never reached her."

"I can't think of anyone big enough or tough enough to get past the officer you had on duty."

"They didn't, which is why the attempt didn't succeed. The guy popped out from behind the door when Bobby, my deputy, went to check on an open window beside Jessica's bed. The perp cracked him on the head, but Bobby didn't go down completely. He was groggy, but still managed to stop the lowlife from taking Jessica. Good thing Bobby's head is as hard as steel."

"You have the suspect in custody?" Sister Agatha asked quickly.

"No, he got away. All we know is that he was about Bobby's height — which puts him at five foot seven — and was wearing a Dallas Cowboys baseball cap. He might be the same guy you saw at the hospital earlier."

"You never saw him?"

He shook his head, reached for the coffee, and took a sip. "I wanted to take Jessica out of the hospital today, but the doctors strongly advised against it. So we now have two guards posted there and I'm still no closer to catching the perp than I was when this thing started."

"Has Jessica been any help — about the intruder, or about the accident?"

"No. I tried talking to her several times, but she's still too unfocused. Not all of her is back, if you catch my meaning. She just can't remember anything from one moment to the next — including my questions. The doctors are pretty optimistic about her eventual recovery, but I can't wait around for weeks for the case to break. I need answers now if I'm going to catch that guy."

"What about the hospital security system? Was the intruder caught on video?"

"The cameras are only for the exits and the front desk. Nothing on the second floor at all. I've got a deputy going over the tapes a third time, but it looks like the intruder saw the cameras and kept his head down."

"That's a tough break. Is there anything I can do?"

"Maybe," he said, lowering his voice to a whisper. "I've questioned the people Jessica works with at Grayson Construction, and I'm getting bad vibes. They're holding something back, I can feel it in my gut. I hauled them in separately, but I still didn't get anywhere. My guess is that they're afraid of losing their jobs." He rubbed his eyes, then took another sip of coffee.

"If they're afraid of losing their jobs, that tends to point the arrows at their boss."

"I've done background checks on the four of them, and that includes Jessica, but they're all clean. My hands are tied at this point."

"Let me check with Smitty to make sure our business is concluded, then I'll go over there and see what I can do," Sister Agatha said softly.

Leaving Smitty's five minutes later, Sister Agatha drove directly to the offices of Grayson Construction. As she stepped inside the reception area, a young brunette sitting at the front desk looked up. "May I help you, Sister?"

Sister Agatha introduced herself then added, "I'm a friend of Jessica Tannen's. I was wondering if I could ask you a few questions about her."

"Yeah, I suppose," she said hesitantly. "What do you want to know?"

"Did Jessica have a best friend here in the office?" Sister Agatha asked.

The woman cast a nervous glance at the

hallway behind Sister Agatha, then answered quickly. "We work so hard here, we don't have time to socialize much. Of course we talk during our breaks but that's about it, unless it's work related."

A tall man wearing a long-sleeved shirt and a bolo tie came through the front door. "I'm Joseph Carlisle, the office manager," he said, looking directly at Sister Agatha. "I couldn't help but overhear your question as I was coming up the hall. Jessica Tannen's auto accident is a matter for the police, or her lawyers. It doesn't concern Grayson Construction and is certainly *not* the business of Our Lady of Hope Monastery."

Carlisle looked at the receptionist. "If you don't have work to do, Cathy, I'm sure I can find something. Sister is just leaving."

"I'm sorry you feel this way, Mr. Carlisle," Sister Agatha said stiffly, although Carlisle had already turned his back to her and was walking away. "But you don't have to take it out on this young woman," she added loudly so he'd hear.

"I'm sorry about that, Sister," Cathy said, an angry look on her face. "He can be a real pain sometimes," she added in a whisper-soft voice.

As she walked out, Sister Agatha had the impression that the receptionist might be more willing to talk to her if she could manage to catch her away from the office.

Sister Agatha drove back to the sheriff's station, and as she pulled into the parking lot, the Antichrysler backfired loudly. One deputy near the entrance spun around, automatically reaching for his gun, while two officers near their units ducked down and peered over the engine blocks.

Sister Agatha got out and gave them all a sheepish smile. "Please, shoot this car. It would be a merciful death."

Before she'd taken another step, Tom came out the door in a hurry, his hand over his holstered weapon. Realizing what had happened from the acrid smell of burning oil and the blue smoke still in the air, he relaxed. "How did it go at Grayson Construction?" he asked, leading her back inside.

"I didn't get anywhere," she said as soon as he'd shut the door to his office. "Joseph Carlisle showed up and wouldn't let the receptionist talk to me about Jessica. In fact, he insisted I leave. But I think the girl, Cathy, will talk to me if I can catch her someplace else. Carlisle really . . . ticked her off."

"If you manage to talk to her, let me know."

"You've got it." Sister Agatha lowered her voice, then continued. "I really need permission to go by Jessica's home again. Natalie likes the doll you picked out for her, but she really wants me to bring her favorite one. She keeps asking me to get it for her, and I can't keep putting her off."

"If someone sees you with the doll . . ."

"I know. That's why I thought I'd go to the hospital straight from Jessica's. If anyone sees me carrying a bag out of the house and follows me, they'll just assume I went to get a few things for her."

He nodded. "Good strategy. And if you manage to get anything out of Jessica that makes sense, especially concerning the attempted kidnapping or the accident, let me know."

"Of course. Shall I check her mail and things like that while I'm at her house?"

"That's a good idea. If you see anything from her ex-husband Henry Tannen, call me," he said, giving her the key Father Mahoney had left with the department. "I've been trying to get an address for him, but so far all my leads have fizzled out. I've had a lot of problems cutting through the red tape, too. I can't even get a mug shot."

"He served time, correct?"

"Yeah, but I don't have any details yet.

Have you been able to learn anything about him from Natalie — maybe something she heard from her mother?"

She told him what Natalie had said. "Do you want me to ask Father Mahoney?"

Tom shook his head. "I've already done that. When I brought up the subject of Jessica's ex, I thought he was going to rip the arms off his chair. I got the feeling Father Mahoney would be more than willing to tie all of Henry Tannen's limbs into one big knot if they ever meet again."

"Father Mahoney is normally a gentle giant, but Jessica *is* his sister." Sister Agatha stood. "I better get going. I've got a lot of things I need to get done before I head back home." Sister Agatha went outside to the parking lot and started the Antichrysler. Another explosive backfire shattered the morning calm, but this time no one even flinched.

A short time later, she pulled into Jessica's driveway. It was a good thing she was going to the hospital next. Subterfuge was impossible when driving a car that sounded like a tank under heavy artillery fire.

Esther Reinhart waved from her window and Sister Agatha smiled back, then ducked under the police tape and headed to the door, stopping by the mailbox first. It was stuffed to the brim, so after picking the bundle up, she unlocked the door and went inside.

Sister Agatha dropped the mail on the kitchen table and walked down the hall. As she entered Natalie's room, she saw the girl's beloved toys strewn on the floor, her clothes scattered everywhere, and two bookcases overturned. Remembering Natalie's description, Sister Agatha searched the floor for the angel doll called Gracie. She found several rag dolls, angel bears, and even a cow angel, but no Gracie.

Seeing more toys near the closet door, Sister Agatha searched the pile there. Gracie was at the bottom. There was no mistaking her. The rag doll's smudged face was so ugly it was actually cute. She wore a pale yellow robe with a rope belt. Attached to that was a small leather pouch — representing a purse — with the word "Gracie" in glitter script.

Putting the doll beneath one arm, she went to Jessica's bedroom and picked up a nightgown. She then placed both items inside a grocery sack she found in the kitchen, nightgown on top, in case anyone took a look inside.

On her way back out, she stopped at the kitchen table and sifted through the letters and flyers. Besides the usual round of bills, there were dozens of letters hand-addressed to Natalie. From the angel drawings and stickers on the outside, she guessed that they were appeals and petitions for the girl's help. One of the last envelopes in the stack had come from Joey Rubio.

It wasn't her business to open it, but knowing what she already did about Joey's missing daughter, she telephoned Tom and told him about it. "Joey is one of our roofers, Tom," she reminded.

"Open it and read it to me. I've got Father Mahoney's standing permission to enter the house and do whatever I need, so we're covered."

She read him the letter, an obvious cry for help from a man with one goal that kept him going from one day to the next — finding his child.

After Sister Agatha was finished, silence stretched out on the line between them. "I'll have a talk with Rubio," he said at last. "But let me handle this. Natalie is being kept away from the windows and areas where she might be seen by the workmen, right?"

"We've done our level best but nothing's foolproof."

"I have the option of pulling her out of the monastery and putting her in protective custody in another community, but Father Mahoney's against that idea. He's sure she'll run away."

"She might. But Joey sounds pretty desperate in this letter, Tom."

"Let me check out something else." She heard a rustle of paper then Tom back on the line. "According to my deputy's report, he couldn't have been the phony nun — his whereabouts that day are accounted for. But I'll go see if he has an alibi for the night Jessica's car was run off the road."

"I'm still going by the hospital to see Jessica before going home. Maybe she's lucid enough now to be able to help."

When she finally reached the hospital, Sister Agatha took Gracie out of the grocery sack. Pushing her quickly beneath the seat, Sister Agatha locked the car and walked to the hospital entrance carrying the bag containing Jessica's nightgown.

Mrs. Johnson, the ICU nurse she'd met earlier, greeted her. "Are you looking for Jessica, Sister?"

She nodded. "I brought her some nightclothes."

"We were able to move her out of ICU. She's in the last room down this hall on your right. You'll see the officers. But if you're not expected, I doubt you'll get in."

"The sheriff knew I was coming," she said. "How's Jessica doing, by the way? Will I be able to talk to her for a bit?"

"She'll know you're there, but things are very confusing to her right now, an effect of the stroke that followed her initial trauma."

Sister Agatha hurried down the hall. Nodding to the officers, who recognized her immediately, she went inside. The room held three beds, but only one was occupied. Jessica lay still, her eyes closed and her face pale, even in the subdued light. A monitor had been taped to her finger and the machine to her right beeped in steady rhythm.

Sister Agatha approached quietly, but as she reached the chair next to the bed, Jessica opened her eyes.

"Do you remember me, Jessica?" Sister Agatha asked softly, placing a gentle hand on her arm.

Jessica's stare was vacant. Sister Agatha wasn't even sure she'd heard her, but when she repeated the question, she got the same response.

"I brought one of your nightgowns," she said, showing it to her, then hanging it up in the closet when Jessica didn't react.

"Natalie is in good hands," Sister added, hoping to elicit some reaction.

"Natalie," Jessica repeated in an unsteady voice.

Sister Agatha saw a glimmer of recognition in Jessica's eyes, but in a heartbeat it was gone.

A young nurse came into the room and smiled at Sister Agatha, then at Jessica.

"You're doing so much better!" she told Jessica cheerfully.

Sister Agatha studied the nurse's expression, trying to decide if she'd really meant what she'd said or if it had been simply for her patient's benefit.

"She really is, you know," the nurse said as if she'd read Sister Agatha's mind. "There's still swelling in parts of her brain, but that'll come down. Before you know it, she'll be back to her old self."

Sister Agatha wasn't sure whether to believe her or not, but from what she could see, Jessica wouldn't be able to help them anytime soon. Sister Agatha had started walking back to the door, paper bag in hand, when she heard Jessica's voice.

"Natalie," she said, more firmly this time.

Sister Agatha remained where she was, wondering if Jessica had actually remembered her daughter or if she'd just parroted the word. Approaching the bed again, she looked directly into Jessica's eyes. Pain and confusion were mirrored there along with another emotion — fear.

"Everything's all right, Jessica. We won't stop praying for you. God's all the backup you need."

The eyes that stared back at her were haunted, but as Jessica closed her eyes, the harsh lines around her mouth eased and a sense of peace seemed to settle over her.

"*Benedicite Domino,* Jessica," she whispered, then hurried down the hall.

15

When Sister Agatha entered the parlor at the monastery carrying the paper sack with Gracie inside, she found Sister Bernarda at the front desk.

"What happened to all the hammering?" Sister Agatha asked, noting the silence around them.

"The insulation that's supposed to go beneath the fiberglass sheeting didn't arrive. Del's now waiting for a shipment that's supposed to arrive either later this afternoon or tomorrow."

Hearing a vehicle driving up outside, Sister Bernarda glanced through the window. "It's the delivery man coming to pick up our last shipment of altar bread," she said, pointing to the tiny labeled box on a side table. "Good thing we've been deluged with e-mail orders for our Cloister Clusters, and Smitty called about an hour ago, too. He's selling at twice the rate he predicted, so he needs another shipment as soon as possible."

"That's great news," Sister Agatha said. "But we're going to need to find more efficient mass production methods. Otherwise, we'll be overwhelmed." From the looks of it, they were becoming too successful for their own good.

Hearing the deliveryman's knock at their door, Sister Bernarda went to open it.

"Good afternoon, Sisters." Mike, their regular Parcel Express driver, was in his early forties and resembled Cro-Magnon man. His beefy hands were surprisingly gentle, however, whenever he handled their altar bread boxes. "I came to make the regular pickup."

"What happened to the new driver, Andrew?" Sister Agatha asked.

"We're sharing this route. Today he's doing residential deliveries in town, so I'm taking care of our commercial accounts."

"Sounds like your company's doing a brisk business," Sister Agatha said.

"It'll get even crazier as the holidays get closer." He pulled a baseball style cap from his pocket and put it on his head.

For a moment, Sister Agatha couldn't get the image of the man she'd seen at the hospital out of her mind. But Mike wasn't wearing a Dallas Cowboys cap, just the brown cap that went with his uniform.

"I bet it's hard to keep all the routes manned, particularly during your busy season. I would imagine you have your fair share of on-the-job injuries with all the lifting that's involved in your work," she said, wanting to follow through on an idea she'd just had.

"Once in a while one of our drivers pulls a muscle or cuts a finger, but injuries aren't as common as you might think."

"What about you? I'm almost sure I saw you at the hospital the other night," she said casually, all the while studying his expression intently.

"Me? No way. Hospitals give me the willies, Sister. I'm a Christian Scientist and we have our own methods of healing. Trust me — the only way anyone would ever get me inside that place is feet first."

Sister felt inclined to believe him. "My mistake."

As Mike left, Sister Bernarda gave her a quizzical look. "What was *that* all about?"

She explained briefly. "I realized the baseball cap was a stretch, but he's one of very few who pays us a visit *and* wears a hat like that." Sister Agatha checked her watch. "It's almost time for None. I'll take over in the parlor so you can go, but first give me a chance to track down Natalie."

"She's with Sister Ignatius. Those two have the most incredible rapport. If you still need to get information from Natalie, I think you should consider enlisting Sister Ignatius's help."

"Natalie talks to *me,* too," Sister Agatha said.

"She may talk to you, Your Charity, but she's also aware that you're working with the police. On the other hand, when she's with Sister Ignatius, she's with a kindred spirit. They're both artists and you know how Sister Ignatius feels about angels."

Sister Agatha nodded. Sister Bernarda was right. As much as she liked Natalie, the rapport between them was forced. Natalie answered her questions not out of any sense of friendship, but out of necessity.

Hearing hushed whispers coming from down the enclosure hall, Sister Agatha listened and heard Natalie speaking animatedly to Sister Ignatius about Gracie. "Gracie's perfect. She's even got her own purse."

"You've given her a very important job," Sister Ignatius agreed, also whispering.

Seeing Sister Agatha across the grate, Sister Ignatius smiled. "We've had a productive day, Your Charity. But the bells will ring for None soon, and I thought it was time for her to come back."

Sister Agatha opened the enclosure door and brought Natalie outside.

"Did you bring Gracie, Sister Agatha?" Natalie asked quickly.

Sister Agatha reached for the paper sack and handed Natalie her doll.

"Gracie!" Natalie gave the doll a hug. "Thanks, Sister Agatha. I really hated not having her around."

"I heard you telling Sister Ignatius that Gracie has a special job. What does Gracie do?"

Natalie averted her gaze. "It's just something . . ." she muttered.

As Sister Agatha walked to the parlor desk, Natalie hurried into her room and closed the door. The rejection stung far more than Sister Agatha ever imagined it could.

Sister Bernarda gave her a long, pensive look. "Whether you realize it or not, the right thing *is* happening between you and that girl."

Sister Agatha gave her a puzzled look. "What are you talking about? Nothing's happening at all."

"Exactly," Sister Bernarda whispered. "Natalie's chosen another confidant and that'll give you the emotional distance you'll need to work on this case with the sheriff."

"I suppose," Sister Agatha said with a nod. "What makes it hard is that sometimes when I look at Natalie, I find myself thinking of her as the child I might have had," Sister Agatha admitted softly. "It doesn't make a bit of sense, but there it is."

As the bell rang for None, a hush fell over Our Lady of Hope Monastery. Sister Bernarda picked up her breviary and went into the enclosure, leaving Sister Agatha alone in the parlor. The nuns began to chant the Divine Office, and the sound of their voices filled the empty corridors. In those moments of serenity, the power of the Divine touched each of their hearts and gave them the gift of peace.

They gathered for Morning Prayers the following day feeling a huge sense of accomplishment. Today was their first public sale, so all the sisters, including the externs, had worked in shifts throughout the night.

Sister Agatha, Sister Bernarda, and Frances Williams would be manning the booth at the local Harvest Festival, and a huge crowd was expected to attend. The externs spent an hour loading every available inch in the Antichrysler with cookies. They had to keep warding off Pax, who'd made it clear he would have loved a chance to steal a box or two. Today they'd also be selling a few of the angels Sister Ignatius and Natalie had made. Since Natalie had agreed to leave them unsigned and put the monastery's crest on them instead, they'd be testing the marketability of those designs today instead of waiting for the Christmas bazaar.

Leaving behind what they couldn't fit into the station wagon for now, they set off for Bernalillo. The drive to the Harvest Festival grounds took less than fifteen minutes, even at the snail's pace that the Antichrysler demanded.

Frances, the rectory housekeeper, had already arrived and set up their booth. "It's about time, Sisters!"

Even before the morning chill had left the air, a crowd had gathered, hoping to get the best selection and bargains. The angels Natalie and Sister Ignatius had made sold out almost immediately, and the Cloister Clusters went two or three boxes at a time. By ten o'clock, the line in front of their booth was the longest one at the entire event.

One of their customers, Chuck Moody, came up to Sister Agatha with a silly grin on his face. Sister Agatha hadn't seen him in the full light of day for a very long time,

263

but now she realized that he hadn't changed much at all except for the attempt at a beard. He was a small man, built chunky like a fireplug, and he had a nervous, kinetic energy that all but demanded that he remain in constant motion.

"Can you leave the booth for a minute, Sister? I've got something important I need to talk to you about."

"Now?" She looked at the long line behind him.

She was tempted to turn him down, but something in his tone warned her that doing so would be a mistake. Sister Agatha signalled Frances, who was unpacking more cookies from the big cartons. "Frances, can you take over for a few minutes, please? I won't be long," she said. Seeing her nod, she walked away from the booth with Chuck. "This better be good," she said.

"Remember what I said the other night? I really do owe you big-time, Sister. You forced me to sober up, and I've got a good life now. But I've still got to make up for some of my past mistakes, and I'm starting with you. That's why I came to offer my services."

"Your services?" Sister Agatha asked, confused.

"I know you work with the sheriff every

once in a while. Some of it has made the newspapers. So right now I'm guessing, you're looking into Jessica Tannen's accident for the sheriff and Father Mahoney." Not waiting for an answer, he continued. "It just so happens that in my new job I hear all kinds of things. So I'm going to be keeping my eyes and ears open for you, Sister."

"I appreciate that, Chuck, but if you hear anything pertaining to the case, shouldn't you take it to Sheriff Green?"

Chuck shook his head. "To them, I'm an ex-con and that's all I'll ever be. They'll never listen to anything I have to say. I'll bring whatever I find to you, then you can decide what to do with it."

"Thanks, Chuck, I appreciate this, but you owe me nothing, truly," Sister Agatha insisted. "Being a good citizen is all anyone expects from you now."

"You're wrong about that, Sister. Prison was a real test for a little guy like me. There were times when I honestly didn't think I'd leave there alive. So I prayed a lot, and made a deal with God. If he got me out of there in one piece, I'd do my best to make things up to the people I'd screwed — er, I mean threatened, or whatever. Then the parole board finally believed that I was serious about going straight and I ended up getting an early parole. So now I've got to keep my deal with the man upstairs. You know what I mean?"

"Yes, I do."

"So here's what I wanted to tell you." He paused for dramatic effect. "Did you know that the monastery's roofing job is the *only* reason Del Martinez's company hasn't gone bankrupt? Joseph Carlisle happens to be Del's brother-in-law and he manipulated Del's books to make it look like the roofing company was running in the black. That made Del eligible to do subcontracting work for Grayson Construction. But Grayson requires an annual audit of all their subcontractors and this year it's happening earlier than usual. Unless Del or Joseph can come up with enough cash to match their phony numbers quickly, they're going to be looking at possible jail time. That's why Joseph and Del are trying to track down Natalie Tannen. One of the tabloid reporters has offered a big finder's fee on behalf of his paper to anyone who leads him to Natalie, and there's a hefty bonus included if the lead includes a photo op."

Sister Agatha stared at him in surprise. Did Chuck somehow know where Natalie was, or was he just trying to warn her since she was working the case with Tom? His smug grin wasn't encouraging. She took a deep breath and answered. "Where did you get all this?"

"One of my old . . . contacts, serves drinks at an establishment that shall remain nameless. She knows I work for a newspaper, so she passes gossip on to me — stuff she thinks might give me a lead to a story. I used to go out with her, and we're still kind of close," Chuck said and winked.

She resisted rolling her eyes — barely.

"You get it now, right?" he added. "Natalie is the only way those two can get money fast — providing they can lead the tabloid guy to her."

Sister Agatha was determined not to let Chuck know how troubling she'd found the news he'd given her. The creative bookkeeping he'd mentioned may have somehow involved Jessica. Had she threatened to talk? She'd have to tell Tom as soon as possible. "Thanks for letting me know about this, Chuck. If it checks out, it may be the break Tom needs to close the case," she said. "But right now I've got to get back to the booth."

"Okay, Sister. If I hear anything else, I'll let you know."

Seeing a deputy, Sister Agatha sent Tom a note then got back to work. Lunch became hot dogs at the booth, but by two in the afternoon they were out of cookies. Sister Agatha sent Sister Bernarda back to the monastery for more.

After hanging up a sign that read, TEMPO-RARILY SOLD OUT, Frances decided to take the opportunity to walk around the grounds and check out the other booths. Alone for the moment, Sister Agatha sat down and took out her prayer book. She could do the afternoon "little hours" while she waited. She'd only just opened the breviary when a dark-haired man wearing round glasses approached.

"Will you be getting more cookies in soon, Sister?" he asked with a friendly smile.

The man looked very familiar, but she couldn't place him until someone yelled out, "How ya doin', Jer?"

Her guard went up instantly. Jerry Dexter was the owner of Bountiful Bakery.

"You've got yourself a winner with those cookies, Sister. But I think I should warn you that going into the retail market can be very risky. The monastery might get more of a benefit from this by selling me the recipe or licensing it to my business. You could then go back to doing whatever it is nuns do, and still get a small percentage of the profits."

"Small? Why small? It's *our* recipe."

"Sure, but all the other expenses, such as overhead, advertising, storage, shipping, and spoilage, would be mine."

"Thank you for your offer," she said coldly. "I'll tell Reverend Mother what you said, but I'm fairly certain that we'll take a pass. Like you, we also have to support ourselves."

"Listen, Sister, you're cutting into my business," he said, lowering his voice. "That bakery's my livelihood, and unlike your monastery, I don't receive donations."

The harshness of his tone surprised her. "Surely you sell more than cookies," she countered.

"Of course we do. We sell all kinds of breads, cakes, pies, and pastries. But our cookies are — were — our best profit-makers. Now even Smitty has cut his whole-sale orders from our ovens. Are you nuns going to be in the cookie business for a long time, or is it just to raise some extra money?"

"I don't expect we'll stop anytime soon. Our expenses still have to be met."

"I've worked too hard to build a business in this community, Sister. If you're going to become my competitors, then expect a fight on your hands."

"Mr. Dexter, there's a place for both of us under God's plan. We have no desire to usurp you. We just want to sell enough cookies to keep a roof over our heads."

"A bakery has a low profit margin, Sister. I honestly can't afford to sit back while you steal my customers."

"Then give them a good reason to buy the other items you bake. We have no desire to hurt any other business in the community. But our Cloister Cluster sales are going to continue, at least for the time being."

As she finished speaking, a backfire in the parking lot told her the Antichrysler had returned. "Speaking of that, I've got to help Sister Bernarda unload some cartons. Please excuse me."

As Dexter strode off, Chuck Moody came up to her. "Sister, I heard him giving you a hard time. Maybe I should go let the air out of his tires. Whadda ya think?"

Sister Agatha looked at him in surprise, then laughed out loud at the outrageous offer. "No, Chuck, thank you, but we don't do things that way."

Just as Chuck moved off, Sister Bernarda hurried up to the booth, carrying a large carton containing boxes of Clusters. "What was Jerry Dexter talking to you about?"

Sister Agatha filled her in, and when Sister Bernarda heard Chuck's offer, she laughed. "I just can't figure out what's bothering Dexter. People go into his shop for bread, wedding cakes, and doughnuts, don't they? He only has one little display case of cookies, if I remember correctly. Surely he doesn't *really* think we're hurting his business."

About an hour later, while Frances and Sister Bernarda were busy with customers, Sister Agatha took a moment to rearrange the boxes on the counter so they'd be within easy reach. As she did, a small white envelope caught her eye. It had been placed at the corner of the narrow counter and weighed down with a rock so it wouldn't blow away. "Did either of you put that there?"

When both of them shook their heads, she opened it quickly, curious to see what it was. Several one-hundred-dollar bills were crammed inside. Sister Agatha counted them quickly. "There's a thousand dollars in here," she said. Seeing a small yellow note between the bills, she brought it out and read it. "It's a donation for the monastery."

"From whom?" Sister Bernarda asked.

"It isn't signed." Leaning over the front counter, Sister Agatha caught the eye of the

271

woman in the booth next to theirs. "Did you see anyone leave an envelope for us?"

"Yeah, that man over there," she said, and pointed. "You were all busy unpacking boxes at the time."

Sister Agatha gazed in that direction and saw a tall, lanky man wearing a blue baseball cap low over his face. Before she could get a good look at him, he disappeared into the crowd.

"Reverend Mother said that we needed one thousand for the down payment on the roof," Sister Agatha said quietly.

"Then it's a gift from God," Sister Bernarda said.

"Maybe Natalie's angel is working for you," Frances said.

For the first time she found herself fervently hoping that they did have an angel in their midst. That possibility was a lot less frightening than the alternative — that their private conversations had been overheard from the day the roofers had first arrived.

16

After morning prayers the following day, Sister Agatha went to Reverend Mother's office. They'd arrived late last night and she hadn't had a chance to speak to the abbess until now. Sister Agatha didn't bother to knock. The abbess, who had taken to wearing her ear protectors now that the hammering had begun again, never would have heard her.

As Sister Agatha approached the desk, Reverend Mother looked up and removed her ear protectors. After the customary greeting, Reverend Mother invited her to sit down.

"Child, you look so worried. Is something wrong?"

"Mother, we may have a problem," she said, telling her what Chuck Moody had said and about the donation. "If they're listening . . ." she said, having to raise her voice because it was the only way to be heard.

"Warn the sisters and our guest to be especially careful," she said, without mentioning Natalie by name.

When Sister Agatha returned to the parlor, she found Sister Bernarda at her desk and Natalie reading softly to Gracie. The scene was peaceful. Then, all of a sudden, several hammers began to pound in unison.

Gritting her teeth, she wrote down the warning Reverend Mother had asked her to pass on, then gave Sister Bernarda the note. Sister Bernarda's eyes widened slightly as she read it and she nodded somberly.

Sister Agatha decided to take another look at the adjoining reception room that had become Natalie's quarters. The windows were covered with thick curtains. Nothing — not even the merest trace of light — penetrated, and there were no vents in the walls or ceiling that could conduct the girl's voice outside.

Wordlessly, she turned and went outside. As she walked over to the Harley, Pax came bounding up to her. Sister Agatha signaled Pax to jump into the sidecar then sped out the gates. The wind felt good against her skin, and seeing Pax happily sniffing the breeze as they zoomed down the road, she allowed herself to relax.

Less than fifteen minutes later, Sister Agatha eased back on the throttle. As she made the turn onto the narrow drive leading to the rectory, she saw the door fly open.

Father Mahoney ran outside, then sprinted down the front end of the small building. "Get him!" he yelled, looking in her direction for a second.

She couldn't see anyone except for Father Mahoney, who'd reached the corner already. Then Pax barked, placing his front paws on the sidecar windscreen.

"No! Stay!" she shouted, afraid he'd try and jump out of the moving Harley and break a bone, or worse. Speeding up, she drove on, trying to see what or who Father was chasing.

At the back of the rectory, the church parking lot continued for another hundred feet, then ended in a six-foot adobe wall. A man in gray coveralls and a baseball cap was running west across the gravel.

She accelerated, hoping to head him off. Making a sliding left turn, Sister Agatha barely missed the row of concrete parking barriers. Pax, still excited and barking at the top of his lungs, nearly fell out of the sidecar. But she was too late. The man raced in front of her, leaped up onto the wall, and scrambled over before she could stop.

"Go around. Try to see where he goes!" Father Mahoney shouted as he caught up to them. He leaped up onto the wall and scrambled over with a grunt.

"Hang on, Pax!" She made a quick turn, then raced back out the driveway, looking for oncoming traffic in the main street, hoping to pull out immediately. But she had to stop for an old pickup. Once it passed, she raced up to the next corner and made a right turn, heading west. This street would take her into the neighborhood where the intruder and Father Mahoney had gone.

"Let's head him off at the pass," she said to Pax, who barked back. Speeding down to the next corner, she realized the road ended there. She slid to a stop and climbed off the Harley. Pax was already out, but unsure where to go.

"Up," she yelled, climbing a weed-covered embankment so she could look around. It took only a few seconds to find the man in the coveralls. He was climbing into a tan pickup a hundred yards to the north, on the other side of the wide ditch. The canal was empty, but the sides were steep and lined with tall brush, and there were no foot-bridges within sight. Even Pax would have trouble climbing up the other side. She was forced to stare in frustration as the pickup roared off to the west. Running up the ditchbank, Pax by her side, Sister Agatha kept the vehicle in sight as long as she could. It reached the next corner and turned south, finally passing out of view behind a house.

Hearing footsteps, she turned and saw Father Mahoney racing up. All she could do was shake her head. "He got away."

Father Mahoney rode back in the sidecar with Pax more or less on his lap. It looked uncomfortable, and Pax jumped out as soon as they pulled up in front of the rectory. Frances came out immediately, telephone still in hand.

"I called the sheriff," she said, looking over the priest. His clothing was dusty and there was a tear in his black trousers, and his hair, usually neatly groomed, had been blown askew by the motorcycle ride.

"Is anything missing from my office?" Father Mahoney asked, reaching for the screen door handle.

"We should wait outside, Father," Sister Agatha said loudly, then realized she still had her helmet on.

"Oh. You're right. There might be fingerprints or something. No, wait — he was wearing gloves, I think." He turned to look at Sister Agatha. "Wasn't he?"

She nodded. "I think I saw them when he climbed over the wall. But we'd better let the experts check first."

"You can wait for the police on one of the benches," Frances said, pointing to the wooden seats in the small garden area between the church and the rectory. "I'm going to go into the chapel and thank the Lord we're all still alive."

A few minutes later, Sister Agatha learned the details of what had happened. Father had come in from the church and greeted Frances, who was in the kitchen. Puzzled, she immediately asked who was in his office. He'd hurried in and nearly grabbed the intruder, who'd overheard and was escaping out the open window. Father had gone around, not able to fit through the window, and that was when Sister Agatha and Pax arrived.

"Well, with the tan pickup, we can make the connection between today's break-in and the attack on Jessica and Natalie," Sister Agatha concluded. "The intruder must have come searching for something that would lead him to Natalie."

"If I'd been a step faster, I'd have had the sorry bas— weasel in my hands. If I ever catch up to him, I'm going to yank his arms right off. The Lord would forgive me, I'm almost certain of that," Father replied. His voice was very controlled and even, a quality that made it even more frightening.

"This kidnapper, or whatever he is, will be caught," Sister Agatha said softly.

Father Mahoney closed his eyes for a moment in what looked like a prayer, then sighed loudly and turned to her. "What brings you here today, Sister Agatha? Good news, I hope."

"Maybe news that will lead us to answers." She told him what she'd learned about Del Martinez and Joseph Carlisle, and the threat that might have posed to Jessica, who'd had access to their bookkeeping. "But my source is far from reliable," Sister warned. "Did Jessica ever mention her boss to you?"

"I got the impression she didn't like Carlisle very much. But if Jessica had discovered something illegal was going on, I'm certain she would have told someone."

Sister Agatha nodded. "Maybe she told the wrong person. Or maybe she kept quiet, afraid she'd get pulled into the mess somehow and end up having all the blame pushed off on her. Could that have been the real reason she was planning to leave town?"

"Only Jessica can tell us that," Father Mahoney said warmly. "But I hate even the thought that the pair would try and cover their behinds by selling out Natalie."

"We need to keep an eye out for that tabloid reporter, whoever he is," Sister Agatha said. "There're a lot of people around here who could use the money he's apparently offering for information on Natalie."

"Unfortunately, some events, like what happened on the night she was run off the road, may never come back to Jessica. That's according to her doctor," he said. "It's all up to Sheriff Green now. I just hope for Natalie's sake that he can track down the man in the tan pickup."

"He's also looking for Henry, Jessica's ex-husband, too, just in case," Sister Agatha reminded.

"In my opinion, that's a waste of time."

"Why do you say that?" she asked as Frances brought each of them a cup of freshly brewed coffee, obviously prepared in one of the church's meeting rooms. The housekeeper stood back in the shade, watching the road for the sheriff's deputy to arrive.

"Henry's been completely out of the picture for seven years, give or take," he said. Shaking his head, he added, "Yet Jessica's always been terrified that he'd return one day and force his way into her life again." Father scowled as if the subject disgusted him. "One of my biggest regrets is that I never knew what he was doing to my sister when they were together. If I had, I'd have put *him* in the hospital." Father Mahoney's eyes were flashing, and for a second he looked more like the man who'd chased after the intruder less than a half hour ago.

Father forced himself to take a deep breath, then calmed down, sipping his coffee briefly. "Sorry, Sister, I find it hard to show any semblance of Christian charity to that bum. Not long after he finally split, I discovered that Henry used to beat the tar out of Jessica. That's why she ended up giving birth to Natalie before her due date. Jessica filed for divorce the day she got out of the hospital with the baby, but he stalked her on and off for more than a year, despite a court order. Then one day he just disappeared. She heard a rumor, later on, that he'd ended up in prison."

He stared at the coffee cup for a moment then stood and walked toward the steps of the chapel's main entrance. After a moment he turned around and faced her again.

"Even if he's out now, I just can't see him trying to get back into Jessie's life — particularly because I'm in the picture now and he knows I'll protect her."

As he fell silent, Sister Agatha got a glimpse of the odd expression on Frances's face, but before she could say anything, the portable phone the housekeeper was still carrying in her apron pocket began to ring. She answered it, then handed the receiver to Father Mahoney. Sister Agatha walked away with Frances into the lobby of the church, giving him some privacy.

Frances's loyalty to Father Mahoney was total, but there was obviously something bothering her right now. "The deputy will probably be arriving any minute, Frances. While we have time, why don't you tell me what's on your mind?" Sister Agatha said softly.

Frances hesitated, then after a moment she answered, "Jessica told me once, not long ago, that if Henry ever heard the stories about Natalie's special 'gifts' he'd come back — that he'd never pass up the chance to use his kid to make money. Jessica was terrified, but not for herself. She was afraid for Natalie. I'd always assumed Father knew that, but maybe not. If Henry's around, I mean if it turns out he's the one who just broke into the rectory, I should mention this to the police."

"Do it anyway when they come." Remembering the man Jessica's neighbor had seen the night of the storm, she added, "What would Jessica have done if Henry had shown up at her door?"

"Called the police," she said, then shook her head. "No, nix that. She was afraid that he'd demand visitation rights or partial custody. My guess is she would have come here, to her brother's."

Sister Agatha thought of Jessica's fateful car trip. It was possible she'd been on her way to the rectory. What if the man who ran them off the road had been Henry?

Thanking Frances for the information, Sister Agatha walked to where Father stood. He was off the phone now.

"The deputy has been delayed, so we can go back into the rectory as long as we stay out of my office. Now what were we talking about?" He opened the door and motioned for her to join him.

Sister Agatha joined him at the kitchen table. "I have a question for you, Father. So far no one's been able to figure out *why* Jessica chose to leave her house during that terrible storm. Is there *any* chance that she was running to you — that maybe her husband Henry tracked her down? Could the man we just saw, the man in the tan pickup, be Henry Tannen?"

Father Mahoney gazed across the room, his expression frozen and his hands clenched into massive fists. "If he lost a lot of weight, maybe. I didn't get a look at his face, so I can't say it wasn't Henry. But if that's the case, then I screwed up and I'm to blame for what's happened," he said, his voice raw. "I kept telling Jessica that Henry was too cowardly to come around again. If it turns out I was wrong and she paid for it . . ."

"You have nothing to blame yourself for. Besides, this is just speculation. We still don't really know what happened."

"But even now I'm failing Jessica," he said in a harsh whisper. "I've visited parishioners dozens of times at the hospital and yet when it comes to my own sister, the ball game changes. I've tried, but I can't even stay for five minutes. It hurts too much to see her this way. Jessica's always been the tough one, really. Even when her marriage to Henry fell apart she never crumbled. She found a job and raised Natalie alone. Next year she was planning to start taking night classes in accounting. Fate couldn't destroy her spirit, so it destroyed her body instead."

"Jessica hasn't given up, and you can't, either."

"I'm a priest, Sister. I'm on the front lines every single day. I *know* hope for what it is. It tempts you to believe in chances, to forget the odds. Better to brace yourself for the worst 'cause that's what usually ends up happening."

"God never said life would be easy," she answered. "He only promised that He'd see us through the hard times, that we wouldn't walk alone."

Father Mahoney nodded, then turned toward the window again and stared outside.

"You don't have a photo of Henry, do you? I'd like to know what he looks like — just in case."

"Not a one, and I don't think Jessica kept any, either. He was an ordinary looking guy, about your height and a bit chunky. Brown hair and eyes. That's all I could tell Sheriff Green when he asked. Sorry."

When the deputy arrived, Sister Agatha gave her statement, then left the rectory. She wished she could have done more, not just to catch the intruder, but also to help Father Mahoney resolve his own conflicts. For those who had chosen the religious life, a crisis of faith — a dark night of the soul,

as St. John of the Cross had called it —
often came with devastating results. It
sapped the heart of the confidence and
courage it needed to follow a path all too
often lined with thorns.

Sister Agatha drove to the sheriff's station
next. The weather had turned overcast and
the temperature had dropped. The chill
outside matched the coldness that had
seeped into her heart. The more time passed
without answers, the greater the danger to
Natalie and Jessica.

When they entered the station a few
minutes later, Pax immediately headed for
the bull pen, and Sister Agatha walked
directly to Tom's office.

He glanced up from a tall stack of file
folders. "Come in and take a load off," he
said, waving her to a chair. "I got the short
version of the incident at the rectory. What
else can you tell me?"

She quickly related the pursuit, and the
intruder's escape in the tan pickup. Then
she added the speculation concerning
Henry Tannen, including what Jessica had
told Frances.

"I've never ruled out the ex-husband, but
none of my inquiries have produced any in-
tel on Tannen's current location. I have my

officers on alert in case his name pops up," Tom said. "Father's right about Tannen being a lowlife. Henry Tannen got involved in some shady stuff about the time his marriage ended. He has a record, and served time — which explains why he's been out of the picture for years. But he got out six months ago and then dropped out of sight. As I told you, I'm having a tough time getting even a photo from his old files. One's finally supposed to be on the way, so I can let you have a look when it arrives."

"What if Henry's completely innocent — at least in this instance? Think of the message on Jessica's machine. Del Martinez and Joseph Carlisle have a motive, and we know where *they* are. Let's concentrate on them while we wait for more info on Henry."

"That's exactly what I've been doing. But we need hard evidence — a witness and a vehicle, certainly something more than an ex-con's secondhand gossip. I've done background checks on everyone in that office and they're all squeaky clean except for a few speeding tickets. I also interviewed the office staff, including Joseph Carlisle, but I've got nothing we can use."

"What about her second job?"

"Jessica works behind a desk checking out books. There's nothing for us there."

"I think I can get Cathy, the receptionist, to talk to me — providing it's outside of work. Do you know where she lives or where she goes to lunch?"

"You should talk to Mike, our day shift dispatcher. He dated Cathy for several months. She told me that herself, but I think they had a hard breakup, because when I questioned her I got the distinct impression she's no longer a fan of the sheriff's department."

Sister Agatha thanked Tom, then went to talk to Mike. After some chitchat, she got to the point. "Cathy's boss is obviously a difficult man to work for, and I don't want to get her into trouble by trying to meet her at the office."

"Carlisle's a jerk, that's pretty clear to me, but Cathy's very protective of her job. It pays pretty well, and she needs the medical benefits it gives her. She supports herself and her mother."

"Does Cathy have a favorite lunch spot?"

"Nah, she usually just brown-bags it and eats at her desk. But I went out for a smoke during my break a short while ago and saw her silver Civic pull into Dr. Woods's parking area."

"The dentist down the street?" she asked, having seen his office.

"Yeah."

"Thanks."

Sister Agatha called Pax, and together they walked to the dentist's office, which was only about a half block away. Leaving Pax at stay just outside the door, she went inside and glanced around. Cathy was sitting against the far wall, reading a magazine.

As she approached, Cathy glanced up and smiled. "Hey, Sister. Got an appointment today?"

"Not exactly. I've been wanting to talk to you and someone said you might be here," she said, deliberately being vague about the details. "Will you be going in right away, or do you have some time now?"

"Actually, my mom's the one with the appointment and it's going to take a while."

"Then why don't you come outside with me? I've got Pax at stay on the sidewalk, but sometimes he intimidates people. I'd hate for him to scare away some of the doctor's patients."

"No problem."

As they stepped outside, Pax stood up and wagged his tail. Cathy bent down to pet him. "I had a feeling that sooner or later you'd come looking for me. You didn't seem the type to give up easily. In that respect you have a lot in common with Jessica."

"Tell me more about her," Sister Agatha asked, strolling down the street beside Cathy and Pax.

"I'm not exactly her best friend, but I can tell you this much. Jessie's a born fighter and as honest as they come. She and Mr. Carlisle have their differences, but she's a good worker and he knows it. That's probably why he's never fired her though they seem to argue all the time."

"What about?" Sister Agatha asked, stopping by the flower shop to admire a display of roses.

"*Everything.* Carlisle makes Jessica crazy by looking over her shoulder while she's working. Most recently they argued about the annual profit and loss statement. She said that he was pulling numbers out of his . . . you know . . . and that the auditor would have a fit when he went over the books. He said she was getting everything wrong and that made her go ballistic. By then, they were in his office. I heard Jessica tell Mr. Carlisle that she wasn't going to take the blame for his mistakes. About that time, Carlisle slammed the door shut and I didn't hear the rest."

"How long ago was that?"

"Last week — no, the week before." Cathy gazed absently down the street. "But it seems so unimportant now, after what's happened to her." Cathy gave Sister Agatha a sad smile. "Jessica never gave up on her dreams," she said, then added, "I really wanted her to make it, too, you know?"

"Because she was your friend?"

"Yeah, but it's more than that. You see, when one of us beats the odds and actually makes her dream happen, it gives the rest of us hope. It's the lottery mentality, I suppose. You hear that someone somewhere won big, like that local guy who got himself a five-thousand-dollar scratcher just two days ago. So you figure that if other people can win, why not you, and you plop your hard-earned buck down for a chance, and for the right to dream, if only for a little while."

Sister Agatha's heart went out to her. "If you want something more from your life, trust God, not chance, to bring you the good you need. That gives everything a brand-new outlook."

Cathy smiled. "Jessica's faith was rock solid, like yours. Personally I think it's a miracle all its own that she managed to keep her job."

"Did Carlisle ever give her a hard time because she was moonlighting?"

"No way," Cathy said. "Mr. Carlisle is for

anything that keeps us from asking for a raise," she said as they returned to the dentist's office.

Seeing a light blue sedan pull up to the stoplight, Cathy stared at it for a second, then suddenly gasped. "Of all the rotten luck! That's Mr. Carlisle. Now the fur's going to fly." She turned and gazed into the window of the dentist's office, hoping she wouldn't be recognized.

"But he knew you'd be at the dentist's today, right?"

"Not for that — for talking to you, Sister. But maybe he didn't notice me. I better keep my back to him until he drives off."

"Tell me one last thing. Did Jessica have a best friend?"

"Not at the office, she didn't." Cathy faced the glass window, monitoring the reflection of traffic in the street. "She did mention an elderly woman she enjoyed visiting. I can't remember her name but she makes and sells goat cheese."

After Cathy went inside the dental office, Sister Agatha walked back to the parked Harley and headed home. She was starting to feel discouraged and needed a visit to the chapel.

As she drove by The Hog, she saw Chuck Moody coming out the door. Surprised to see someone who professed to be on the wagon at a bar this early in the day, she made a quick left turn, pulled into the parking area, and caught up to him just as he reached his car.

"Hey, Sister! Just the person I was looking for!"

"I thought you'd given up drinking, Chuck," she said sternly.

"I have. I'm just doing a little undercover work for the paper."

She gave him a skeptical look.

"It's true," he said, lowering his voice. "I just had a coke, no booze. But I'm glad you're here 'cause I've got something for you. I looked into Jessica Tannen's background and found something interesting about her ex-husband, something in his past that probably wasn't in the official police files the local sheriff would see. Henry served time in Colorado, but got paroled after testifying for the prosecution concerning some prison incident he witnessed. It was gang related, so his testimony made him some powerful enemies. Now he's got some major bad guys trying to track him down. When I started asking questions about Jessica and him, I stirred up a hornet's nest. So watch your back."

"Why would *I* have to do that?" she asked.

As understanding dawned over her, she stared at him, aghast. "Did you tell people *I'm* looking for Henry?"

He stared at the ground and shifted from foot to foot. "I think my exact words were that you were hot on his trail," he muttered. "But I was just trying to get them to loosen up and give me something you could use. Not even gangbangers would go after a nun."

"Please, Chuck, *don't* help me so much next time," Sister Agatha snapped. Sensing her mood, Pax growled at Chuck and he took a step back.

"Sister, what are you worried about? You've got Attila the Dog there. Like I said, no one's going to hurt a nun. Most of the bad guys in this area were probably raised Catholic anyway."

"*What* are you saying?"

"Oh — I didn't mean any offense. Most of the people in this town *are* Catholic, right? Even the cops."

Swallowing back her irritation, she forced herself to take a deep breath. "I'm going back to the monastery to pray that God will send you some brains and, me, a pair of eyes for the back of my head."

On her guard now, Sister Agatha took a quick look around. Two hardened-looking men standing beside their motorcycles seemed extremely interested in Chuck and her at the moment. When a third one came out, a man wearing a black leather jacket and a red bandanna around his head, Sister Agatha placed her hand on Pax to reassure herself.

"Do you know any of the people who are out here right now?" she asked Chuck, keeping her voice low.

"No," he said, glancing around furtively. "My guess is they aren't attorneys or accountants, Sister. But maybe they just like the Harley."

"I'll be seeing you, Chuck."

Sister Agatha started the bike quickly and pulled out of the parking area. Although no one seemed to be following her, she remained on her guard until she finally drove through the monastery gates. She now knew why Henry Tannen had dropped out of sight. Two minutes later, she was on the telephone, telling Sheriff Green the news.

Sister Bernarda was pacing in the parlor, rosary in hand, as Sister Agatha came in. "Their nail guns remind me of boot camp," she shouted to Sister Agatha. "A little while ago, I could have sworn I was back on the rifle range."

"Where's Natalie?"

"In the crafts room. She's created an angel design that's absolutely gorgeous. She calls it a pocket angel. You should go see it."

Sister Agatha stepped inside the enclosure and went to the crafts room. Sister Ignatius saw her arrive and immediately held out the small figure. The angel was about the size of her thumb but remarkably detailed. The figure was kneeling in prayer, flowing robes around it. But the truly stunning effect came from the fact that the angel had a golden sheen. "Is this metal or clay?"

"It's a special clay that some of the Pueblo tribes use. It has mica in it. I had Uncle Rick find us some. Do you like the angel? It can be put on a chain or used as a Christmas decoration." Natalie was beaming with pride.

"It's beautiful, Natalie. I think this'll do great at the bazaar. We sold the other ones you made for us almost immediately, and this one is even prettier."

Natalie stared at the angel critically, her lips pursed.

"Is something wrong?" Sister Agatha asked.

"I like it, but real angels don't look like this," Natalie said crossly, then shrugged. "But I guess that's what people expect."

Sister Agatha smiled at her. "Tell me what an angel *really* looks like."

"Well, they're not all the same, you know. Samara doesn't look like the one who protects the monastery. I've seen him a few times, too." Suddenly her gaze fixed on a point just behind Sister Agatha.

Pax, who'd been sitting next to Sister Agatha, turned around and lay down, ears pricked forward, expression alert, staring at the exact same spot Natalie was focused on.

Sister Agatha's skin prickled as she glanced at Sister Ignatius, who looked back at her, eyes wide.

"There he is now. Wow. I've never seen him this clearly before. He's as tall as the ceiling! He's wearing a white robe with a gold belt and has a huge sword with jewels. His hair isn't as long as Samara's but it's even whiter, and he's as bright as the sun. He's so beautiful," Natalie whispered.

Sister Ignatius dropped down to her knees, but Natalie turned to her quickly. "No, don't do that! He doesn't like it. He says that only God should be worshipped. Angels are just His servants and messengers."

Sister Ignatius stood up reluctantly, but her head remained bowed.

Sister Agatha squinted, straining her neck

forward. Suddenly she realized how silly that was. Squinting couldn't help her see what wasn't there.

Natalie turned and glanced at Sister Agatha. "He says that you shouldn't worry if you can't see him," she said, then gave her a sad smile. "Someday I won't be able to see angels either. When I get older, they'll fade away."

"The loss of innocence," Sister Ignatius whispered.

Sister Agatha nodded slowly. Innocence, like childhood, was a path traveled only once.

"He's leaving now but he wants me to tell you that although the monastery will face great dangers he, and others like him, will always be here to protect the sisters from harm."

"Does he have a name?" Sister Agatha asked, still searching for proof.

"Tah— Tazuriel," she answered.

Sister Ignatius crossed herself. *"Deo gratias,"* she whispered.

Instinct told Sister Agatha to pray, but the words got jumbled in her head. Suddenly remembering an old story, she began whispering the letters of the alphabet.

"He's gone," Natalie said softly.

Sister Ignatius looked at Sister Agatha, a

bewildered expression on her face. "Were you whispering the alphabet, Your Charity?"

She nodded and gave her a hesitant smile. "There's an old story about a man who always received what he asked for from God, though he'd never memorized any formal prayers. Others came to find out how he appealed to God, and he told them that he simply recited the alphabet and let God put the letters in the right order." She smiled. "I did the same, and added 'Amen' after the Z. Not exactly brilliant, but I think God understood."

17

It was three thirty in the afternoon, the time for manual labor, when Sister Agatha went to Reverend Mother's office. Unable to disturb the abbess earlier, who'd been on the phone with some supporters of the monastery most of the morning, her report of the incident with Natalie and the angel had been put on hold until now.

The abbess listened to Sister Agatha in silence. "And your impression?"

"I looked up the name Natalie gave us. I believe she meant Tzuriel. It comes from the Hebrew and means 'God is my rock.' There's no angel by that name, but there's an archangel by the name of Uriel. She could have simply added a 't' sound to it and, pardon the pun, winged it."

"So you're not convinced."

"Mother, I believe that Natalie's been given a gift to foretell certain events. But the rest . . . I just don't know. She believes in the angels she sees, that much I do know. But they may be her way of coping with her ability and making sense of it all."

Reverend Mother gave her a long, calm look. "The church officially says that we're free to believe her or not and I've chosen to believe Natalie. Her words bring me comfort and I see no harm in them." The abbess stood in front of the statue of the Blessed Mother, lost in thought. "But what we need right now is closure to the events that brought Natalie here. Help the police find answers, child. Natalie has brought us a blessing, but she belongs on the outside, not in this monastery."

"I'll keep trying, Mother."

Sister Agatha walked back to the parlor. Her past as a journalist had placed a heavy burden on her shoulders. The monastery counted on her far more than it did the other externs when it came to resolving problems like these. Now fear of failure dogged her footsteps.

Moments later, Sister Bernarda listened to her as Sister Agatha explained that she might need to be away for longer periods of time.

"Why are you so troubled? You have a talent for this kind of work," Sister Bernarda responded. The hammering had moved to another part of the building and they could speak at normal levels.

"What if I can't find the answers? A child's life is in our hands."

"Her life is in God's hands. It was never in ours."

"You're absolutely right," Sister Agatha said after a pause. "Pray that I'll always remember that we *serve*, we don't command — not even the situation," she added with a grateful smile.

Sister Agatha rode back to the sheriff's department with Pax. Tom would be her best source. Once she arrived at the station, she went directly to his office. "Come in," he said, glancing up.

Sister Agatha filled him in on what she'd learned from Cathy. "I want to talk to this friend of Jessica's that Cathy mentioned, but who the heck makes goat cheese around here? Do you know?"

"No, not off the bat," he said, "but I know someone who might. Maria Fuentes. Do you know her?"

"No, I don't think so."

"She's a very competent defense attorney. She takes quite a few pro bono cases, and I've dealt with her several times. She opened a new office a few months ago and invited me to stop by — kind of an open house deal. While I was there, she offered me some crackers and goat cheese and said that it was locally made. The stuff wasn't half bad."

"I better go speak with her then. Where's her office?"

"Just around the corner, two doors down."

Sister Agatha called Pax and they walked to an office building less than a hundred yards from the station. The newly lettered shingle on the door read, "Maria Fuentes, Attorney at Law."

Seeing that the door was partly open, Sister Agatha stepped inside, Pax with her. There was no receptionist, but a short, middle-aged woman came out from the back office to greet her.

"Sister Agatha?"

She nodded. "You're Maria Fuentes?"

"That's me. The sheriff just called to say you were coming." Maria smiled at Pax and invited Sister Agatha to take a seat. "What can I do for you?"

"I wanted to know where you bought the goat cheese you served at your open house," she said.

Maria smiled. "I get it from an elderly woman who lives on the eastern side of town. There's a lot of nonsense gossip claiming she's a witch — or crazy — but she's neither. Her name is Elena Serna."

Sister Agatha smiled and nodded. "I've met the woman, and you're right. She's a decent lady."

"Her goat cheese is the best I've ever tasted — actually, it's the only goat cheese I've ever tasted. Jessica Tannen brought some to my office in that huge purse of hers once. I smelled something odd, said something, and out came a plastic container of cheese and another of crackers." Maria laughed. "Elena needs some business, so Jessica was helping her by carrying samples to give out at lunch. Of course that purse of hers is huge and has pockets for everything, so it was perfect. When I teased her, saying that she could hide just about anything in that small suitcase she called a purse, she laughed and said that when it came to hiding places she was an old-fashioned girl. She said she believed in vaults — like Capone."

"I didn't know she had a vault."

"I think she was joking, Sister. I mean I assumed she was."

"Are you and Jessica close friends?"

"I handled a few legal matters for her and we have a good professional relationship, but that's it. I think she's pretty close to Elena Serna, though."

"That's such an unlikely duo. How did they ever meet, over the goat cheese?"

"Yeah, I think so. When Jessica found out how people shunned Elena, she befriended her almost immediately and became her best customer and advertising rep. Jessica's always on the side of the underdog."

"Although I didn't know about Elena's cheese, I do know the woman. She allows people to think she's a witch because, in a way, it protects her."

"An elderly woman who lives alone needs any edge she can get," Maria agreed with a nod.

Five minutes later, with Pax in the sidecar, Sister Agatha headed out, driving east across the railroad tracks, through a wash, and into the countryside. Elena Serna's low adobe home was visible beside a small spring that spilled out from among several big boulders. A dozen goats grazed on small tufts of grass in a low spot beside the road.

A curtain next to the living room window moved as Sister Agatha pulled up in front of the house, letting her know that the elusive Elena had seen her arrive.

Elena opened the door just as they stepped up onto the porch. "Hello, Sister Agatha. I was wondering how long it would be before your latest investigation led you here."

Sister Agatha went inside and sat down on the well-worn couch. There were candles everywhere and cryptic symbols painted onto the concrete floor. But she'd learned a long time ago that Elena had only put them there for dramatic effect — psychological decoration.

"How's Natalie?" Elena asked her.

"I've been told she's well," Sister Agatha said casually.

Elena smiled. "Sister, I'd be willing to bet my last goat that she's staying with you at the monastery. But you don't have to comment. I know Natalie and figured she'd end with the sisters because it was the safest place to hide her. I heard that there's a tabloid reporter named Springer looking for Natalie, so stay on your guard. Has anyone been lurking around the monastery?"

"Not that we know of." Unless that was the guy who'd disguised himself as a nun. Deciding not to mention that, Sister Agatha waited, letting the silence between them stretch.

"I know why you're here," Elena said at last. "But I don't have the answers you need. I don't know who ran Jessica off the road. What I can tell you is that Jessica was terrified that Natalie had become a target for loonies. All Jess really wanted was a normal life for her kid. I tried to explain to her that being different can have its advantages, too, but I don't think she really understood me."

"You made it work for *you*," Sister Agatha said, nodding.

"Exactly. Boys used to come by and throw things at my goats, or ruin my garden with their pickups. The sheriff back then wasn't much help, so I came up with a way to help myself. I drew a big star on the side of my house and stained the biggest rocks outside with red paint thinned out with water. It looked like blood and worked like a charm. When the kids saw those, they started getting worried about the crazy old woman who lived here. The rumors about me started, and eventually people left me in peace."

"But it must be hard to be so alone," Sister said.

"I have friends. My goat cheese has become popular in recent years with all the growing interest in natural foods. Jessica and Natalie love my southwestern flavored one. That's how Jessica and I got to be friends."

"It sounds like you two had a lot in common."

"Living alone can make you vulnerable

and I know what that's like. But I've never been in the type of mess Jessica was in," she said, leaning forward in her chair and looking directly at Sister Agatha. "Someone was trying to frame Jessica for something, and she was terrified that she'd end up in jail unless she could get evidence to substantiate her innocence. Once she got that she was planning to leave town with her daughter and go someplace where she and Natalie could start fresh."

"Framed for what?" Sister Agatha asked, thinking of Joseph Carlisle and her conversation with Cathy.

"I honestly don't know. I asked Jessica, but she was very closemouthed about it. She said she wasn't going to put anyone else in danger. I assured her I could take care of myself but she told me she could handle herself, too, and that I shouldn't worry. She said she was a great believer in insurance and that she'd be getting all she needed soon."

"What insurance — I mean, against what?" When Elena shrugged, Sister Agatha gave her a long, thoughtful look, then added, "You haven't told the sheriff about this?"

"No, I knew you'd be coming by soon, so I wasn't worried."

This put a whole new light on the investigation. Father Mahoney had not been told the real reason for Jessica's planned departure, apparently. Sister Agatha considered calling Tom immediately, but after reaching for her cell phone, she put it back into her pocket. "I'll go see the sheriff right now and tell him about this in person."

"I wouldn't leave without a plan, if I were you," Elena said, calling Sister Agatha's attention to a glimmer of reflected light playing on the far wall. Elena went to the window, peered outside, then glanced back at Sister Agatha. "There's someone parked at the end of my road, watching the house."

"Who?"

"Let me take a closer look." Elena pulled a pair of binoculars out of a drawer and began to zero in, adjusting the focus wheel with a scrawny finger.

Sister Agatha laughed softly. Those were good binoculars, not the toy store kind.

"I could tell you that I'm a bird watcher, but that would be a tall pile of manure." Elena turned her head and smiled. "I'm snoopy — so there. What else is there to do? My closest neighbor is a quarter mile away, so these have to be quality."

Sister Agatha bit her lip and tried valiantly to keep from cracking a smile. "What's the driver doing?"

"Sitting in a white Ford Escort, watching us. And he has his own binoculars." She turned around and handed her pair to Sister Agatha. "Here, take a look. The focus is in the center."

Sister Agatha stood by the side of the window, trying to hold the heavy instrument steady enough to get a good look at the man. "I don't think he's got binoculars. It looks more like a camera with a telephoto lens," she said, then added quickly, "Uh-oh, I think he just spotted me looking at him."

A few seconds later, they heard the sound of an engine revving up. "I want to get his license number," Sister Agatha said, running to the door. "Call the sheriff and let him know what I'm doing."

Sister Agatha raced out to the motorcycle, Pax at her side. She had to know if the man was really a reporter — which seemed likely because of the camera — or one of the gang members searching for Henry Tannen. Chuck Moody's warning was still fresh in her mind, though she couldn't imagine some image-conscious gangbanger in a white Ford Escort. Either way, she would not be used by anyone — crook or reporter — who wanted to harm another human being.

Sister Agatha climbed onto the Harley as Pax leaped into the sidecar. In a heartbeat she shot after the fleeing car, going through the cloud of dust the other driver had left in his wake.

By the time they reached a paved road, the fleeing car had increased its lead. Sister called Tom, pushing the phone beneath her helmet and giving him the location and direction of the chase, along with the license number and a description of the car.

"I'll handle this. Back off," he ordered.

"I'll just keep him in sight until you show up!" She disconnected the call before he could argue with her.

Sister Agatha stayed behind the Escort, maintaining pace. She didn't want to catch up to him — that was Tom's job. But she'd make sure that Tom would be able to find the car and driver. Moments later, the car entered Pueblo land and headed north to the giant parking lot around the casino.

Forced to slow nearly to a halt for a truck loaded with bales of alfalfa, Sister Agatha lost sight of the white Ford for several seconds. By the time she turned into the parking area, the Ford was gone. She began driving up and down rows of parked vehicles, surprised at how many small white cars there were. After several minutes she found the car again and passed by close enough to see it was unoccupied.

Once again she called Tom and updated him. "It's got a rental sticker on the back bumper," she said.

"And he was on Elena Serna's property?"

"Inside the fence line, yeah, so you can get him for trespassing. Her property is posted."

"Okay, hang tight. I'll need to work out the jurisdictional protocol because the vehicle is on Pueblo land now, but I'm on my way."

"Good. I'm staying right here. He's either ducked into the casino or is hiding out in the parking lot. Sooner or later, though, he'll have to return."

Less than ten minutes later, Tom caught up to her. A tribal policeman was with him.

"Where did he go?" the patrolman asked her.

"I don't know, but I suspect he's inside the casino. I figured that Pax and I would wait him out. I want to know if he was following me or just keeping an eye on Elena, which makes him a potential stalker."

"I'll go inside, talk to casino security, and see what I can find out," the tribal patrolman said.

"I'll stay here beside the vehicle, officer. If

he returns, I'll hold him," Tom said.

As the tribal officer left, Sister Agatha told Tom what Elena had said about Jessica and her concerns at work. "She did the accounts receivable and payable, Tom, and this corroborates what Cathy said about Joseph Carlisle. Something was going on in that office for sure."

"That might be right, but I can't touch him without more to go on. Without physical evidence or Jessica's own testimony, it's all hearsay."

As Sister Agatha drove back to the monastery, she kept a sharp eye on the rearview mirror. Moments later, as she passed through the open gates, she breathed a sign of relief.

When she went through the parlor doors, Sister Agatha was greeted by Sister Bernarda, who was in the parlor, just getting off the phone.

"How are things here?" Sister Agatha asked, noting the little girl was in the next room.

"Smitty just called. He's increased his order again. He wants to carry even more of our cookies. Apparently they're flying off the shelves."

"The income that'll generate will be a blessing," Sister Agatha said, though she was beginning to see that there was such a thing as being too successful. They were working round the clock as it was.

When the bells for Vespers rang, Sister Agatha, alone in the parlor, locked the doors. Natalie was still in the adjoining room quietly sketching.

"Sister Agatha, why don't you go to Vespers? I'll stay here and watch Natalie."

Sister Agatha looked at her, tempted, but not wanting to take advantage of Sister de Lourdes. After all, she and Sister Ignatius and Sister Bernarda had watched Natalie most of today. "Are you sure you don't mind looking after her a while longer?"

"Not at all. Go. We'll be fine.

Sister Agatha walked down the enclosure and took her seat in the chapel. Thinking of her sisters here and the people in town who struggled daily to make the world better, she opened her heart, holding them all in a spiritual embrace, and prayed. "You are in our midst, O Lord, and your name we bear . . ."

After Mass and breakfast, Sister Agatha went directly to Reverend Mother's office and brought her up to date on yesterday's events.

"The fact that our intruder may have been

one of those tabloid people makes me very uneasy," the abbess said. "They usually show no regard for the privacy of others. But I'm relieved to hear that it may not have been Henry Tannen at all. That man sounds dangerous."

"I'll see the sheriff later on. I'm hoping he'll have more definite news for us by then."

As she left Reverend Mother's office, Sister Agatha felt the dull pulsing ache in her hands that usually meant she was in for a bad time with her arthritis. Before she could try to figure out when she'd taken her last pill, Sister Eugenia met her in the hall. The infirmarian held a glass of milk in one hand and two pills in the other.

"I won't have you leaving without taking these, Sister. I placed two tablets in your cell last night, but you didn't take them."

"I didn't even see them," she admitted. "I had cookie baking duties that didn't end till three this morning. By then, I was too tired to even see straight. I just fell onto my bed and never moved again until this morning."

"These will help you out today. But you *have* to take them on a regular basis. You and Sister Gertrude are such terrible patients!"

"How is Sister Gertrude?"

"She insists on helping with the cookies, just like you. But we can't let her get too close to the ovens because of the heat, and mixing the dough in the large bowls is physically taxing. So last night before your shift in the kitchen, she led us in the rosary while we worked. However, she didn't take her heart medication, and by the time I discovered what she'd done, she'd missed one cycle of pills. This morning she had chest pains, so I'm insisting that she remain in the infirmary today."

"Take good care of her, Sister Eugenia. I wish, for her own sake, that she could still be our cellarer. She was such a whiz at taking care of the monastery's accounts, and we all need to feel useful. Working is as vital to a nun as breathing."

"Yes, but Sister Gertrude's health requires her to be free of stress. That's why Reverend Mother reassigned the task to Sister Maria Victoria. Unfortunately, number crunching isn't her thing. She's been trying to balance the monastery's checkbook for three days now."

"It might not be a bad idea to have Sister Maria Victoria and Sister Gertrude share cellarer duties," Sister Agatha said with a burst of inspiration. "That might be the best medicine we can give Sister Gertrude. Will you consider suggesting that to Reverend Mother?"

"Absolutely. I think it's an excellent idea. All things considered, it might do Sister Gertrude a world of good."

Saying good-bye, Sister Agatha headed outside and called Pax to her, eager to get started today. They were close to finding answers now. She could feel it.

Enjoying the crispness of the autumn morning against her face, Sister Agatha drove into town. A brilliant burst of red and orange leaves lit up the path before her. What an irony it was that nature was always at its most beautiful when it sang its last dying song before the onset of winter.

18

Sister Agatha entered the station a short time later.

"I was just about to call you," Tom said, meeting her in the hall. "I've got some news. We tracked down the man in the Ford Escort, a tabloid reporter named Jack Springer, and brought him in for questioning. He was released with a warning, but not before we discovered he's done some serious research on Jessica and Natalie. Springer is convinced that you know where Natalie is. He's been keeping an eye on you, apparently, though always at a distance. But he got too close over at Mrs. Serna's. Claims he thought he was on public land, and she won't press charges."

"Who does Springer work for?"

"The National Inquisitor."

Sister Agatha scowled. "Great. So he was planning to stick a story about Natalie and her angel between the feature about crocodiles in the Washington sewage system and NASA's cover-up of that Elvis face on Mars?"

"Yeah, all the news that's sick to print. According to Springer, anything concerning spirits, especially when healing and apparitions are involved, is front-page material. He's hoping to get a photo of the angel."

"You're joking?"

"No, and if he doesn't, they'll probably fake one to go with his story. Springer is really eager for an interview. Desperate, maybe, because he wants to get the exclusive."

"I can almost sympathize with him. But I was never *that* eager as a journalist . . . was I?" Sister Agatha asked.

Tom smiled. "Of course you were. By the way, Springer denied sneaking into the monastery in that nun disguise, though he's our best bet so far. Just make sure you continue to keep a sharp eye out for any reporters. And keep Natalie out of sight. We have to protect her from danger of all kinds now, including kidnapping."

"She's safe and will remain that way. Anything new on Jessica's boss, Carlisle?" she added, changing the subject.

"He's so clean, he squeaks. And the paint scrape we got off Jessica's car doesn't match his vehicle at all — not to mention that we've established the hit-and-run vehicle was a pickup and Carlisle doesn't own one. We've got a boatload of smudged fingerprints from the surfaces of Jessica's car, some partially washed away, and it's taking a lot of time to process them all. So far, most are Jessica's and Father Mahoney's. He helps her with maintenance and oil changes."

Sister Agatha said nothing for several moments. "I have an idea that might get us something on Carlisle." Reminding him what Jessica had told Elena about insurance and then telling him about her conversation with Maria Fuentes about hiding places, she added, "Have you checked to see if Jessica has a safe deposit box?"

"Sure, a while back, and the answer is no."

"I think it's time to look for the insurance Jessica spoke about. My guess is that she hid it in her home somewhere. It's the only place left for us to search."

"Agreed. Let's go over there right now. I'll have to ask Father Mahoney's permission on the way since I already released the scene."

"He won't mind."

"I still have to ask, particularly now. He's had some trouble over at Jessica's. People have been stealing little things out of the yard that Natalie might have touched — the door to the mailbox, a flower pot from the front porch, even a sprinkler. At least there haven't been any more break-ins that I've heard about."

As they drove to Jessica's house, Sister Agatha followed the sheriff's vehicle in the Harley. They were halfway there when she caught a brief glimpse of Chuck Moody as he passed by. Although he merely waved and then drove on, she had a feeling that Chuck was still trying to keep an eye on her. Working hard to forgive him for being such an irritating man, she kept her eyes focused on the road.

When they arrived at the Tannen house five minutes later, Sister Agatha left Pax sitting on the porch and went inside with Tom. Dividing the house into sections, they searched everywhere — even inside food containers. Finally, ninety minutes later, they returned to the living room.

"I looked inside the light fixtures and even sifted through the soil in the potted plants. There's nothing here," Tom said, disappointment evident in his tone. "Maybe Jessica was bluffing — or she never got the insurance she intended."

"I don't agree. Remember what Jessica

told Elena. There's something here — it's just well hidden."

"Gut feeling?"

"No, logic. If Jessica thought someone was framing her, she would have done whatever was necessary to protect herself. There's no way she would have risked getting arrested and being separated from Natalie."

"That makes sense, but if she buried something in the backyard, we're going to be here a *long* time."

Sister shook her head. "Outside, anything could happen to whatever she was protecting. She has a fence back there, but it's not enough to isolate the yard. My guess is that we're overlooking something here, inside, a place where she would have quick access."

They'd taken all the human steps possible. Now it was time to turn the matter to God. Sister Agatha said a silent prayer asking for guidance then slowly looked around the room, taking in every detail. Finally, after several moments, she spotted something she hadn't seen before.

"Look at the power strip attached to the outlet by the TV," she said, standing. "She's got a gazillion things plugged in there."

"Yeah, so what's your point?"

"Why have all those attachments there when you have another unused outlet a few feet away behind the table lamp?"

Tom glanced where she was pointing, muttered an oath, then went to move the lamp aside. Crouching down, he studied it. "This is one of those fake outlets you can buy from catalogues." Pulling it open from the top revealed a small hiding place and a floppy disk in a plastic case nestled inside. He took it out gingerly. "I think we just found Jessica's insurance. Let's go back to the station and find out what's on here."

It took another hour of waiting and pacing at the station before Tom came out to meet her. "The disk has a letter explaining the contents as well as all the proof we need to bring criminal charges against Joseph Carlisle. On a phony spreadsheet, the amounts Carlisle withdrew and pocketed showed up as cash used to purchase construction materials, goods later listed as stolen from work sites so they didn't have to be accounted for in inventory or as part of client structures. Jessica has no idea what Carlisle did with the money, but notes that he must have discovered her password or he couldn't have doctored the spreadsheet files. Jessica kept a second set of backups on a floppy, which contradict the records Carlisle sent to the head office. She found out what was going on when the accountant at

323

the head office called to question an entry."

"But that won't exonerate Jessica. It could be argued that *she* did the doctoring."

"True, but now that we have a case for fraud we can subpoena bank records for both Joseph Carlisle and Del Martinez. My guess is that the money Carlisle took from Grayson Construction's business accounts ended up in Martinez's books."

"But all that establishes is fraud. Can you tie Carlisle or Martinez to Jessica's car accident?"

"Not yet. Let's see what happens when I question Carlisle," he said. "Why don't you stick around? You can stand outside the interview room and observe through the two-way glass."

"Thanks, I'd like to do that. But if he doesn't have a truck . . ."

"Carlisle still could have borrowed someone else's vehicle that night. Let's see what kind of alibi he has."

Thirty-five minutes later Sister Agatha stood on one side of the glass while Tom questioned Joseph Carlisle. The man stonewalled completely at first, but Tom was tenacious.

"We have *physical evidence* that you were embezzling funds. Jessica Tannen kept another backup disk, as you probably discovered some time ago. Once we subpoena your bank records and get delivery records from your suppliers, I think we can prove those construction materials you reported stolen never existed. My next question is this — what do you have that'll convince me you're not also guilty of attempted murder? Prove to me that you weren't the one who ran Jessica Tannen off the road and tried to kill her."

"First of all, I don't have to *prove* anything — you do." Despite his bravado, Carlisle's face had paled considerably. "But why would I want to kill Jessica?" he challenged. "Even if I were guilty of embezzling — and I'm not admitting anything — why kill Jessica? If she had evidence that could be used against me, I'd have been better off pressuring her to tell me where it was."

"Where were you the night of her accident?"

"I was home alone, God's truth, watching the football game. I went to bed early, as soon as the game ended." He paused. "Look, if you don't believe me, ask me anything about that game."

"That's no good. Ever hear of a VCR?"

Sister Agatha watched Carlisle's brows knit together as he struggled to find a way out of his situation. He hadn't admitted to embezzlement, but he seemed pretty desperate to clear himself of attempted murder.

"Wait. I remember something. With all the thunder and lightning, my neighbor's dog was going nuts and barking like crazy. I called to complain, but they didn't answer so I left a message on the machine. Ask them."

"You could have called them from Budapest. That's no good."

"How would I have known the dog was barking? My other neighbor could corroborate that, I'm sure. Just ask him. The dog was really going crazy. Or check the phone records. They'd show I made the call from my house, right?"

"That would only work *if* the call was made at the time of the accident, give or take fifteen minutes. How lucky do you feel, Carlisle?"

"I'm not going to confess to a crime I didn't commit!" he roared then stood up.

"Sit down," Tom said, his voice low and deadly.

Carlisle eased back into his chair.

"Anyone you know have a tan pickup?"

Carlisle thought about it a moment. "My neighbor down the street, and my brother-in-law," he answered, then shrugged. "A lot of people own light-colored trucks. What's your point?" He stared at Tom with the desperation of an animal fighting for its life. "There are paint scrapes from the collision, right? Well, my car's blue. And my brother-in-law's truck has been in the shop for nearly a month waiting for a new axle. And neither one has a scrape on it. Check that out yourself."

Tom came out of the room a few minutes later. "I've got a good case for embezzlement, but the rest . . ." Tom shook his head.

"What about Del Martinez? It was his company that raked in the benefits of the embezzling scheme, if our informant is correct, so he has to know something about where the money came from."

"All true, but that doesn't tell us what part — if any — he played in what happened to Jessica. I'm going to bring him in for questioning and see where it goes."

Sister Agatha stayed in the hallway with Pax as Carlisle was led away to booking. As he walked past her, he shot her a venomous look. "You're responsible for this mess. Damned crow!"

Millie, the desk sergeant, came up and stood beside Sister Agatha until he was out of view. "Don't let him get to you. They all trash talk when we bring them in."

"Thanks, Millie," she said, touched that the deputy had backed her up.

"By the way, Sister, I wanted to tell you that the Coconut Clones the Dexters are baking are no match for the Cloister Clusters. They're such an obvious attempt to rip off the monastery's fund-raising efforts, some people are boycotting the bakery. The Clones' only advantage is that they're cheaper," Millie said, and quoted her a price.

Sister Agatha gasped. "How can they afford that? They couldn't possibly be using the same ingredients!"

"They're not. For one thing they use coconut flavoring instead of coconut flakes. Makes them a lot less chewy," Tom pointed out as Millie stepped away to answer the phone.

Sister Agatha stared at Tom. "I'd like to wring the Dexters' necks. That's not very charitable, but there it is."

He laughed. "Go ahead. Vent. Do penance later."

"Are you going to be bringing Del Martinez in yourself?" she asked, wanting to stick around if he was.

"I've sent two deputies to pick him up." Seeing Millie come up again, he shifted his attention. "Problem?"

"Yeah. I just got a call from Officer Marquez. Del Martinez can't be found. The roofers at Our Lady said he left about an hour ago without a word. Another deputy went by his home, and Del isn't there, either. According to a neighbor, Del came home, five minutes later threw a suitcase in his car, then took off in a hurry."

"Get a judge. We need warrants to search his home and business office."

"What's going to happen to our roof now?" Sister Agatha asked as Millie stepped away. "The workers will need to complete the job, but if their boss is skipping town . . ."

"Don't jump to conclusions. The neighbor may have misconstrued what he or she saw. Hang tight and keep this under your hat — or veil."

When Sister Agatha returned to the monastery, Sister Bernarda was back at the parlor's desk.

"How's it going here?" Sister Agatha asked her.

"We've had some good news. Justin Clark, the construction crew foreman, said that they'll be finished with our roof ahead of schedule," she said, giving Sister Agatha the details.

"That *is* good news."

"It's almost one, time for our midday meal. Why don't you go ahead and join the sisters in the refectory? I'll handle things here," Sister Bernarda said. "I've already eaten."

Today's lunch at the monastery comprised a vegetable casserole that Sister Clothilde had concocted and a small bowl of potato soup. Both tasted delicious and neither the human skull on the table beneath the cross at the far end of the room, nor the martyrology recounting the death of one of the saints, could put a dent in Sister Agatha's appetite.

Afterwards, she helped Sister Clothilde pick up, all the while doing her best to postpone talking to Reverend Mother. Sister Agatha looked around the refectory as the other sisters filed back into the kitchen for another round of cookie baking, coupled with prayer. People on the outside sometimes thought that the monastery protected them from life. But that wasn't so. They weren't immune to hard times. The biggest difference was that, here, it simply meant that they'd be leaning on God even more.

The words said during Morning Prayers came back to her now. "Lord visit this house . . . may your holy angels dwell here and keep us in peace . . ." Somehow that prayer had never seemed more appropriate.

19

Sister Agatha reluctantly walked to Reverend Mother's office. She had no desire to add another burden to the weight the abbess already shouldered, but there was no way to avoid it.

Sitting across from Mother's simple desk, she presented her with all the facts about Carlisle and their roofing contractor, Del Martinez. Since the workers were at the other end of the building now, there was no need to shout.

"If Mr. Martinez is arrested and his company shuts down, all those men outside may be left without jobs right before the holidays," Reverend Mother said. "And we'll be left the problem of finding someone who'll complete the work at a price we can afford."

"There's only the metal trim and crown to complete, Mother. Maybe Grayson Construction will take care of them and us,"

Sister Agatha answered.

"I'll tell the sisters to begin praying for an equitable solution for all," Reverend Mother said. "And I'll reread our roofing contract."

"There's more, Mother." She saw the lines on Reverend Mother's face deepen. "It's about our Cloister Clusters," she said, and explained what the Dexters were doing. "It should have occurred to me before to get a patent, formulation, copyright, or whatever they call it, for our recipe. But since we haven't, I think we should, and as quickly as possible."

"We're extremely short of cash, child."

"I may be able to get around that, Mother. Let me see what I can do."

Sister Agatha left for town a short time later with Pax. She'd go talk to Maria Fuentes, and with luck enlist the attorney's help.

As Sister Agatha drove past Bountiful Bakery, the Dexters' shop, she saw a group of women picketing out front. Surprised, she pulled up and heard the picketers chanting, "Cloister Clusters can't be beat — Coconut Clones are the devil's treat!"

As she and Pax walked up to the picket line, one of the women came up to her. The young brunette's ponytail bobbed up and down as she walked.

"I'm Melodie Robles, Sister. Our parish group is going to protest outside the bakery until they stop making Coconut Clones. The Dexters are practically taking food out of the mouths of the sisters."

Unsure of what to say, Sister Agatha paused for several moments. "Maybe there's another way to work this out. Reason can work wonders sometimes and if —" Sister Agatha got cut off suddenly by an explosive backfire that rocked the air. She flinched, and Pax let out a bark of surprise.

Turning her head, she saw Sister Bernarda pulling up in the sputtering Antichrysler. Sister Agatha hurried to join her. "What's happening at the monastery? Did you come looking for me?"

"Yes. We've had a bit of a problem." Sister Bernarda lowered her voice. "Sister de Lourdes was taking care of the parlor. Natalie was in her room reading with the door closed, so Sister began doing the Little Office of Mary at her desk. When the doorbell rang, she went to answer it, and Andrew, our Parcel Express delivery man, came in. He saw Gracie in the parlor chair where Natalie had left it."

Sister Agatha cringed. "What did Sister say?"

"That it was a donation for St. Francis's

pantry. But unfortunately that doll is very distinctive. Reverend Mother thought that, under the circumstances, you should tell the sheriff. None of us know if Andrew can be trusted."

"I'll go there next."

While Sister Bernarda headed back to the monastery, Sister Agatha drove directly to the station, leaving the problem with the picketers to the Dexters. As soon as she walked in, two deputies stopped her. "Put us down for two boxes of Cloister Clusters each," they said, before heading out to their squad cars.

"Me, too," Millie piped in.

Tom came out of his office. Seeing Sister Agatha, he gestured silently for her to follow him.

"I've got bad news," Sister Agatha warned as soon as he'd closed the door to his office. She told him what had happened at the monastery with Natalie's doll, Gracie. "We don't know what — if anything — we should do next. If we say anything to Andrew, it would only confirm where Natalie is."

"We'll need to find a backup hiding place for Natalie soon. Leave that to me."

"I have to pay Maria Fuentes a visit, but on my way back I can stop and see what you've come up with."

"Good idea."

Sister Agatha sat down in Maria's office and the attorney offered her some crackers and cheese from a plate on her desk. Sister took one, and continued, "I needed to ask you a question," she said. "How much would it cost us to take out a patent on Sister Clothilde's cookies?"

"It's mostly paperwork, but with a recipe it's probably not the best solution. You should trademark the name 'Cloister Clusters.' That's simple, but legal mechanisms like patents lead to full disclosure, which is why the big corporations won't go that route. They prefer to keep their recipes to themselves, trusting their employees not to give out their formulations and secret ingredients. Of course, they have employee rules and confidentiality agreements to back them up. But that shouldn't be a concern at the monastery, right?"

"Of course."

"I know you're worried about the competition, but I doubt the local bakery has the resources to get your cookies analyzed, and even if they approximate your recipe they'll still have problems beating your costs without substituting cheaper ingredients.

Remember, they have to pay for their labor. In the long run, I don't think you have anything to worry about. I'll take care of the paperwork and give you a call when it's ready."

Sister Agatha thanked her and left for Tom's office. She found him on the telephone as she reached his open door. Tom waved for her to come in, and hung up a few seconds later.

"I've come up with a really good idea, but successfully pulling this off will require planning and perfect timing."

"I'm all ears."

Sister Agatha was in the parlor talking to Natalie when Andrew, the Parcel Express driver, came by to make a scheduled late afternoon pickup of Cloister Clusters for shipment. Sister Agatha closed the door to Natalie's room and borrowed Gracie, keeping it with her.

"Hello again, Sister Agatha," he greeted pleasantly. "You still haven't taken that doll over to the toy box at St. Francis's Pantry, I see. I don't blame you. It'll probably scare the other dolls."

Sister Agatha smiled. "We've already found a recipient for the doll. Sister Gertrude's niece has been visiting this afternoon and will be heading home shortly. We've decided to give her the doll when she leaves as a present. It apparently caught her eye."

"Kids have really weird tastes, but it's nice to have them around," he said pleasantly. "They really light up a room, don't they?"

"Do you have any children?" she asked casually.

"A daughter," Andrew said with a nod. "She's a great kid, but I don't get to spend as much time with her as I should. I'm always working nowadays."

"You're doing a fine job for Parcel Express," she said. She noted he was the same general height and body type as the man with the tan pickup. But the description would fit one man in four, probably. She'd also observed that Andrew seemed tired every time she'd seen him. He obviously worked very hard at his job, and she wondered if he'd have the energy reserves to run as fast as the intruder she'd seen trying to escape Father Mahoney.

Once the deliveryman left, Reverend Mother gave her okay to put the plan into motion. Sister Agatha, Natalie beside her, waited by the door for Sister Bernarda to bring the Antichrysler around. Natalie was wearing a bright yellow dress over rolled up jeans and a T-shirt, and black dress shoes on loan from St. Francis's Pantry.

"You'll be taken from the monastery by Sister Bernarda," Sister Agatha said. "Halfway down the road Sister Bernarda will pull behind some cover. You'll slip out of the dress and black shoes and get out wearing your jeans, T-shirt, and sneakers, with your hair tucked up into a baseball cap. The daughter of one of the deputies will get into the car. You'll go with the sheriff and pass yourself off as one of his sons. The other girl, your same size, will be wearing the dress and the black shoes and continue to the bus station. She'll go on a ride to Santa Fe with her mom. Hopefully that'll confuse Andrew or anyone else who might suspect that you've been hiding here with us. We expect Sister Bernarda will be followed, so the switch will have to be made fast and in a spot not easily observed, but those are details the sheriff has already worked out."

Natalie looked inside the purse she'd been given which contained the baseball cap and sneakers. "This is exciting!"

A minute later as they hurried out to the car, Sister Agatha could see that at least two of the roofers had seen them. So far it was going according to plan.

"What's going on, Sister?" Justin Clark, Del Martinez's foreman asked. "You've added babysitting to your fund-raising projects?"

She laughed. "No, our guest is the niece of one of our sisters. She's been allowed to visit and see the monastery but now it's time for her to go home. Sister Bernarda will give her a ride to the bus station."

As soon as the construction foreman walked away, Sister Agatha went back to the parlor. Sister de Lourdes was already there at the desk, her eyes filled with tears.

"This is my fault. If anything happens to her . . ." Her voice almost broke, and she seemed reluctant to make eye contact.

"You were praying fervently at the time and God rewards devotion. Hold to that."

"That's almost what Natalie said to me. She said that the angel had a message for me. 'We know that to them that love God, all things work together unto good.' "

"Romans eight, verse twenty-eight. That was part of today's Office . . . and very appropriate."

Sister Agatha, accompanied by Pax in the sidecar, drove out of the gated area. There was enough daylight left for everyone to have seen the girl in the dress leave.

By the time she passed Sister Bernarda on the road, the switch had been made. Trusting Tom and his deputies, Sister Agatha drove to the sheriff's station to wait there. A while later, Tom hurried in through the back door, Natalie in tow.

"That was really fun!" Natalie said. "We made the switch with the girl pretending to be me. She was almost my size, and her hair was the same color, too. Then the sheriff and I sneaked away through the trees. After that we ran to his squad car then drove around real fast making sure nobody was following us. It was so *Spy Kids!*"

Sister Agatha smiled. Natalie was a bright girl, but a child nonetheless. The danger hadn't registered.

Natalie smiled brightly at Tom. "How do we get back to the monastery? Can I see Mom first?"

"I'll sneak you back into the monastery, but we can't go back to the hospital, not yet. We don't want *anyone* to know where you really are, Natalie."

"I wouldn't stay long," she said, but then saw that his expression was set, and sighed.

"Millie?" Tom called out.

The sergeant came over from where she'd been working and took Natalie with her into the lunchroom.

"One of my deputies reported that Sister Bernarda had at least two people following her all the way to the bus station," Tom said, as soon as they were alone. "Then they saw our double, Meredith, realized they'd been set up, and left."

"Where'd they go?"

"One's staking out the monastery right now," he said. "The other one slipped away."

"You *lost* him?"

"We're not certain it was a tail, but, yes, we lost him," he said, biting off each syllable.

"Do you know who's watching the monastery?"

"Yeah. It's Springer, the reporter from the *Inquisitor.* A real die-hard."

"If he's watching everyone who comes in, how are you going to get Natalie back to us? Our original plan won't work now."

"It will, but I'm going to need your help. Go confront Springer face-to-face and take Pax with you. Convince him that you're just as interested in finding Natalie as he is. Maybe you can say that Sister Gertrude's health is failing and talking to an angel would give her peace."

"Where will you be?"

"I'll take Natalie back in an unmarked car. Unless Springer changes location, I'll drop her off about thirty yards from the back wall, inside the bosque. Sister Bernarda can meet her and lead her back to the monastery. It should be a piece of cake for her. Didn't she used to be a Marine?"

"That was a while back."

He grinned. "Once a Marine, always a Marine."

20

Danger was pressing in. If they didn't get Natalie back unseen, they'd be leading a potential kidnapper right to the monastery's door.

"What you've got in mind will require Reverend Mother's permission and Sister Bernarda's consent. Mother won't force this on her," Sister Agatha said.

"I'll leave that to you while I take care of the other details."

As Tom left her alone in his office, Sister Agatha called the monastery and spoke to Sister Bernarda. She detailed Tom's revised plan, then added, "If you're willing to do this, we'll need to talk to Reverend Mother."

"Can do on all counts. I'll go talk to Mother right now."

"Call me back as soon as you can."

Permission was granted and the plan set in motion less than fifteen minutes later.

"Make sure that you've got Springer's

undivided attention for at least five minutes — more, if possible," Tom said.

"Count on it. But what about the other guy who followed Sister Bernarda, the one still unaccounted for? Do you think it might have been Del Martinez, or someone working with him?"

"To what end? I've got every officer in three counties watching for Del. He's not leaving this area easily."

"My point exactly. Getting hold of Natalie might give him the leverage he thinks he needs."

"Anything's possible, but I don't think he'll be focused on Natalie. The finder's fee he might get from the *Inquisitor* wouldn't be of much use to him now. In either case, we'll have to play this out with the cards we're holding. I'll have people watching your back — and mine."

Tom gave Sister Agatha precise directions to the spot where Springer had set up his surveillance. "If you get into trouble, bend down as if you're brushing something off the hem of your skirt. We'll move in."

Sister Agatha signalled Pax, who'd fallen asleep by Tom's desk, and hurried outside with the suddenly alert animal. Pax jumped into the sidecar and sat bolt upright, now as tense as she felt.

They got underway, and before long she drew close to the spot where Tom had told her Springer would be. With the brightness of a full moon she spotted his car easily, parked just beneath an old cottonwood. Anyone crouching low beside the tree would have a clear, unobstructed view of the monastery.

She turned off the engine, letting the motorcycle coast to a wide spot in the road out of sight from Springer. The Harley made a distinctive sound, but she'd been moving quite slow, and fortunately the breeze had carried most of the noise away from the reporter.

She took Pax on his leash, silently cutting across a field and approaching Springer from behind. Had she remained on the road the man would have seen her coming at least a hundred yards away. Moving quietly, something that was practically second nature to her, she came up within fifteen feet of him, still undetected. "Can I help you?" she asked, clearly and distinctly.

Springer, who'd been using the hood of the car as a support for his camera, jumped and spun around. The camera slid halfway off the car before he managed to grab it, cursing.

"You trying to give me a heart attack,

Sister?" He placed the camera back on the trunk of the car, making sure it was secure. "I'm Jack Springer from *The National Inquisitor.* I'm on public property, and photographs are legal from here."

She remained in the same position, forcing him to look at her rather than at the monastery, now at his back. "Exactly what are you after, Mr. Springer? An exposé of the monastery after dark? I assure you, it's not going to be much of a story, unless your readers want to see nuns in a chapel."

Springer, a lean man of average height in jeans and a sports coat, with tightly cropped hair and a single gold earring, gave her a mirthless grin. "I'm just a journalist trying to do my job. My readers are inspired by photos of special people — like Natalie Tannen."

Looking down, she noted that the left heel of his sneaker left a track with a diagonal slash across it. Springer had been their nun. Too bad she couldn't prove it.

"I don't see what that has to do with us," she argued, remembering a time when she'd been the one working on a story, pressing for information, and struggling with an impending deadline. But it was hard to be sympathetic with methods that pushed the limits when children were involved.

"You know why I'm here. All my leads point to you — an extern nun who often works with the police *and* has connections with the family. *You're* hiding the kid who sees angels. And that's not right. Think of all the people who desperately need to have their religious faith supported by hard evidence. That girl's ability is a real gift. One way or another, I'm going to get photos and an interview with Natalie Tannen."

"You're obviously on a mission. Maybe we should join forces."

"We should what?" he narrowed his eyes.

"You've been wasting your time hanging around here. In spite of my connection to the family and the parish, we don't have her. The girl who visited the monastery wasn't Natalie."

"Why should I believe you?"

"Because I need to find Natalie even more than you do. One of our nuns is ill. If the angel said to be accompanying that child can comfort our sister in any way, or, even better, intercede on her behalf, then Natalie needs to pay a visit to our monastery as soon as possible."

"So you're telling me they've sent you to track down Natalie Tannen?"

"Not 'sent.' I'm doing this on my own because I know it's the right thing to do," she said flatly.

"If Natalie Tannen isn't at your monastery, where is she?"

"I don't know. That's why I'd like to make a deal with you. If you find Natalie before I do, let *me* know where she is. I can take our sister to her, and you can take photos of the meeting — and whatever else happens at that time. You'd have an exclusive," she said, then added, "you can't lose — and neither could we."

"Sister, quit snowing me. You know *exactly* where Natalie is. I've read up on how you've worked with the sheriff before. I'm guessing you had a hand in this from the beginning."

"Mr. Springer, if you've really done your homework, you know that Our Lady of Hope is a *contemplative* order. We spend our lives in prayer and we need solitude and quiet to do that effectively. Does that sound like a place we could stick an eight-year-old girl? Kids are seldom silent. If we had her, someone would have heard her by now, don't you think?" she demanded, hoping he wouldn't stop to consider the noise the roofers made.

He said nothing for a long time then finally spoke. "An *exclusive,* right? With photos?"

"Yes. You probably know I was a journalist before entering the order so I understand your position completely. You can't go back to your editor empty-handed or wait for table scraps after someone else breaks the story. I'm sure you don't want to end up cranking out alien abduction stories the rest of your life," she said, playing on his need to deliver to *his* boss.

"Okay. You've got yourself a deal. But I need your help to root out the kid. You grew up around here. Where do I start looking?"

"I'm assuming you have access to good resources, so you might want to find out if social services was contacted and which foster homes are open and able to take in another child on short notice. Look into church retreats and residences for clergy in this area, too. Maybe a deal was cut with another denomination just to throw off the press. Natalie could be living in a Methodist minister's rectory, for instance."

"That's a possibility. What else?"

"You might want to check for cabins or weekend retreats owned by local law enforcement people, like the sheriff or retired deputies. They could have made arrangements to sock her away someplace like that."

"If you're conning me, Sister, *your* photo is going to make the front page." He brought up his camera and snapped a shot, the flash blinding her for a second.

Pax growled and stepped forward, positioning himself in front of her.

Sister Agatha grabbed his collar. "He's getting crabby," she said. "I better take him home and feed him dinner before he decides to gnaw on a camera — or your arm."

"Good idea, Sister," he said, backing away from her very slowly.

Sister Agatha and Pax hiked back to the Harley, then returned to the monastery. She'd just finished parking when her cell phone rang. Reluctant to interrupt the Great Silence, she stayed outside as she answered.

"Yes?"

"It's Tom. Natalie's already inside the grounds. Your timing was perfect. And whatever you said to Springer worked. He stowed his camera and is now headed back to Bernalillo."

"Thanks for the update."

Sister Agatha hurried through the building and out the back door, then waited there in the darkness. After a few minutes, she saw Sister Bernarda and Natalie putting away the ladder they'd used to climb over the monastery wall.

"Ran into a problem," Sister Bernarda

351

said, ushering Natalie inside.

Sister Agatha locked the doors behind them. "What happened?" she whispered quickly.

"Let's go to Natalie's quarters and get her squared away first, then I'll fill you in," Sister Bernarda said.

"Sister saw a coyote! Isn't that cool?" Natalie whispered, her words coming out in a rush. "I wanted to stay and try to get closer, but she wouldn't let me. We had to get over the wall quickly so nobody could see us."

As soon as they reached the parlor, Sister Agatha gestured to Natalie. "Go get ready for bed," she said softly.

Natalie nodded wordlessly, well acquainted with the Great Silence by now, and went across the hall into her room, closing the door behind her.

The moment Natalie was out of earshot, Sister Bernarda pulled Sister Agatha aside. "We need to call the sheriff. Just about the time he sent Natalie through the trees toward the wall, I *felt* someone watching us, and not a coyote. I kept out of sight and scanned the perimeter. Just below the crest of that high levee to the west I saw a brief glint of light. As a Marine, I would suspect a sniper, but it was probably just someone with binoculars or a telephoto lens. In either case . . ."

Sister Agatha didn't wait. She reached for her cell phone, called Tom, and relayed what Sister Bernarda had just told her.

"Sharp eyes," he said. "Sister Bernarda probably saw one of my deputies. John was in that area watching for activity. Hang on." He put her on hold for a few minutes, then finally returned. "John says that he wasn't below the levee, but maybe Sister Bernarda's directions were a little off or she just saw a reflection from a broken beer bottle tossed off the levee. We're going to check the area just in case. I'll let you know tomorrow if we find anything."

Sister Agatha gave Sister Bernarda the gist of what Tom had said, then went to tuck Natalie into bed.

Natalie smiled as Sister Agatha came into the room. "Don't worry, Sister. From now on, I'll take Gracie with me everywhere. I won't let her out of my sight again."

"Good. I'll hold you to that."

Sister Agatha turned off the light, then walked back to the parlor.

"I'll stay here tonight," Sister Bernarda said. "And Sister de Lourdes will take over for me at daybreak."

Sister Agatha walked silently down the

hall. She'd missed Vespers, Compline, and Reverend Mother's *Noctem Quietam* blessing before bedtime. The Liturgical Hours and the customary of the monastery weren't duties to be followed blindly. They were threads that, woven together, formed the fabric of a life devoted to God alone. Without the wellspring of support that gave her, she felt cut off.

Being an extern was a privilege, but it was also the hardest duty of all.

21

Sister Agatha rose at the sound of the bell rung faithfully at four thirty each morning. Matins had to be sung before daybreak. It would be followed by Lauds — the hour of pure praise at dawn — then Mass and breakfast.

As she went by the parlor, she found Sister de Lourdes had already taken over for Sister Bernarda. Since the Great Silence wouldn't be broken until after Morning Prayers — what had once been called Prime — Sister de Lourdes pointed to the chapel, then quickly wrote a note.

Sister Bernarda will attend the morning Office. You can, too. I'll stay here with Natalie and wake her up for breakfast at six thirty.

"Thank you," Sister Agatha mouthed noiselessly.

Matins was a prayer meant to counter the evils that seemed to grow stronger in the absence of light. As the nuns' voices rose in chant, a welcoming peace settled over her. Here and now, she was in the sweet presence of God. He was faithful. He had promised to be with those who believed — always. This was the peace he'd offered — that when they prayed as one, His presence would fill their hearts.

Her courage renewed, she was ready to face the day. After Mass and a quick breakfast she hurried to the parlor. Sister de Lourdes and Natalie had already gone to the crafts room and Sister Bernarda was at her post alone.

"I can take over for you this morning, Sister Bernarda. You've been putting in long hours as portress," Sister Agatha said.

"Thanks. I'd really welcome time for silent meditation in chapel. By the way, I was told by Justin Clark, the foreman, that they'll finish the roof today for sure. Although Del Martinez hasn't been found, Grayson Construction has guaranteed the work and the workers their paychecks."

"Amen to that."

"He also answered another question that has been puzzling us," Sister Bernarda said. "The one-thousand-dollar donation we received apparently came from one of the roofers. He won the New Mexico lottery the other day — five thousand dollars —

and left the money for us because he wanted to make amends."

"For what?"

"According to Mr. Clark, the roofer was responsible for dropping the debris that nearly clobbered you. It was an accident, but he was afraid to say anything because he thought he'd get fired. Still, he wanted to make things right, so he asked Saint Joseph, the patron saint of working men, to show him how. A few days after that he won the money. He paid off some overdue bills and gave us what was left after taxes."

"Who was he?"

"Mr. Clark promised not to reveal his name, but the man asked that we forgive him for his carelessness. I told Mr. Clark to tell him he could consider it done."

When Sister Bernarda opened the doors to the enclosure, ready to go now that Sister Agatha had agreed to take over as portress, the acrid scent of smoke drifted into the small room. Sister Bernarda and Sister Agatha exchanged quick glances, then both ran down the hall, searching for the source.

As they ran through the refectory, they saw Sister Clothilde and Sister Maria Victoria opening windows as a choking, heavy smoke poured out of one of the ovens in the kitchen.

"Is everyone all right?" Sister Agatha asked quickly, looking around to make sure no one had been burnt.

"It's our old oven. It went into meltdown," Sister Maria Victoria said. "I'm not at all sure what we're going to do. We still have our new oven but with only one we won't be able to keep up."

"This is partly *my* fault," Sister Bernarda muttered. "We're supposed to turn the other cheek, but I've always stunk at that," she said softly. "When the bakery in town started making their version of our Clusters, I asked God to let the fires of hell rage in their ovens. But now it's *our* oven that burned itself to a crisp. I don't think it's coincidence. I think God's trying to tell me something."

Sister Agatha understood guilt better than anyone. "Well, a little penance wouldn't hurt, but the monastery's oven is older than dirt. This was bound to happen with the stress we've been putting on it."

"As far as I'm concerned this is a wake-up call — for all of us," Sister Ignatius said slowly. "We got so busy trying to help ourselves — running a business and making money — that we forgot that it's God who provides for us, in the right way at the right time."

One could avoid the truth, but never escape it completely. Once confronted, truth ripped apart any illusion or pretense that had stood in its path.

"You're right. We've put too much emphasis on the business side of the scale and not enough on God's," Sister Agatha said.

Reverend Mother, who'd come up to stand behind them, cleared her throat. "I tried to guard against that, but it happened anyway when we weren't looking. Have all the sisters gather in the recreation room. It's time to reestablish our priorities."

Twenty minutes later, with the distant sound of hammering overhead, Reverend Mother presented the problem to all except Sister de Lourdes, who was with Natalie.

"Our Rule stipulates that we live by the work of our hands, but our priority is to serve God. We can't continue our current work schedule and still honor our primary duty," she said. "That's why I'm considering licensing our recipe to the bakery in town — providing we can get a good price. If not, we'll continue to bake the cookies here — but only during the times we normally set aside for manual labor. Does anyone object?"

When no one spoke, Reverend Mother

continued. "Very well then. This is God's house. Let His will be done."

A brief prayer closed the meeting, but a new spirit had been kindled in them all. As Sister Bernarda returned to the parlor, Sister Agatha took the opportunity to go back to the chapel. Alone, she prayed without words, letting her love for God and His Son speak in a language that came from the heart and needed no other form of expression.

After Sext, the sixth hour of prayer, Sister Agatha walked to the crafts room and watched Natalie fashion another clay angel while Pax lay at her feet.

Sensing her, Natalie looked up and smiled. "This one's special. Would you like to see?" she asked, stepping back.

Sister Agatha looked down at the sculpture. The folds in the figure's long robes gave the impression that it had been walking, while the mica in the clay gave an ethereal quality to the angel's facial features. "It's really outstanding, Natalie," she said honestly. "No wings this time?"

"This is the angel who watches over the monastery — or as near as I can sculpt him. He doesn't have wings."

Sister Agatha pointed to a small, shaped

piece of clay on Natalie's right. "And that?"

"It's the sword he carries, though his is made of light." Natalie looked up at Sister Agatha and smiled. "It's my present to the monastery. I'll be leaving here pretty soon." Her smile faded. "Mom and I will move to a new place where nobody knows us."

"Your angel told you this?"

She nodded. "It'll be lonely for a while, but I'll have Samara, and Mom, and Gracie."

"And you'll still have all of us here. Our prayers will follow you wherever you go."

"I won't forget any of you. I always remember my friends. Thanks to Gracie, I won't even forget my dad, even though I've never met him."

"Now you've lost me. Are you saying that Gracie looks like your dad?"

She laughed. "No, Sister. Gracie's just a doll. She doesn't look like anyone except Gracie. But Mom gave me a photo of Dad she'd found in the bottom of a drawer a few years ago. She'd thrown the rest out and put that one in the garbage, too, but I found it and cleaned it off so she let me keep it. It's in Gracie's purse so Mom won't ever have to look at it." She paused, then added, "That's been Gracie's job — keeping Dad's photo. Mom said that a dad is one who sticks around and takes care of you, so he wasn't really my dad. But I still wanted to know what he looked like. Wanna see?"

She nodded, wondering why neither she nor Tom ever asked Natalie if *she* had a photo of her dad.

Natalie reached into the doll's purse and handed Sister Agatha the photo, which had been folded in half. It was crumpled and damaged, something Sister Agatha assumed was from its brief stay in the garbage. The man's face was slightly out of focus, but he looked familiar somehow. He had a full face, brown hair, brown eyes, and a mustache, but no distinguishing features. Only his chunky upper body was visible as he rested in a chair, beer bottle in his hand.

It was far from an idyllic pose, and not likely to inspire Natalie's fantasies about her father. Maybe that was why Jessica had allowed her to keep it.

"Natalie, will you let me borrow it for a few hours? I promise to take very good care of it," Sister Agatha said.

Natalie hesitated. "Why do you want it?"

"Now that your mom's not well, the sheriff's been trying to find your dad. This photo might help," she said, bending the truth. The fact was she wanted to give herself a chance to figure out why it looked familiar.

"Okay, go ahead, but give it back. It's my only one."

"I promise. And I'll leave Pax with you in the meantime so it's more like a temporary trade. How's that?"

Natalie smiled and hugged the dog. "Great."

When Sister Agatha walked into the parlor a few minutes later, she saw Mr. Dexter, the owner of Bountiful Bakery, there with Sister Bernarda. "Mr. Dexter is demanding to speak to Reverend Mother," she said coldly.

Sister Agatha gave him a level gaze. "And this in reference to . . . ?"

Mr. Dexter took a deep breath, then let it out again. "Look, I'm only here to call a truce," he said.

"Mr. Dexter, I assure you that we're not behind the picketing or the boycott of your bakery."

"Effective immediately, we're no longer baking Coconut Clones," he said, not responding to what she'd said. "Please tell everyone involved so we can settle this. Cookie sales *are* an important part of our business, but I'd rather give them up completely than lose my bakery. That boycott has really been hurting us."

Sister Agatha thought about the situation and, remembering Reverend Mother's plan, said, "Mr. Dexter, I have a business proposition for you. Earlier you offered to license our cookies and give us a 'small' percentage of the profits. But we need the income this provides, so we can't afford to just give this away. If you're willing to make us a *fair* offer, I think we can come to terms. Are you interested?"

"Absolutely."

"Then get an offer ready and take it to Maria Fuentes, our attorney."

As soon as Mr. Dexter left, Sister Agatha turned to Sister Bernarda. "I need you to tell Reverend Mother about this. I'll contact Maria later and bring her up to speed, but first I've got to go see the sheriff."

Sister Agatha arrived at the station twenty minutes later, and as she climbed off the Harley, Sister Bernarda called her on the cell phone. "Reverend Mother says that if the attorney agrees to take her fee from the sale you should go ahead and complete all the arrangements."

"Okay. Thanks for letting me know," Sister Agatha said.

Once inside the station, Sister Agatha

went directly to Tom's office, but he wasn't there. Seeing Millie Romero, she went up to meet her. "I've some news for Tom. Do you know where I can find him?"

"We got a break on the Jessica Tannen case and he went to make an arrest. Apparently Springer — the reporter from *The Inquisitor* — had rented another vehicle before he got the car he's using now. It was a light-colored pickup and Springer returned it damaged. Springer claimed to have scraped a fence post, but that, coupled with an alibi that can't be verified, convinced Sheriff Green to bring Springer in. We have people checking the rental pickup. If the damage and paint flakes match Jessica Tannen's vehicle, that'll give us something we can take to the D.A."

Sister Agatha thought back to her meeting with Jack Springer. He'd been eager to get the story, but why would he have stuck around if he'd been the one to cause the accident? He would have known that the rental truck's paper trail would lead back to him. In that situation, an intelligent person would have made sure the pickup was stolen or burned to a crisp, knowing the rental insurance would protect him. Something wasn't right.

Sister Agatha took the photo of Henry

Tannen out of her pocket. "Millie, will you do me a favor? Can you run this photo through one of those computer imaging programs that can, say, remove the mustache, and maybe alter the hair color?"

"Sure. The scanner and software for that are on one of the lab computers. But I better warn you that the results won't be spectacular. This photo isn't very clear."

"Just do your best. I'll leave the photo with you while I go see Maria Fuentes on monastery business. I won't be long."

"Sounds good."

Maria was saying good-bye to someone on the telephone as Sister Agatha stepped inside the attorney's office. Sister Agatha sat down and filled her in on their business with the Dexters. "Can you negotiate the terms and do the paperwork for us? We can pay you from the proceeds."

She nodded. "I'll get back to you once I speak to Mr. Dexter, but I'm sure I can get you a good deal."

"Thanks, Maria. We really appreciate that. Call me whenever you're ready."

Sister Agatha walked back to the station, eager to see how successful Millie had been in using the computer imaging program. As she walked inside, Millie came up to meet her, several printed images in hand.

"Here we go, Sister. No mustache, and each one has a different hair color."

Sister Agatha sorted through the photos, but still couldn't figure out where she'd seen Henry Tannen before, or if perhaps he just resembled someone she knew or had known. "The man spent several years in prison and may have gained or lost weight. Can you make his face a little heavier, then thinner?"

"Hang on. I'll give it a try."

She returned a minute later with two more printouts. "Here you go."

The first one, with the extra weight, wasn't much help, but as she studied the second photo, showing sharper features and more prominent cheekbones, she realized why the face was vaguely familiar. If Henry Tannen had lost weight and cut his hair much shorter, he would now resemble Andrew.

She studied it more carefully. "I'm not sure if I've got something here or not, but this photo makes him look a bit like our new Parcel Express deliveryman, the same man who saw Natalie's doll . . ."

"I'll pass this information on to the sheriff."

Sister Agatha went out quickly to the Harley, then decided to go visit the Parcel Express office on Albuquerque's west side. The drive seemed interminable as new questions and potential connections began to stack up in her mind. When she finally arrived, thirty minutes later, she hurried inside. A young man wearing a light brown uniform greeted her from behind the counter. "I bet you don't remember me, Sister! I'm Michael Reyes. My dad was the handyman at the church in Bernalillo for many years."

"Sure, I remember you." Seizing the opportunity, Sister Agatha continued. "Michael, I need your help. I need to ask you a few questions about our new driver, Andrew. I don't know his last name, but he's got short brown hair, brown eyes, is about thirty-five, and a bit shorter than you. He's also more slender."

"I know who you mean. What's the problem?"

"I'm worried about him. He does a good job and carries all the packages, even the real heavy ones, but he always looks so tired, even early in the day."

"Yeah, it's sad. The job is wearing him down because he's got the big C. Lost a ton of weight, so he said. He hasn't been working here long enough to be eligible for medical insurance, either. But you've got to admire his upbeat attitude. He tells everyone that he's going to turn this thing around pretty soon."

"A good mental attitude is important," Sister Agatha said slowly. "Could you check and see if he's supposed to make a delivery or pickup at the monastery today?"

"I don't have that info on my terminal, so give me a sec to check with the dispatcher," Mikey said, picking up the telephone and pressing a button. A few moments later, he hung up. "Your regular driver is running late, so Andrew took the afternoon run to the monastery. He's probably on his way there as we speak."

"One more question, Mikey. Do you happen to know what kind of vehicle Andrew drives after work?"

He thought about it a moment. "A pickup?" he asked, not expecting her to answer. "Yeah, a tan F-150, I think."

"Is it parked outside?" she asked, moving to the window and tipping her head toward the lot. "I'd sure like to see it."

"It's back in the employee parking lot. But why do you want a look?"

"I'd rather not say. Trust me, I wouldn't be asking if it wasn't important."

"Okay, Sister. Come on. Let's check it out."

Mikey waved to another employee who came over to take the counter, then they went outside through a side door. Against the back fence of the property were a dozen or more vehicles. One was an old tan F-150. As she approached she saw the long dent on the passenger's door and front fender. It had been washed and scrubbed, but traces of blue were still fused into the tan paint where the damage was most severe. Inside, on the passenger's seat, was a Dallas Cowboys baseball cap.

"Thanks a lot, Mikey, I've seen enough. I've got to go now, but I'll be in touch later. Don't let anyone — including Andrew — take this vehicle anywhere. The police will want to look at it first, I'm pretty sure."

"The police? What did Andrew do?"

"I'll tell you all about it later, I promise."

Sister Agatha ran to the Harley. Taking out the cell phone, she dialed the sheriff's station. "You'll need to check the paint scrape," she added, after telling Millie all she knew about the vehicle, the cap, and Andrew. "Right now I'm on the way to the monastery, and I'd like you to send a deputy to meet me there."

"Sister Agatha, you're on the wrong trail. Sheriff Green found out that Springer was driving in the area at the time of the accident. A charge slip for gas at a local station confirmed it. Springer has a motive, and we now also have his rental pickup with the damage on the passenger side. He's already in custody, and if the paint is a match . . ."

"Is the damage at the right height to match up with Jessica's vehicle? And what about blue paint flakes on Springer's pickup. Were any there?"

"The rental company had the door replaced. All they kept were some photos for legal purposes, and those won't be any help now. We're still trying to find out what the body shop did with the old door. But there's *no* doubt Springer was in the area at the right time with a vehicle that matched the witness's description. Sheriff Green's planning on turning the paperwork over to the district attorney if we can track down the missing door and verify the physical evidence. The monastery and Father Mahoney were given the news just about ten minutes ago, and the officers working on the case have been pulled."

"Millie, I've got a strong feeling and some physical evidence that suggests Springer is innocent. I can't prove it yet, but the person behind all this could be Henry Tannen — driving a Parcel Express truck and using the first name of Andrew. Would you call the sheriff and tell him what I just told you?

Meanwhile, I'll call the monastery and warn them that they still have to keep a close eye on Natalie."

"Okay, Sister, I'll relay everything you told me."

Sister Agatha hurried back out to the Harley. Everyone's guard would be down, and now that the roofers weren't there anymore, Natalie was more vulnerable than ever. She tried to call the monastery several times, but kept getting a busy signal.

Sister Agatha made the trip back in less than fifteen minutes. As she pulled through the monastery gates, she saw the large Parcel Express van parked next to the parlor entrance. Fear pounded through her, decimating her courage, as she watched Sister Bernarda innocently holding the door open for Andrew, who was carrying a large box inside.

As Sister Agatha hurried inside after them, Pax and Natalie came out into the hall, playing tug of war with a knotted piece of rope.

Andrew, who'd just set the box down, turned toward the girl, pulling a pistol out of his pocket as he did. "Hold onto the dog's collar, Natalie," he ordered. "If he gets loose, I'll have to shoot him."

Pax snarled, but Natalie grabbed onto his collar with both hands, then tried to cover his back with her body, shielding Pax as much as she could. "No! I won't let you hurt him. He's my friend."

"Pax, stay!" Sister Agatha ordered.

The dog continued snarling at him, but didn't move.

"You don't want to hurt the girl. Put your gun away," Sister Agatha said firmly.

Sister Bernarda was subtly maneuvering closer, apparently thinking of disarming him, but Andrew noticed and turned the weapon on her. "Stop right there, Sister."

Natalie kept a firm hold on the dog, but Pax was oblivious to her, his gaze fixed on Andrew. His fangs were bared and a low, deep growl was coming from his throat.

"Shut that dog up, Sister Agatha, if you want him to live."

"You're mean. Just leave!" Natalie yelled, her voice trembling. "He doesn't want you here — nobody wants you here!"

Andrew's face softened as he looked at her. "Natalie? Don't you know who I am?"

"No! And I don't care. You're scaring all of my friends. Just go!" she said, hugging Pax at the same time she glared at Andrew, tears flowing down her cheeks.

"I'll go if you come with me," he said.

"No! Just go *away!*"

"Sweetheart, I can't leave without you. I'm Henry Tannen — your father."

22

Sister Agatha stepped closer to Natalie, causing Henry's deadly gaze to shift.

"Stay where you are, Sister. I don't want to hurt anyone," he said, "except that fool dog."

Though Pax continued to growl, Natalie hugged him even closer. "I won't let you hurt him."

"You're not taking that girl anywhere," Sister Agatha said flatly. "You'll have to shoot Sister Bernarda and me first, and if you try, the dog will be all over you. If you really do love your daughter, you'll leave and stop endangering her."

"I won't hurt Natalie. I want her with me, safe and sound."

"You've got a funny way of showing it, Henry Tannen. You nearly killed her and her mother, and now you charge in here, waving a gun and threatening us all."

"I didn't mean to hurt Jessica that night,

it was just an accident. I was only trying to get her to pull over so we could talk. I didn't mean to bump into her — swear to God. When she ran off the road and crashed I turned around and went right back to help. But then another car came up, so I had to get out of there. I can't go back to prison. I'd be killed for sure."

"Didn't you know Natalie was in the car, too?"

"Yeah, but she ran off. I went after her, but there was no time with that other car about to stop. I'd heard Jess shouting for her to run away from me. I expected her to go right back to her mother once I left."

Sister Agatha shook her head, but before she could comment, Henry continued.

"Jess tried to make sure I'd never find her or Natalie again. But once Natalie became a celebrity, I knew I had to meet her," he said, giving his daughter a quick smile. "I got a job with Parcel Express because I know Jess is a heavy catalog shopper. That's how I tracked her down. The night of the storm I came to her house, but Jessica saw me and met me outside. She told me to leave, that her neighbor was watching and would call the police if I caused any trouble. She said she needed time to talk to Natalie and that I should come back in an hour. I waited down the street, watching the house. But Jess took off with Natalie, so I followed." He paused and looked at Natalie. "I just wanted to see you."

"The courts will have to decide if that can ever happen. Right now, you need to end this. Turn yourself in. The sheriff is already on his way here," Sister Agatha said flatly.

Henry shook his head. "No way. I have a scanner that listens in on police calls. The sheriff arrested some reporter and called off the deputies who were watching the monastery. I wasn't fooled when you took Natalie out of here, switched her with another girl, then sneaked her back in," he said. "And forget about the phone. I cut the line a half hour ago."

"That's old news. *I* know about your tan Ford F-150. It's the third one in the back row of the Parcel Express employee parking area, by the fence. There're still traces of blue paint on it that you couldn't rub off. And I called the station just a few minutes ago using a cell phone and told them who you were. Check the scanner if you don't believe *me.* This is the end of the line."

"You're not *my* dad," Natalie said, furiously. "I have a picture, and you don't even look like him."

"Maybe you've got one of my old fatty

pictures, honey. I've lost over fifty pounds since then — from cancer. That's why I came to find you. I need your help raising money for doctors and cancer treatment. People would pay to have you ask your angel about their dead relatives, or just to have you pray for them. And reporters will offer big money just to take pictures of you. Come with me, Jessica, I really need you now."

"I don't need *you!* I want to stay here," she shouted.

"If you have any feelings for your daughter at all, you'll leave right now, Henry," Sister Agatha pressed. "Or turn yourself in."

"Sorry, Sisters. Step into that other room. I'm going to lock you up for a while. Don't make me have to shoot both of you and the dog. You want Natalie to have that on her conscience?"

Sister Agatha and Sister Bernarda inched toward Natalie's room, still stalling for time.

"No, don't hurt anyone," Natalie said. "Leave them alone and I'll go with you."

As Henry turned to face his daughter, he lowered his weapon slightly.

"Rex, *packen!*" Sister Agatha shouted, using Pax's police dog name.

The dog broke away from Natalie and lunged, biting down on Henry's sleeve.

Henry yelled, slipped his arm out of the jacket, then tossed the fabric over Pax's head. He clubbed Pax with the pistol. Pax yelped, then sagged to the floor.

Henry grabbed Natalie's hand, waving his pistol at the sisters. "Get in there. *Now.*"

Since there was no lock on the interior parlor door, it had only taken several good shoves to dislodge the chair Henry had jammed against the doorknob. By then, Henry and Natalie were gone. Sister Agatha raced for the Harley with Sister Bernarda, and in seconds they were speeding down the gravel road, searching ahead for the Parcel Express step van. Sister Bernarda was crouched down in the sidecar, cell phone at her ear. They were only a few minutes behind Henry and Natalie.

"The sheriff is already on his way from town, and the main roads have been blocked. I doubt Henry will reach the highway before he meets up with deputies," Sister Bernarda shouted over the roar of the motorcycle.

"Good! Keep watching driveways and side roads in case they turn off. They'll leave a trail of dust," Sister Agatha shouted back. Neither had helmets on — there hadn't been time — and that made communication a lot easier.

Her eyes were trained on the road, her fingers gripped tightly to the handlebars and throttle, but Sister Agatha's prayers were for Natalie — and Pax, who she'd left alive and stirring when they'd left the parlor. The other sisters would do what they could to treat him, and were undoubtedly asking for the Lord's help, just as she was doing right now.

Her heart skipped a beat as they rounded a curve and she spotted red and blue flashing lights in the distance. Sister Agatha slowed the Harley. Either Henry had reached the highway and encountered the deputies, or he'd seen the lights and turned to find a hiding place. He'd made deliveries in this area, so he probably knew there was no other route to the highway, except on foot. But he'd have to hide the truck first.

"Dust! Turn left!" Sister Bernarda yelled, pointing to a side road. It led to the deconsecrated adobe church Natalie had hidden in after the accident days ago.

Passing through a low cloud of swirling dust, Sister Agatha slowed the motorcycle to a crawl on the bumpy path. "Call the sheriff. He knows this place," she said to Sister Bernarda.

"Already on it," the nun in the sidecar said.

The narrow, tree-lined lane opened up at the far end into the parking lot, but no delivery truck was visible. Stopping the cycle at the end of the road, they looked at the ground. A set of large vehicle tracks circled to the right.

"He's parked behind the church," Sister Bernarda announced, looking around the site, enclosed by fences and trees in every direction except for the lane. "Let's block the road so he'll have trouble getting the truck back out."

Sister Agatha turned off the engine and climbed off the bike, keys in hand. "I'll get the flashlight in case they're hiding inside the building," she whispered, unfastening the leather strap on the saddlebag.

Sister Bernarda had already stepped out of the sidecar and was watching the grounds. "I doubt they had the time to break in," she said, coming up beside Sister Agatha. "The front doors are chained shut."

A dog somewhere to their right suddenly started barking, then there was a loud curse.

"That sounded like Henry," Sister Agatha said, looking in the direction of the noise, where a fence separated the former church property from the neighboring farm. Figures

381

emerged from high brush at the perimeter, and she saw Henry dragging Natalie along by the arm at a run, heading toward the church.

"Henry, stop! Let Natalie go!" Sister Agatha shouted.

He waved the pistol in their direction.

"Down!" Sister Bernarda shouted, crouching.

He didn't fire; instead he kicked in the boards covering one of the church windows. By the time they reached the opening, he and Natalie were inside.

Sister Agatha waited while Sister Bernarda passed the information on to the sheriff via the cell phone, then she ran over to the window.

Sister Bernarda, right behind, grabbed her arm. "The sheriff said we should stay outside," she whispered.

"And leave Natalie alone with an armed lunatic?"

"You're right." Sister Bernarda brushed past her and stepped over the low windowsill into the building, pushing a loose board aside.

"Wait for me," Sister Agatha grumbled.

The interior of the church was brighter than they'd expected, illuminated by the late afternoon sun passing through the round, stained glass window. But there were enough dark corners and long shadows to hide a dozen criminals. They stood against the inside wall in the shadows and listened for movement.

A minute went by, the only sound coming from sirens in the distance, slowly increasing in volume. Help *was* on the way, Sister Agatha realized, thanking God.

The rattle of metal coming from the back of the church caught their attention. Sister Agatha turned on the flashlight, revealing Henry and Natalie standing just inside the main entrance, in the alcove. The door was chained and locked from the inside, as well. Even from a distance she could see the dark stain on Henry's sleeve. Pax had drawn blood before being laid out.

"You're trapped, Henry, wounded, and losing blood. Please put an end to this and let Natalie go. You can leave if you want. We won't stop you. Just leave Natalie with us," Sister Agatha said.

Henry was moving toward them now, one hand holding Natalie tightly, the other used to aim the pistol at them. "Get that light out of my face," Henry growled, stepping around them, leading Natalie by the hand.

Sister Agatha lowered the beam, but kept the light on, providing enough illumination to read his expression as he stood by the window. Blood was dripping to the floor from his arm, puddling at his feet. He definitely needed medical help, and would soon become light-headed. Time was on their side, if they could just stall a little longer.

"Henry, you're bleeding. Let us help you," she whispered.

Henry cursed, then tried to swing Natalie around to the window. But the girl suddenly resisted, not moving an inch despite his efforts, and in the process he nearly lost his balance. Angrier now, Henry tugged hard at her hand, but somehow Natalie remained rooted to the spot.

Sister Agatha looked at Natalie, aware she wasn't looking at her father or them. Her gaze was focused on something or someone to her right only she could see.

"Come on, kid." Henry yanked her arm, but he slipped on the blood and staggered, hitting the wall with his shoulder and losing his grip on Natalie.

In a heartbeat Sister Agatha grabbed the child and swung her around, protecting Natalie with her own body.

Sister Bernarda moved, too, but in the opposite direction, taking the offense. The ex-Marine delivered a high kick, knocking the gun out of Henry's hand. He made a grab for the weapon and Sister Bernarda sent another kick to his side, hurling him back into the adobe wall. He struck his head, then crashed to the floor.

The rustle of footsteps diverted their attention momentarily, but it was Sheriff Green at the window, a deputy by his side.

"Don't move, Tannen," Tom growled, climbing though the opening, then standing over the dazed man, his weapon out and directed at Henry's chest. "It's over."

"What kept you, Tom?" Sister Agatha said, reaching for Natalie and discovering both their hands were trembling.

After Henry had been taken away in an ambulance, under guard, Sheriff Green came up to Sister Agatha, who was sitting on the front steps of the old church. He held the pistol Henry had used against them in an evidence pouch, tagged and labeled.

"I don't know if this will make you feel any better, but the gun is only a very realistic replica. The cylinder turns and the trigger works, but the bullets are fake. It can't hurt anyone."

Sister Agatha exhaled softly, tired and glad it was over. "Made a good club, though. Ask Pax. What'll happen to Henry now?"

"Once he's stitched up, we'll put him in a cell. It'll take months for the courts to decide what comes next, and we'll have to deal with Colorado. Agencies there have been protecting him as part of a testimony deal, sitting on his records and doing their bureaucratic stall. We should have been told about his situation from the very beginning, especially after Henry became a kidnapping suspect. But at least in the meantime he'll get medical care for his cancer."

While they were making their statements, Father Mahoney arrived. For the remainder of the process, he refused to leave Natalie's side.

As soon as Sister Agatha was finished with her account of the events, she went to join the priest and his niece. "I'm glad you're here, Father."

"It's only temporary. I'm going on sabbatical," Father Mahoney replied. "You'll have a new chaplain soon."

The news should have surprised her, but for some reason it didn't. "You're setting your duties aside for a while to take care of Jessica and Natalie?"

He nodded. "They have no one else, so they'll be my priority for as long as they need me."

"And Jessica? I haven't seen her for a few

days. How's she doing?"

"She's improving slowly. We'll be leaving town in a few days, if her doctors give us the okay, but I'm not sure where we'll end up yet. I guess I'll figure things out as I go." He stood up. "Keep us in your prayers, Sister."

"We all will, Father. Come back to us soon."

Later that evening, just after sunset and during recreation, Sister Agatha walked outside with Reverend Mother. The temperature was cool and pleasant, and for a while they were content to stroll in silence.

At long last they stopped by the statue of the Blessed Virgin. Reverend Mother glanced down at Pax, who'd accompanied them. "He looks no worse for wear," she said.

"He's okay. He may be sore for a while, and the cut will have to heal, but nothing's broken," Sister Agatha said, glancing down at him affectionately.

"I'm very concerned with how easily he responded to your attack command. Is it safe for us to keep him now after what he went through today?"

"Absolutely, Mother. He obeys the police commands he was taught, but not indiscriminately, and the command has to be given *in German.* All things considered, the monastery couldn't ask for a better canine friend."

"You're right," Reverend Mother said, nodding. "And now he's just Pax again." She smiled as the dog came up and put his nose into her hand, asking to be petted. "Things have worked out well."

"Yes, they have, Mother," Sister Agatha answered. "And I have some other good news. Sister Bernarda received a substantial offer from a collector for any angel figures or art Natalie completed while she was our guest."

"Sell the smaller ones, but we'll keep Tzuriel."

"The angel who guards the monastery," Sister Agatha said. "Good choice, Mother."

Sister Ignatius approached and fell into step beside them as they continued to walk. "I'm going to miss baking our altar breads and cookies."

Reverend Mother smiled. "We're getting excellent terms for licensing the cookies to the bakery, and expect a steady return from the profits. But we'll have to find something that'll allow us to fulfill the rule requiring us to live by the work of our hands."

"I've been praying that God will lead us

to the right thing," Sister Ignatius said. "As a sign, I've asked He send us a gentle, peaceful light, one that is present where no other light shines," Sister Ignatius said.

"That leaves a lot of room for interpretation," Sister Agatha said with a tiny smile.

They'd only walked a few more feet when Sister Ignatius gasped and pointed across the river to the west. "There's our sign!"

For a split second the three of them saw a glowing cloud that shimmered in the fading light.

A sudden flaring up of flames from burning leaves, Sister Agatha concluded, or maybe headlights shining into a cloud of dust generated by a vehicle. In the time it took her to blink, the haze vanished.

"Did you see it?" Sister Ignatius said in an excited voice.

Reverend Mother smiled. "You're right, child. It was a gentle light. We can expect our answers soon, then."

As the bell for Compline sounded, Sister Agatha bowed her head and hurried to the chapel, along with the sisters and Reverend Mother. Another day was done and, under His wings, they would find refuge from the night.

ABOUT THE AUTHORS

Aimée and David Thurlo are the authors of more than forty novels and their works have been published in more than twenty countries. They are best known for the Ella Clah novels and the two previous novels, *Bad Faith* and *Thief in Retreat,* featuring Sister Agatha. The Thurlos live in Corrales, New Mexico.

Visit the authors' Web site at www.aimee-anddavidthurlo.com.